PACKED AND READY TO GO

PACKED AND READY TO GO

Jacki Kelly
Copyright 2014 by Kelly, Jacki
Smashwords Edition
ISBN: 978-1-942202-03-5
First Edition Electronic December 2014
Published by Yobachi Publishing, LLC

This is a book of fiction. Names, characters, places and incidents either are the product of the author's imagination or are used fictitiously. Any resemblance to actual persons, living or dead or events or locales is entirely coincidental.

Other Books By Jacki Kelly

THE SWEET ROAD SERIES
The Sweet Road Home
The Sweet Road To Love
The Sweet Road Back

DATING JUST GOT SERIOUS
Blind Date
One Date At A Time
Date Me
A Single Date
Speed Date
Dating Just Got Serious – Box Set

WOMEN'S FICTION
Packed and Ready To Go
Going Backwards

For Gregg, Kimberli and Kellen

The cruelest lies are often told in silence.

Robert Louis Stevenson

Chapter One - Tracy

The day I realized my marriage was in crisis started like any other day. I can look back at it now and see all the fat cracks and gaping holes. Back then, I saw nothing through the haze of busyness.

Like so many other mornings, the sun rose over our deck, baking off the morning fog. I got to work early, attended every scheduled meeting, and paid just enough attention to grasp the details being presented.

I stopped at the grocer on the way home to pick up a rack of lamb, baby white potatoes, fresh broccoli and French bread. Walter and I needed a special night. This weekend was going to be different. My sole goal for the evening was to pause our world long enough to remember what he smelled like, tasted like, felt like.

I pulled into the garage, hurried into the house to set the atmosphere for our special evening I had planned. By the time the delicious smell of garlic, butter and grilled meat filled the house, and the mellow sound of Paul Taylor's saxophone, I ran upstairs to slip into my shortest, sexiest, silky nightie. Dinner was ready and so was I.

The snug fit did little to boost my confidence. Dropping twenty-five pounds would make me look like one of those women who always turned Walter's head. I pulled the teddy over my hips and headed downstairs.

The wine, the music, the smell of good food all helped to relax the knots in my shoulders.

Walter promised to be home by seven. I set the oven to warm and curled up on the sofa to wait. And wait.

By eight o'clock the lamb had dried out, the wine had warmed, my anxiety rose, but I waited some more.

My entire relationship with Walter wasn't measured in special events, but in time.

How long would it take for him to notice me?

How long would it take him to ask me out?

How long would it take for him to propose to me?

Now I sat at home waiting on him, crippled with fear while our marriage continued to crumble.

I swirled the merlot around in the glass. No matter how close it came to the rim, I managed to not spill it. Walter and I must have thought we could do the same thing, push our relationship to the limit, hoping not to rip it apart. We took everything for granted. Even each other.

At nine o'clock, I ate dinner.

Alone.

The flavors lay on my tongue like overprocessed leather. After two mouthfuls, I wrapped the leftovers and tucked them into the refrigerator already stuffed with other meals, I'd cooked that he hadn't eaten. He'd probably come home and pass out instead of eating.

The band constricting my heart tightened, trapping my breath in my chest. I didn't recognize my own life.

At nine-thirty, I heard Walter's keys in the door. I forced my anger down before I unfolded my legs, placing my feet on the floor. Running to greet him had ended years ago, just like his morning good-bye kisses and coming home on time to eat dinner with me.

"Tracy, I'm home."

I stayed in the family room, listening to him open the oven. I downed the last of the wine before walking into the kitchen with the biggest smile I could muster.

"Did you cook dinner tonight?"

"It's good to see you too, honey. I thought you were coming home on time, tonight." I parked my butt on the barstool and dropped my chin into my palm, bracing for our nightly tug-of-war.

"I had to make a stop, Tracy. Right now, I just want to eat and go to bed." He pulled a plate from the refrigerator and peeled back the aluminum foil. He loosened his tie and placed his jacket on the back of the stool. The creases along the sleeve of his baby blue shirt were still sharp. He looked like he'd dressed just moments ago, instead of early that morning. Walter prided himself on his impeccable sense of taste and style.

"Why didn't you keep it warm in the oven?"

"Why didn't you tell me you were going to be late?"

He stuck the food into the microwave. Without looking at me, he punched the buttons then poured a glass of wine. His shoulders rose and fell without the audible sigh that usually accompanied his gesture.

He pressed his hip against the counter, grinning like a child on Christmas Day. "I bought a new car today."

His statement didn't register right away. I was waiting to hear why he was late, and his response to my question shouldn't have started with something he purchased.

"What did you say?" I shook my head and tried to focus.

"That's right. A new car."

I pushed off the stool, made my way to the garage and flipped the light switch. Next to my car, a shiny, new, top-of-the-line Lexus, gleamed under the harsh fluorescent overhead light. The Lexus laughed at me for not being in on the joke that was my life.

My trek to the kitchen and back to the stool was a long, long journey.

I didn't blink.

I didn't swallow.

I didn't move.

I just stared at Walter. Forced myself to breathe in, breathe out.

Seethe in, seethe out.

"What were you thinking? Crystal's graduation and wedding are coming up. You couldn't have waited a few more weeks?"

From the way he looked at me, I was the bitch trying to steal his joy. Why couldn't I just walk over to him, kiss his cheek and forget about it? That's the wife I wanted to be.

"I work every day. I don't need your permission to spend my money."

"It's not about permission. We had an agreement to discuss large purchases. A dishwasher, a blender, hell-even a new sofa-wouldn't need to be discussed, but a car that costs thirty-thousand dollars—"

"It was a lot more than that." His tone was so casual he could have been discussing the purchase of sweat socks. "And, we struck that deal when we first got married, when money was tight and we had to be careful. But now, I wanted the car. I bought it."

My life was slipping through my fingers and I didn't know how to close my hands around it.

I nodded. Not in agreement, but with acceptance. I accepted the shift in our marriage, from what I thought was true, to the reality staring across the counter at me.

Chapter Two – Tracy

The morning sun streamed through the bedroom window, warming Walter's empty spot in the king-size bed next to me. His declaration from last night had left me spinning, like he'd abandoned me on a deserted island. The rift between us oozed through the house like a red wine stain, in the things he said and didn't say.

Ignoring the signs wasn't the smartest move, but we'd faced hurdles before. Every married couple did, I reminded myself. Like the other times we'd managed, and we would this time, too.

The sound of Walter's heavy footsteps coming up the stairs brought me fully awake. When we were first married, he used to bring me coffee in bed. I lay there waiting in hopes that he'd come bearing a hot steamy mug to make up. I positioned myself on my elbows, hoping to look sexy enough to entice him back into the world where we loved and cared for each other.

"If we're picking up your parents and planning on arriving to the graduation on time, you need to get up." Walter stood in the doorway, holding a mug in his palm.

I swung my legs over the edge of the bed. "Is that my coffee?"

"No. You don't have time to drink and dress, or we'll be late."

Without commenting, I left him standing there before I could develop my pre-caffeine response. Lucky for him. The words forming in my head were as ugly as his behavior.

Chapter Three – Walter

Tracy strolled across the room, her slinky nightie rose just enough to catch my interest. Getting out of the bedroom was the best option for us both. Her perky breasts and full hips always stirred my lust. My body jerked to life, every cell warming to the thought, but the idea had trouble scrolled across it.

There used to be a time when I couldn't keep my hands off her, but then all the dull, routine stuff got in the way. All the had-to-dos got in the way of want-to-dos. The talk about mortgages, grocery lists, or bills were the staples holding us together. I used to be the focus of her attention, but when Crystal came along, she abandoned me, leaving me with too much time and too much pent-up sexual energy.

As I reached the base of the stairs I heard Tracy turn on the shower. After a few seconds, I pulled my cell phone from my pocket and dialed.

"Isn't the graduation today? I didn't think I'd hear from you." Sasha cooed into the phone, instantly making me ache for her.

"I have a few minutes before we leave and I wanted to hear your voice. I'm expecting the rest of the day to be bogged down in ritual."

"If you sneak over here before going I'll give you plenty to think about."

"I bet you will, you always do." I dropped my voice, before glancing upstairs. "I do have something to talk about with you—"

"I have something to tell you, too."

"I don't like surprises. Tell me now." I moved towards my office.

"Oh no. It can wait. I really miss you, Walt." She sweetened her voice, like she always did when she wanted to wrap me around her pinkie.

My resolve to break up with her circled my heart. The idea seemed absurd, but I had to stick with it this time, even if it meant limiting my sexual thrills to no frills. Returning to faithful husband should have made me happy, instead I felt like a man marching towards the guillotine.

Finding excuses to feed Tracy was exhausting, and Sasha wanted more. I saw it in Sasha's eyes every time we talked, the way she clung to me when it was time for me to leave, and her unexpected visits to my office. Designer handbags, diamonds, and trips were easy, but time, commitment, and relationships were not.

With the threats of major lay-offs at the company, that meant I'd have to cut back on the money going out. Which meant I couldn't keep lavishing expensive gifts on Sasha. Which meant my twenty-something exquisite lay would be moving on to someone more age-and-funds appropriate. Which meant I'd have to settle for what I had, at least until everything settled down at work.

I cupped my hand over the mouthpiece. "I'll try to stop by before the weekend is over. After the graduation, things will settle down."

"I'll be waiting with no panties, just the way you like me."

I disconnected the call, entered my office, and dropped into my leather executive chair. I'd tried to resist Sasha. What was supposed to be a routine book purchase from her bookstore had turned into three trips. I knew she was baiting me by playing hard-to-get, but I liked a good old-fashioned cat and mouse game. Especially when the prize was young, single, and undemanding. Giving up Sasha wouldn't be easy. She was a fun distraction from the routine, a link to my youth. Being with her was like being back in college with fast girls and quick sexual encounters. When sex was just about sex and not about securing a future or paying a mortgage or raising children or grocery lists or where to vacation. With Sasha, I didn't have to pretend to have all the answers because she had so few questions. As long as I satisfied her in bed and brought her a few baubles, she was fulfilled.

Someone else would eventually take her place, but until then, I could be happy with Tracy. She wasn't as imaginative in bed as she used to be, but she was always willing. Maybe when I got older, the everyday sameness wouldn't be so detestable. Tracy seemed to thrive on routine. How she managed to be happy with the dull regimen amazed me. But I'd give it another try. The next time, I'd cross my fingers tighter and try harder to keep my dick in my pants. Tracy deserved better.

Chapter Four - Tracy

I wanted to be mad at Walter for buying the car and breaking one of our marital canons, but I couldn't hold on to the anger. Watching our daughter receive her hard earned, expensive degree pushed everything else aside.

When the ceremony ended, the graduates filed out of the auditorium. I came to my feet and took long strides to catch up to Walter. Once in the aisle, his progress came to a halt. A crush of family and well-wishers inched out of the auditorium, like a slow wave of cold molasses.

The unhurried egress benefited my parents. They moved like snails. I turned around to find they'd fallen well behind Walter and me. With his long legs and easy gait, Walter pushed towards the fresh air outside. I grabbed his arm.

"We need to wait for my parents." I stepped aside to allow the flow towards the exit to continue. A bead of sweat dangled between my breasts. I swiped it away and willed my parents to pick up their pace before I melted.

"Is everything okay?" I asked when they caught up.

"We're fine." My mother shuffled alongside my father, her lips pulled tighter than a length of thread. "Your dad's a little slow, that's all."

"Don't listen to your mother. She likes to make mountains out of mole hills."

"Look at how slow you walkin'. Ain't nobody making mountains. You can barely keep up."

"Frances, I'm fine. What's your hurry anyway? Go on ahead. I'm right behind you." My father waved his hand like he was shooing flies.

"We'll talk later," my mother mouthed to me.

Inches away from the main exit, I felt the promise of less humid air. I used my hand as a fan to dry the perspiration beading on my forehead.

We stepped outside. The temperature was only marginally better than the auditorium, but at least there was room to move around and the air didn't feel used. Walter crossed his arms over his chest and glared down at me. His sharp jaw and pronounced cheekbones caught the sun, reminding me how much I loved his fierce good looks.

"Are we heading home now?" he asked.

My stomach pummeled. The rosy expectations I had for the day vanished like pixie dust.

"Don't you want to see Crystal and Max? We need to take some pictures to remember this moment...the whole graduation thing."

"Can't we do that later?"

Before answering him, I drew a deep breath. His debonair style, nor my need to make him happy, wouldn't change my mind about leaving him this time. The car was the nail that bit me in the ass and sealed my decision. I reached for my reservoir of patience, using just enough to get through the moment, because I knew I'd need more before the day was over.

"It won't be the same later. I want to capture this moment, not some made-up moment. And after the pictures, we're taking them to dinner to celebrate."

Instead of answering, he sighed and repositioned his arms.

"We're going out to dinner," I said again. "Our daughter just graduated from college. We talked about this a week ago and you agreed." When he didn't respond I continued, "Carla and Ursula are coming too."

"No! Not the loud mouths. I've got to deal with your parents, and now you're throwing your two friends into the mix. Is Carla bringing that talkative Javier, too?" His eyes followed the lines in my dress down to my shoes. "Besides, I thought you were dieting again?"

Again.

He said again.

And he said it loud enough for everyone within earshot to hear. I sucked in all the air my lungs could hold. His comment was like a sucker punch. My weight was not open for discussion. Not ever. In fact, never. Even if I got tent big.

My favorite pair of Jimmy Choo shoes and the new Ellen Tracy dress didn't make me look like the svelte girl he married, but I didn't need his help counting calories or to remind me of the weight loss promises I made and failed to keep.

"Yes, Carla's coming, and I'm sure she's bringing Javier. He's her husband. And Ursula might bring a friend too." He looked pained. Ursula was coming alone, but I threw that comment out to rile him.

"I thought we were going to have something at home. At least then I could watch television or get some work done."

"Having something at home means you get to sit down and I get to do all the shopping, all the preparing, and all the running around." I paused, trying to find a level of Zen to get me through the day. "There will be no television tonight. We're going out to dinner in your new car and I hope my parents don't piss in the back seat."

The stricken look on his face let me know I'd hit my target.

My parents weren't incontinent, but getting back at him for the diet comment rumbled through me like a child well past nap time.

"Fine, Tracy. Where are we going?"

"We talked about this, Walter. Don't you remember?"

"I've got a lot on my mind. You know, with work and all." He shoved his hand in his pocket.

"I made reservations at Ruth's Chris at the Baltimore Inner Harbor."

"That means I have to pick up the tab for your parents, your friends and Crystal *and* Max?" He punctuated each word. "Damn! Why did you pick such an expensive restaurant?" I expected him to stomp his foot like a child.

"Walter, please, not today. This is supposed to be a happy day. Where do you think we should celebrate—McDonald's? You weren't thinking about money when you bought that new car. Besides, you made it clear we don't have to consult each other on expenditures. Right?"

He clenched his jaw.

"Fine." His curt tone and rigid stance indicated he wasn't fine.

His right eye twitched, a telltale sign that my position chaffed him. We needed quality time, and soon. When we're in sync little things like this didn't ruffle us.

Walter towered over me by a foot. Even at forty-two, his stomach remained flat and his thighs were as solid as iron rods. His salt and pepper hair gave him a distinguished appearance. More than twenty years of marriage and I still adored him. But we were out of rhythm and I was out of solutions. Other women gave him long hot looks. He didn't think I noticed, but I noticed everything. Everything.

Crystal rounded the corner of the brick building, her gown flowing behind her and her arm linked in Max's. The huge grin on her face made me smile, too. Even the corners of Walter's mouth tugged upwards.

After a few photographs, Crystal and Max dashed off to take more pictures with friends. Walter retrieved the car and huddled us in. The drive to the Inner Harbor started out quiet.

"Well, Walter, you must be very proud today. Your baby girl graduated from college with honors, she's getting married to a fine young man and you're married to a beautiful woman. Life has been good to you." My father's slow southern drawl pierced the silence. From the back seat, he laughed and slapped Walter on the shoulder.

"I'm real proud, Carl," Walter replied without expression.

My father chuckled. I wondered if he detected the sarcasm in Walter's words.

"This sure is a nice car. You got all the bells and whistles I see. Nothing beats the smell of a new car. How much did it set you back?"

I jerked around in my seat. Perspiration dotted my father's forehead. "Dad, you don't ask people that question," I admonished him.

"Carl, you know better," my mother chimed in with a disapproving look.

"Oh, I didn't mean no harm. You ain't mad are you, Walter?" My father rubbed his stubby index finger along the plush leather seat.

"It's alright Carl, don't worry about it."

"I don't believe you," my mother hissed.

"Aw Frances, if Walter ain't mad, don't get your knickers in a knot." He patted my mother on the knee. "You gonna tell me what you paid, Walter?"

"Not in front of Tracy. She's already having a fit about this car."

"She don't like it?"

"It's a fine car, Dad," I said. "Now let's change the subject." The last thing I wanted to talk about was the expensive vehicle and the problem it'd unleashed.

My father sat back in his seat, content to be quiet now that he had caused a sufficient stir.

"Dad, you're sweating, do you want me to turn up the air conditioner?"

"No, honey, I'm fine." He pulled a handkerchief from his breast pocket and mopped his forehead.

"You see, it's not hot in here, and you're sweating like you stole out the church offering basket." My mother's southern drawl had an added dose of concern.

"Oh Frances, don't go starting that. Not now."

I turned back around. From the corner of my eye I watched Walter gnash his teeth.

I reached over and squeezed his thigh. "Hang in there, baby. In a few weeks, you and I will get away and really relax. Just the two of us."

Chapter Five - Tracy

Walter's cell phone chimed while we waited for the restaurant valet to park the car. He snatched the phone off his belt loop and looked at the display.

"I thought you didn't like silly ring-tones. Whose ring is that? It sounds childish." I asked, trying to ignore the sudden chill washing over my body.

"One of the salesmen—a royal pain-in-the-ass. I gave him his own ringer so I'd know when he called."

"You promised you weren't working today."

"Tracy, I'm always working. What can I do?" He accepted the call, then covered the mouthpiece. "Why don't you and your parents go in? I'll end this call and be right there."

I searched his face for a moment, not sure what I expected to see. Happiness. Disappointment. Love. He blinked twice before looking away. I opened the car door and stepped out.

It took several seconds before my eyes adjusted to the dim lighting inside. A server rushed by, carrying a large tray of drinks balanced on the palm of her hand.

I made my way to the hostess stand and gave her our name.

"Your table will be ready in a few minutes. Your party can wait in the bar if you'd like. I'll come find you."

I signaled to my parents, and followed the carpeted path to the wide oak bar. I dropped my clutch on the counter and signaled the bartender. Without hesitating, I ordered a sour apple martini, then turned to my parents. "What would you like?"

"Let's see." My father scratched his chin, as if stimulating his brain. He always ordered scotch and water, but I played along with him.

"I'll have a white wine," my mother piped up while my father continued to stroke his chin.

"I want scotch and water," he said.

"Yeah, I knew that's what you wanted." I poked his ribs with my index finger. He kissed my cheek and winked. Being an only child gave me special moments with my father. But the secret winks made me feel most special. Like we shared a secret my mother would never be privy to.

Walter walked into the bar as the server returned with our drinks. He ordered a glass of ice water. I closed my eyes, hoping he wasn't being cheap, but rather a responsible designated driver.

This day needed to be special. I wanted to imprint it on my memory as the day our daughter began her new life, and so did Walter and I. Unlike some women, I didn't need to be beautiful to everyone, having them turn around to adore me as I passed by. I just wanted to be beautiful to Walter. For him to be happy he chose me. For him to rush home at the end of the day, to be with me. For me to be the only one for him.

My parents moved to the far corner of the bar and sat at a small table with cushioned seats. I climbed onto the padded barstool. Walter shoved his hands into his pockets, his attention focused on the door like he wanted to bolt. There was probably a sports games competing for his attention.

The shy college sophomore I fell in love with had morphed into such a dashing man. Back then he couldn't get enough of me. We had snuggled in the twin-sized dormitory bed, talking until the early morning hours. I thought our love would last forever. How naïve. Now we were strangers and no matter how I tried, I couldn't seem to stop thinking about my co-worker, Marco. Bits of conversations with him popped into my head at odd times. Often late at night while waiting for Walter to come home, images of Marco lying next to me kept me entertained. But, they were only fantasies, nothing I'd ever act on.

"When will Crystal and Max get here? And where are your friends?" The edge was gone out of his voice now, as if he'd accepted his fate for the evening.

"Crystal and Max will be here soon. They wanted to say good-bye to their friends. This is a big day for them." I patted the bar stool next to me. "Come, sit and taste this. It's delicious." I pushed my martini toward him.

He sat and sipped the drink. "It's good." He hunched his shoulders, then placed his hand on my knee, making slow circles with his index finger as his hand inched up my thigh. That was him, distant one moment, loving and caring the next. All we needed to do was stretch the meaningful minutes into a lifetime. Could I gloss over the distance between us and look forward to some speck in the future filled with hope? Could I forget the loneliness of the past, cross my fingers and hope for something better? Did I want to?

His hand continued to inch along my thigh. This was the reason nothing ever got resolved with us. We ignored our problems, afraid to peek behind the curtain because maybe there were no answers there.

It had been weeks since we'd shared any intimacy. My fulfillment wouldn't take place in the bar, but that didn't stop the warm feeling from growing between my legs. My love for him always betrayed my common sense. My pulse sped up, roaring in my ears like a blender.

"Somebody must be feeling better now," I whispered.

"I'm fine. Why'd you say that?" His hand felt warm against my flesh.

"You've been a bit of a grouch."

"After this week, my schedule should settle down." The heavy sound of his voice stroked my already warm body.

"Tonight maybe we can finish—" Before I could complete my sentence, Carla and Javier walked into the bar. Carla's flaming red hair fell to her shoulders. Every eye in the bar turned to take in her sexy black halter dress.

"Hi, girl." She kissed my cheek. Carla could have been a model. Her flawless caramel complexion made her the most beautiful woman I knew. We had been friends since college.

I craned back on the stool to find Javier. His white shirt and khaki pants made him nearly invisible in the muted colors of the bar. But Mr. Personality's hazel eyes danced with mischief as he leaned in and embraced me.

"Hey beautiful," Javier said to me.

"Get outta here." I swatted at his chest, but couldn't help feeling embarrassed.

"Did you cry?" Carla asked.

"Here we go." Walter slid off the bar stool and tried to recede to the far corner of the room. Before he reached the end of the bar, Javier grabbed his hand and shook it. I hoped he filled Walter's ears with whatever had made his smile so bubbly today. Then I turned back to Carla.

"No. I haven't cried yet, but the night is young."

"Do whatever you feel you need to do. It's okay, girl, it's even expected." She climbed on the stool vacated by Walter. "So what's up with him? He didn't even speak to me." She waved at the bartender and ordered a cosmopolitan.

"Who knows what's up with him? It changes from day to day. Today he's complaining about how much everything costs." I took a sip of my drink. "He's complaining about expenses, and yet last night he came home in a brand new, top of the line Lexus. We used to talk about large purchases. Now, we don't discuss anything."

Carla glanced over her shoulder at Walter. "Wow. I guess you don't approve of the car? And, from the grim expression on his face, I take it he's still angry over your reaction."

"You guessed right." I drained my glass and then ordered another.

"Do you want to talk about it before you get drunk?" Carla asked.

"Nope. I'd rather get drunk."

"I aim to please." She raised her glass and took a gulp. "What time is Ursula coming?"

"She should be here soon. You know we can't have a celebration without both of Crystal's godmothers."

"Will we get to meet Ursula's mystery man tonight? She's been dating him for weeks. I want to see the man who's held her attention this long."

"She's still keeping him a secret." I sipped the martini the bartender placed in front of me.

"Do you think he's married?" Carla asked.

I hunched my shoulders. "That's the first thing I asked. Maybe she wants to make sure she'll keep him around." I caught a glimpse of Walter at the end of the bar. "How's your hubby?"

Javier stood at the end of the bar, trying to hold a conversation with Walter. My husband's grip on his water glass and his blank stare indicated he wasn't listening.

I turned to find Ursula standing behind us. "Are you talking about Javier again?"

"Of course." I pulled her into my arms and gave her a tight squeeze.

"Are you alone?" Carla looked past Ursula toward the restaurant's entrance.

"Yes, I'm alone. And you're being nosey," Ursula responded, and then turned to me. "What's the matter with you? If your face were any longer it would be in your drink."

Before I could reply, Crystal and Max came through the restaurant door.

"It's nothing," I replied. "We'll talk later." It was time to be happy.

During dinner champagne flowed, crab appetizers and an assortment of salads filled the table. I ate a loaf of bread smeared with butter while we reminisced about Crystal's childhood and her crazy antics.

Max released a hearty laugh, then planted a kiss on Crystal's lips. I couldn't remember the last time I tasted Walter's tongue. We managed a dry peck before running out the door some mornings. That was the extent of our romance. At night, we fell into bed too preoccupied with our days to pretend we cared about our marriage. I was half tempted to stick my tongue in Walter's mouth, but I couldn't. He abhorred public displays of intimacy.

I glanced across the table at Carla, needing to focus my eyes away from the pure lust I saw in Max's eyes. Javier leaned on Carla's chair, whispering something in her ear. She smiled and squirmed in her seat. Javier must have had his hand under her dress. At forty-one, Carla acted like a teenager. I wanted an ounce of her bravado, then I would contemplate a brief, satisfying moment with Marco.

Ursula twisted in her seat. "Get a room," she said loud enough for everyone at the table to hear.

I covered my mouth to cackle. My mother's mouth was slightly open with disapproval.

"Crystal, I think we've got everything in place for your wedding soiree. It's going to be a night of total decadence." Carla straightened in her chair, forcing the attention back on Crystal.

"There won't be male strippers, will there?" Max asked.

"Max, you know we have more class than that." Ursula placed her hand on her chest.

"Okay, Ms. Tracy, what's up for the evening?" Max turned to me for an answer.

"I have no idea. This is Carla and Ursula's show. They're just using my house."

"And remember, Walter," Carla warned. "No men allowed, so make other plans that evening."

"Don't worry about me. I have no intention of being there." Walter propped his elbow on the table.

My stomach churned and for once I couldn't blame it on hunger. Losing my daughter and my husband all at the same time fanned the fire brewing in my stomach.

***

After dinner, we drove my parents back to Philadelphia. The drive from Baltimore to Philly contained no more chitchat about Walter's new car.

My mother and father still lived in their modest home in Fairmount Park, where I grew up. From the curb I could see the red tulips and golden yellow daffodils in my father's garden against the front of the house.

"Double park here and I'll walk my parents to the door." I unbuckled my seat belt and grabbed the door handle.

"How long are you gonna be?" Walter asked.

"As long as it takes. Turn on your expensive satellite radio while you wait."

I helped my father climb the stairs, and glimpsed up the street at the house where Ursula grew up, where I spent so much time. I half expected to see her skip down the street with her doll in one hand and her pink and white hula-hoop over her shoulder.

"Good night, Mom, good night, Dad. I'll call you in the morning." I kissed them both. "Thank you for sharing today with me and Walter."

"I wouldn't have missed it for all the money in the world," my father said. He touched my arms. "I'm exhausted and maybe a little tipsy. Don't be too mad at Walter about the car. He works hard, so let him have his toy. A good wife lets her husband have at least one toy."

"Yeah. I know, Dad. And I'm a good wife."

He held my glance for a moment before nodding and going inside.

My mother grabbed my arms as I started down the stairs. "Sweetie, it was a good day. A proud day." She tightened her hold on my arm.

"Yes, Mom, it was. Go on in now, it's late."

She lowered her voice and looked over her shoulder. "We didn't talk about your father."

"Mom, it's late. Not tonight?"

"I know. And today with so much going on we couldn't, but we need to."

"It's late—"

"Well, it don't have to be right now, but don't forget."

I detected concern in her voice. I glanced over my shoulder; Walter was tapping the steering wheel.

"I'll call you tomorrow."

She gave me a doubtful look.

"I promise. Tomorrow."

She dropped her hand and stepped inside. I waved before she closed the door. I'd never seen her look so worried but between exhaustion and Walter's impatience, I couldn't handle any more. I dashed down the stairs and jumped in the car. Walter rolled his eyes at me as he pulled away from the curb.

"What does that look mean?"

"It's late, and you and your Mom are yakking it up."

"We weren't yakking. She wanted to talk to me about something important, but I asked her to wait until tomorrow because I could see you glaring at me."

"Do you know how much the dinner check was?" His jaw tightened.

"Let's not do this tonight."

"It was over fifteen hundred dollars, Tray. You guys were buying bottles of wine like they were water. One thousand dollars," he ground out. "Do you know how much we're spending on Crystal's wedding? Do you ever add the money up?"

"Did you add up the money before you bought this car?" I yelled, forgetting my father's advice.

"Damn it, Tray. I was driving a four-year old car. If you can drive a new one, why the hell can't I?"

"I didn't buy a new car behind your back. We talked about it. Remember? And giving Crystal a huge wedding was your idea, too. You were the one who said you wanted her to have the wedding we didn't."

"Who could blame me? You couldn't stand in the front of a church with your belly plumped up, now could you?"

I fisted my hands and placed them in my lap. "You still think I did it on purpose don't you?

Getting pregnant in college wasn't my goal, but you own fifty percent of the responsibility, too. You could have worn a condom."

"I told you I didn't like them."

"Then stop complaining. Shit happens."

We drove a few miles in the heavy silence. He glanced at me. "Why do we have to talk about everything? I knew what car I wanted, so I got it."

"Walter, it's my money too. Did you forget I work every day? I make good money. I'll give you a check for the dinner as soon as we get home." I rubbed my temples and closed my eyes.

"I don't want your damn check. Stop spending money like we have an endless supply of it."

"We just dropped my dad off at his house. So stop acting like my father. I'm not a child. You don't need to tell me what to do."

He huffed and changed lanes.

"This isn't about the money. What's really bugging you?" I asked.

"I told you."

"You're upset about the check? That's it? The check?"

He didn't respond as he weaved into the passing lane. For several miles, neither of us said a word.

When my anger subsided, I tried to focus on happier thoughts. "Can you believe Javier? He and

Carla might as well have made love right there at the dinner table."

Walter snorted without looking at me.

"Are you jealous?" I inquired. "At least somebody is making out."

"Hell no, I'm not jealous. Are you?"

I shifted in the seat. "A little bit."

He gave me a dismissive look and readjusted his hand on the steering wheel. I almost told him about Marco, but he'd find some way to tarnish one of my bright spots.

I wanted passion in my life, someone to look at me like I mattered, for their eyes to light up when I walked into the room. Most days I felt like I was standing in the shadows watching other people live their lives. I couldn't remember the last time Walter and I made hot passionate love, or even lukewarm love. My body ached for his touch, to feel the warmth of his hands caressing me. I wanted to be folded into his massive arms and reassured that life would be good again.

A few weeks back, we had a quickie one evening when he finally came home from work. I threw myself at him before he could fall asleep. He performed his duty, without touching my heart.

Most days, I spent hours daydreaming about Marco Ferrara, my good-looking co-worker who warmed the icy patches left behind by Walter. Marco mixed Italian words with English in his deep sexy voice. If I left Walter, I could have lusty, frenzied sex with Marco. I crossed my legs and tried to suppress my guilt. Good wives never thought about other men. What would my parents or daughter say if they knew how much I thought about Marco? Just thinking about him made me feel guilty.

For the rest of the drive, I pretended to sleep to avoid arguing with Walter. By the time we pulled into the garage, it was one-thirty in the morning. Once inside the house, Walter went straight upstairs without another word.

I stopped in the kitchen and stood in front of the open refrigerator door. The cool air from inside drifted over me. After gulping down a glass of merlot, I kicked off my shoes and rubbed my toes together. My thoughts swam together as I poured a second glass of wine. I didn't want them to stop, because then I would have to do something. A nagging feeling plucked at my brain. Could Walter be having an affair? Again?

My knees buckled. I grabbed the chair to keep from losing my balance. The sound of my heavy breathing flooded my ears. I straightened up, then rummaged in the kitchen cabinets until I found the bottle of pills. I needed them to get through the upcoming hectic weeks.

Walter was already snoring when I climbed the stairs. I wasn't sleepy. Instead, I could still feel him rubbing my knee and inching his hand up my thigh. I undressed, dropping my clothes into a heap on the floor. I climbed into bed and kissed him on the lips. I pressed kisses on his chest as my hand moved to his groin.

"Not now, I'm tired," he barked.

"Come on Walter, you started something earlier. Don't you want to finish?"

"Not now." He didn't even open his eyes.

"Are you still mad about the money? We'll cut back." I stroked his penis until it hardened in my palm.

"Stop it, Tracy." He pushed my hand away.

"I think you want to." I planted a kiss on his chin.

"I can get hard watching a pretty girl walk down the street. It doesn't mean I want to make love."

"Why, Walter? What's bugging you now?"

He pulled away. I gave up and sat on the edge of the bed.

Even though I was twenty pounds overweight, men still eyed me. Weeks ago, some young guy had stopped me on the street to offer me a personal hello. He told me how nice I looked before scribbling his phone number on a piece of paper and pushing it into my hand. That number was still wedged into the corner of my wallet, as if I might call it one day. I'm sure he only wanted sex, but that counts.

I took validation from anywhere. If Walter didn't find me appealing, Marco Ferrara, with his smooth husky voice certainly did. The way he smiled at me at work was enough to make me happy.

"Do you ever wonder how long we'll be married?" I asked in a voice that was almost inaudible.

"Why? What do you think?"

"We're always at odds, arguing about little things that wouldn't have mattered to us years ago."

"People change. They don't always see eye to eye. It means nothing. So please come back to bed."

"So is that a no or a yes?"

"What do you think, Tracy?"

I didn't answer right away. It felt like a no, but saying it aloud made it real.

"Sometimes I think we will, and other times, we don't seem to have the energy to care what happens to us."

"I'm going to sleep." He pulled the sheet over his head.

Was I asking for too much? I only wanted life to slow down long enough for me to catch up. It seemed like Crystal grew up overnight, and now the only thing waiting for me was a long stretch of deserted road. That nagging feeling skidded across my brain again. I closed my eyes, but I couldn't ignore it.

"Are you having an affair, Walter?"

Chapter Six - Walter

I pretended to be asleep right through Tracy's questions until she turned off the light. When her breathing became slow and soft, I pulled to the edge of the bed and slept.

The next morning, sunshine filtered through the shutters, bathing the room in a warm light. Tracy backed into me and wiggled her ass, even though she was asleep. My penis pulsed to life. I turned away from her and pressed my erection with my hand. I couldn't have sex with her, not today. Today was reserved for Sasha. And before I broke it off with her, I planned to have an afternoon of unadulterated bliss between her legs.

Last night's dream about my mother was still fresh in my mind. Tracy had triggered it by drilling me with that question. How the hell did I know if we were going to stay together forever? Tracy often set nightmares about my mother in motion. They were always disturbing and left me flapping in the wind like clothes on the line during a Georgia storm.

I woke up with my heart pounding. Even after a full night of tortured sleep, I was exhausted. My mother lived two hundred miles away and no longer ruled my life. But she was always in my head, trying to find a place she hadn't poisoned yet.

The clock read 6:43 a.m. Sunday morning. I didn't need to begin the day by jumping out of bed and dashing off to work. Sales forecasts, profit objectives, or second quarter earnings didn't matter. I promised myself not to set foot in my home office to check email or faxes or stock prices. If the sales team needed pricing approvals, then they had to wait until Monday.

Being the vice president of Global Sales sounded interesting on paper but, in reality, the job never ended. Seeing Walter Baptiste engraved on the gold nameplate used to thrill me. That wore off when I realized it meant babysitting an uninspired sales team in a downward market. Someone always needed to talk with me, meet with me, or wanted me to solve a problem of their making.

But Sundays belonged to me. No one else ordered my steps. Least of all, Tracy.
She slept and the house was quiet. For a moment I enjoyed the sound of nothing. The absence of noise. Tracy turned over, her eyelids fluttered. My wife was beautiful. No matter what else was going on between us, her beauty captivated me. I admired her ability to be optimistic in almost every situation. Her perpetual smile still made me stare. Her hazel eyes should have been enough to keep me enthralled for the rest of my life, and after today, I would recommit.

Give our marriage another chance.

Even with the extra pounds, she still had curves. The extra weight didn't bother me as much as she thought it did. Nothing on her looked forty; she could claim thirty and no one would question her. Her face wasn't etched with fine lines from everyday living. Even though her beauty was beyond question, my love for her wasn't.

Without making a sound, I climbed out of bed and tiptoed down the hall to the bathroom at the opposite end of the house. The pure pleasure of silence was worth showering and dressing without turning on CNN.

I wanted to get out of the house without waking her. I craved the quiet time. The last two years of my life were a blur. Daily activities told me when to run, when to sit, and when to sleep. But more than anything else, when to come and go. Life choked me. I only controlled my trips to the bathroom, that's all. Every day since I was a barefoot boy in Georgia, somebody, usually a woman, told me what to do.

I tried to be quiet as I crept downstairs to make a strong pot of coffee. Stronger than Tracy could stand to drink. By the time she got up, all that would be left was an empty pot.

I walked out on the balcony with my cup of coffee and took a deep breath of fresh air. Tracy had to have this huge colonial on two wooded acres. Somebody cleaned it, somebody mowed the lawn, and somebody painted the rooms. This was her dream. Not mine. Weeds had taken over the flower garden she'd insisted the gardener dig. This patch of land was all she could talk about when she saw this big lot. All I could think about was the additional work and upkeep. It reminded me of the huge piece of land I'd had to mow back in Georgia.

No question, my life was a snarled mess. I had no original ideas to put the company earnings back on track. My personal life was a mess. My stomach bubbled constantly. The elephant sitting on my chest refused to move his big ass. I felt like I was being buried in mud.

I stepped back into the house and listened for footsteps. Still quiet. I thought about leaving a note telling her I was going to the club for a round of golf. Instead, I smirked; she really didn't want to know. I placed the cup in the sink and walked out the door.

Before backing out of the garage, I tuned the car stereo to the smooth jazz station, and programmed the settings on the driver seat. Blaming Tracy for waiting to buy a new car wasn't fair. She was a good woman; she never denied me anything, which only made me want everything. I'd waited to buy this car because I'd wanted to pay off the other car first. The one she didn't know about.

I arrived at the Country Club just minutes before my tee time. The next four hours belonged to me. For eighteen holes, the constriction in my chest wouldn't invade the serenity I found hitting that little white ball down the fairway. Golfing with Jay was always a great way to release some tension, and his car was already in the lot.

Jay was the Global Vice President of Marketing and a good listener. As much as any white man could understand the struggles of being the only black VP in a large company. Jay was a straight up guy. He was the only person I'd told about Sasha. I could count on him to keep my confidence.

Jay also knew someone on the board. So anytime I needed information on office politics, he had the answers. Today, I planned to pump him for information on the company's plan to downsize.

"I was wondering if you'd show up. You usually beat me here." Jay stood on the tee box, swinging his driver.

"I haven't missed a game in years. I had no plan to miss today."

I strapped my bag in the golf cart before warming up with my putter.

I swung it from right to left to loosen my back. "What's the latest word on the lay-off?"

"It's going to be more massive than they first thought. Raw material prices are dropping, which is encouraging more imports. I heard our departments will be hit pretty hard."

I placed the club back in the bag. "I'm already cutting back. Tracy wants to go all out for Crystal's wedding, and trying to rein her in isn't easy."

"You didn't look like you were cutting back when I saw you in the Lexus showroom with your Sasha."

"Yeah, well, I made a promise I needed to keep. Thank goodness for the healthy bonus this year. It might be the last one for a while."

Jay cleared his throat. His neck and cheeks turned red. "Last week there was quite a bit of buzz when Sasha flounced out of your office."

"Did the head office have a shit fit?"

"They heard about it." He lowered his voice, which meant he was sharing company secrets. "Thompson claims he heard the two of you, and went running upstairs. You can expect something will be said." He avoided looking at me, pretending something on the fairway was more interesting.

Jay's comment felt like someone had taken a drill to my lower spine. I tried to remain cool, hoping Jay didn't see the perspiration popping up on my forehead. "Well, today I plan to break it off with Sasha. Between showing up unannounced, asking me to take out the trash and snake the bathroom drain, I think the romance is over. If I wanted to do stuff like that, I could stay home, right?" I tugged on my golf glove.

"Man, you like taking chances, don't you? I couldn't keep all the names straight." Jay pushed a tee in the ground, took several practice swings then drove his ball down the center of the fairway.

"I bore easy. But this time, I'm going to try harder to be faithful." I stepped into the tee box, repeated Jay's actions, and drove the ball twenty yards further than him. "With the lay-offs, do you think my little episode will hurt me?"

He shrugged his shoulder. Not a good sign. I didn't want to press him for more details. I already had a craw full of regret. We climbed in the golf cart and headed down the fairway.

For the balance of the course I stayed away from the topic of business. Sport scores and handicaps better suited the pressure on my chest. On Monday morning I'd find a way to smooth things over with Thompson.

After the game, I jumped in the car and backed out of the parking space. All I could think about was getting to Sasha. The sooner I ended things, the sooner I could put my life back together. Even though I planned to break it off with her, a few hours of lusty sex would ease the pain.

***

Sasha opened the door as soon as I pulled in the driveway. I could see her happy smile from across the yard. She was so different from any of the other women in my past, and from Tracy. Sasha was petite and curvaceous. She wore her hair long, full and curly. Tracy preferred her hair short and cut to precision. Even their eyes were different. Sasha's almond-shaped dark eyes looked like raw coal, Tracy's big expressive eyes contained flecks of hazel. Sasha was only a few years older than my daughter. Tracy was only a few years younger than me.

I followed Sasha across the lawn. Her short dress blew in the breeze and hugged her body. She ran into my arms, making me feel welcomed and wanted and wonderful. Her full breasts peeked through the low cut neckline.

"Hey." She planted a kiss on my lips, darting her tongue in my mouth. "I love the car. It's like mine."

"I told you, after I paid for yours, I was getting one too." I ran my finger along a vein in her neck.

"Now we have a matching pair." She squealed. Her eyes sparkled. "It's even the same color. I don't believe you did that." She giggled.

"Yep. Told you."

"You did. You're a man of your word." She kissed me on the cheek and whispered. "I missed you." The way she pressed against me wiped away the worry of lay-offs, Tracy and the limited time we had left.

My guilt vanished as my body heated up.

"I still don't believe you bought a car." She shook her head in disbelief.

"I wanted to surprise you."

She peeked inside the driver-side window. "How was the graduation?" She sounded nonchalant.

"Nice until we had to go out to dinner with Tracy's loud-mouth friends."

"Ursula and what's her name?" she asked.

"Carla."

"Did Carla bring her hot Spanish husband?" Sasha shielded her eyes from the sun with her hand.

"She never leaves home without him."

"How are Crystal and Max? I guess they're excited about the wedding."

I took her hand and held her still. "Everything was fine, sweetheart. But you know I don't want to talk about my weekend."

"Forget I said anything." She laced her fingers through mine and led me inside. The house was small enough to feel like home, and far enough across town that being discovered wasn't a worry.

I was going to miss this place, where I could put my feet on the coffee table in the living room and no matter what, Sasha thought I was perfect.

"You said you had something to tell me." She gazed up at me. Her eyes blazed with excitement as if all news was good news. Sasha had a vulnerability that was never evident in Tracy. With her parents dead and no relatives on the east coast, Sasha looked at me like I was her super-hero. If Tracy could make me feel so vibrant, I would be more content at home.

"Not now. We can talk about that later. What did you want to tell me?"

She reached under my shirt, pressing her warm hands against my ribs. "Later. I've missed you so much. It seems like you haven't been here in weeks." She pushed up on her toes and kissed me. Slow at first, but the intensity increased when I responded.

I pinned her against the wall and kissed the small of her neck. She smelled like fresh spring flowers. Her flesh was soft and yielding. I wrapped her slender legs around my waist, and unzipped her dress. She threw her head back when I kissed her collarbone. I pulled her dress over her head; she wasn't wearing anything underneath.

"You were expecting me?"

"Always," she whispered.

My breathing came fast and hot, my heart pounded in my chest. She made me feel twenty years younger and I wanted to be inside her.

I held her up against the wall and found her breast with my tongue. Her nipples hardened when I drew on them. She made a small gurgling sound as I slipped my fingers inside her, stroking her moist center, gently until her breathing matched mine. She tightened her arms around my neck and panted my name.

When she went limp in my arms, I released her legs, but held her for a moment until she could stand on her own. I slipped my tongue into her mouth. The sweet taste slowed me down. Then she fumbled with my belt until she unbuckled it. In the dim hall, she shoved my khakis to my knees. I stepped out of my pants and boxers at the same time and she grabbed my stiff penis with both hands.

"You are gorgeous," I whispered with my hand tangled in her hair. She held my gaze, her eyes intense and penetrating. I picked her up and carried her into the bedroom we shared. On the bed, I kissed her stomach in several places, savoring her smell and the way she felt. She pulled my shirt over my head, then rolled from under me and kissed my neck, my chest, and my abdomen. She took my penis in her mouth, moving up and down with a practiced slowness she'd perfected.

Nothing else mattered.

Nothing else was important.

Nothing could tear me away from that moment of pure bliss. Not even the threat of Tracy finding out.

"My God," I moaned when she released me and pushed her tongue in my navel. I wanted to be inside of her so badly I ached. I pulled her up into my arms and straddled her.

"Well?" she asked in a low whisper that was barely audible, her earnest eyes boring into me.

"What, Sasha? I want you. Now."

"Wait. You know what I'm asking." She stopped me before I could enter her. "How long?"

"I kept my promise. I didn't sleep with her. I haven't slept with her in weeks." I said as I slipped inside her. We moved together, slow and in unison at first. Her warm core tightened around me and a flash of light popped behind my eyelids. I wanted to stay inside her the rest of the day, but she bucked her hips and wrapped her legs around my waist, drawing me in deeper. Each thrust grew harder until I exploded.

Afterward, I sprawled limp on the bed, unable and unwilling to move. Sasha rested her head on my chest and made small circles along my arm with her index finger.

My mother's disapproving snarl flashed in my mind as I luxuriated in the aftermath of our lovemaking. I smirked at her disfavor for, at the moment it couldn't touch me. Nothing could. This was all mine.

My brothers and I had rebelled in some way or another against the strict female household we grew up in. My oldest brother, Allen, never held down a full-time job for longer than a few years, opting instead to borrow money from family members and mooch off girlfriends. My younger brother, Robert, worked so hard he never had any time for a private life. He'd sacrificed two wives and four children for the seventy-hour work week that fed his insatiable need to be fruitful and make money. And I refused to keep my dick in my pants. We were a sorry lot of brothers.

I held Sasha tighter. The moment I told her I was ending our affair she might cry and lash out and act like all the others. Not because I was foolish enough to think she loved me. She wanted me, and the life style I could provide.

I appeased her by pulling out my checkbook and writing out a few figures. Giving her more time required some wrangling and I was running out of excuses to offer Tracy.

"Why are you so quiet? What are you thinking about?" she asked.

This was my opportunity to tell her. Tracy was asking too many questions and my absences were becoming too frequent. Sasha was like a drug. I couldn't get enough of her. I was being selfish. Sasha deserved better, and so did Tracy. The thought of losing Tracy was more painful than saying goodbye to Sasha. Sasha was like a trip to an amusement park, for a while the wild rides were fun, but I couldn't do it forever. Tracy was home, familiar, stable, and reliable. The kind of girl you took home to Mom.

Instead of telling Sasha the truth, I swallowed my speech. I'd tell her later. "Absolutely nothing. I'm fine."

She gave me a long look. "Okay. Then let me give you something to think about."

She mounted me, grinding her hips into me. Her breasts taunted me to touch them. No matter how hard I tugged, she never complained. Sasha had no inhibitions, which gave me the freedom to live out every sexual fantasy I ever had.

And I did.

I lifted her up and pulled her down onto my erection. "Baby you feel so good."

Instead of responding, she moaned, and then captured my mouth. I held her hips and together we rocked the bed until I couldn't hold back.

Chapter Seven – Walter

I wanted to stay in the bed for the rest of the day, making love to Sasha again and again. Instead, she sat up, kissed me hard on the lips, and walked out of the room. I rolled into her empty place and buried my head in the scent she left behind. This life style had many up sides. Very little was required of me.

When I heard Sasha preparing dinner in the kitchen, I pulled myself out of bed, slipped on my pants, and headed downstairs. No matter how much I wanted to pretend differently, this was a fantasy that had to end. We had done all the things lovers do, experienced the highs, the giddiness of exploring each other, whispering together in the night. Now it was time to cash in.

She was too young.

And I was too old.

In the kitchen, Sasha's back was to me. She pushed spinach around a sauté pan.

I stood behind her and kissed her neck. The loneliness facing me in the coming weeks was already riding my shoulders. But the familiarity of being with Tracy was comforting, like slipping on a pair of well-worn slippers.

"Stop it before you start something." She pushed my hand away.

"Nothing I can't finish, that's for sure."

"Well, at least let's eat first." She stepped around me and spooned the spinach in a bowl.

"What smells so good?"

"I cooked your favorites, grilled sea bass with mango and apple salsa, sautéed spinach, and garlic herb crispy potato pancakes. If the bookstore ever goes under, I'm going to open an upscale restaurant."

"I'll be your busboy." I grabbed her butt.

"Don't tempt me, Walter. If it would guarantee me more of your time, I'd set up shop tomorrow."

"I spend as much time with you as I possibly can." I leaned over and kissed her to stem this flow of conversation.

After dinner, I sat at the table, too full to clear the dishes or to move. The aroma of grilled food hung in the air around us. She ran her hand along my arms without saying a word. Her full lips pursed.

"What?" I asked. I knew she was poised to say something and fishing for the words. "You had something to tell me, so now is the time."

"It's almost nine." She shrugged her shoulders. "Since you haven't talked about going…does that mean you're staying tonight?"

The soft glow from the chandelier illuminated her face. I curled my fingers around her hand and kissed her palm.

"Is that what you wanted to ask me?"

"Well—"

"What is it, Sasha?" I knew when something was on her mind because her bottom lip twitched. "I don't want to spend the rest of the night trying to draw the details out of you. Tell me what you need, money? Something for the bookstore? I'm staying the night, so there must be something else."

A smile spread across her face and immediately her eyes darkened, but she didn't release my gaze. She tightened her fingers around my hand.

"I'm pregnant." She sounded like she didn't want to say the words, as if they left a bitter taste in her mouth.

Her comment didn't register immediately. It washed over me so slowly I didn't see it coming. Like a head-on collision. I was too numb, too helpless, too stupid, to get out of the way.

My chest constricted. I managed to keep my mouth closed while I struggled to breathe. For one agonizing, torturous moment, we sat in silence while her words clubbed me over the head. My clumsy silence emphasized the awkward moment.

I wanted to push away from the table and rant, but her pleading eyes nailed me to the chair.

She expected me to be gallant, sure with my response. I couldn't do either. I was inches away from her, but it felt like miles. How did I let this happen?

I groped for something to say.

The right reply.

My chest ignited with a bolt of pain that ran up my arms, across my shoulder and settled in the base of my neck.

This couldn't be happening.

Not now, when I was inches from getting out.

"Whew, I-I, huh. I wasn't expecting that." I managed to say, hoping she couldn't see my distress. "Aren't you on the pill?"

"I am. But remember a few months ago, when I had to take antibiotics to clear up my sinus infection. You wouldn't wear a condom. The medicine could've lessened the effectiveness of the pill." She shrugged.

"It was only once. You couldn't have—"

"What does that mean?" There was anger in her voice, an unspoken accusation.

"I don't know. I wasn't thinking..."

"I can read your face and see what you're thinking." She smacked her hand on the table. "I thought you would be happy. You've said your marriage was dull and your wife didn't understand you. How many times have you said you wanted to leave?"

"I…I…said it, but we've been married for a lot of years. You can't pack up a twenty-some year marriage in a paper bag and walk out."

Sasha pushed back from the table with such force the chair fell over. "Walter…I am not some jump off. I thought we were in a relationship with a future. You made me believe it was only a matter of time before you divorced you wife."

"I never said I was divorcing Tracy." I stood up. Heat gathered under my collar. Life had a way of always returning to the same place. "If you misunderstood my intentions, I'm sorry."

"Oh, you're sorry. Well that makes me feel so much better." The level of sarcasm was new for her. "Now what should I do?"

"You have options, Sasha. This isn't the end of the world."

Her mouth contorted into a sneer, daring me to develop the rest of my sentence.

"Okay, look. We're both a little off right now. Maybe we need to take a moment before we say things we can't take back."

"Before *you* say something else reprehensible."

The numbness of her news oozed over me like warm slime. I needed to be chivalrous. I knew what she expected me to say, how she expected me to act, and how she expected this whole ordeal to end. She wanted me to protect her, say everything would be fine, but the thought of a baby pushed me toward a full-scale nightmare.

Our idyllic relationship swirled down the drain. A child, even with an undemanding woman, turned our charming lifestyle into a hellish inferno that resembled all the other mundane relationships swirling around me, and threatened to suck the life out of me.

Long after the right moment had passed for me to provide the emotional support she needed, I stood up and walked up behind her as she placed dishes in the dishwasher. I placed my hands on her stiff shoulders and kissed her neck.

"I'm sorry." The words sounded weak, spoken like a man given a life sentence.

With tears in her eyes, she turned and kissed me. "What now?" She placed her hand on my cheek.

"I can't do anything until after Crystal's wedding. You know that."

She nodded and pulled away to stand in the middle of the kitchen. With her hands at her sides, her petite frame ramrod straight, she looked so young. She took a deep breath and I was afraid of what her next comment would be. We've had this conversation before.

"You'll tell Tracy you're leaving her? Because I'm already three months and I'll start showing soon." She grinned as she ran her hand over her flat stomach. "I don't feel ashamed that I'm carrying your baby."

Of course she didn't. She had nothing to lose. Life was a yellow-brick-road for her, all rosy and cheerful. I contemplated asking to see the pregnancy test, but I'd already made a mess of things. There would be time.

My shoulders slumped. I hoped she didn't notice the change in my posture.

I couldn't leave Tracy.

"I'll tell her right after the wedding." I made the promise even though I had no intentions of keeping it. That's what Sasha needed to hear. I had six months to figure out something.

And I would.

It wouldn't be simple or easy, but I would have promised her anything to move past the moment.

My phone rang and I looked at the number. My whole Sunday had turned to shit. "Hello Mom," I said without enthusiasm.

"Boy, wasn't Crystal's graduation this weekend? You didn't call me. You know I wanted to be there," my mother spewed into the phone like a rat chewing on my ear.

"Mom, you know you're not up to driving the distance. We talked about it."

"You could've picked me up. Any decent son would have. Now what am I supposed to do? I missed it. If I leave it up to you, I might miss the wedding too. You are a disappointment to me, Walter."

"Mom, I'm busy. I don't have time for this." If I let her get wound up I'd be listening to her all night. I needed a week away from reality.

"What do you need, Mom? You only call and complain when you want something." Everybody wanted something, picking me clean like buzzards on a bone.

"Don't talk to me like that, boy." Her voice held a firm tone that no longer controlled me.

"If you need something you better tell me now because I've got to go."

"I need two thousand dollars." Her words came out in a whoosh, as if hurrying through an unpleasant moment.

"I'll put money in your account tomorrow. Now I've got to go." My mother's call completed my day from hell.

"You never have time for me. You're so much like your brothers. Let me speak to Tracy."

"I'm not home right now, I'll have Tracy call you later. We'll make sure you get up here for

the wedding." I looked at Sasha, but couldn't read
her expression.

"Yeah, okay. I hope you keep your word."

I ended the call and rubbed my chin. Sasha
returned to loading the dishwasher. She chatted
about the pregnancy and how she planned to turn
the small bedroom into a nursery. I handed the
soiled dishes to her, but my thoughts weren't on
another baby.

"What will you tell Tracy?"

"I have no idea. I'll think of something."

"I don't mean about the baby, I'm talking
about tonight. You can't say you're working on a
Sunday night."

"Don't worry about it. I'll think of
something."

I turned away from her and massaged my
chest. It felt like my heart was being squeezed in
my mother's fist.

Chapter Eight - Tracy

Walter slinked out of bed, and later I heard the garage door close. I pretended to sleep because I knew he relished quiet mornings. And if silence would improve his mood, then I could be still for a few moments.

I'd done it before. I was good at placating him. He never seemed to know what I needed.

He had no idea how good I was at hiding my feelings. He probably thought I was happy in our marriage, too. I wasn't. But I could wait.

I scooted to the middle of the bed and stretched. I fished the remote from between the sheets and turned on the television. It felt sinful to watch *The Today Show* in peace. Usually I hurried out of bed to get to church, but after the late night, I needed the rest.

Thanks to the martinis, and more martinis, and the bottle of wine before bed, the sting of Walter's rejection wasn't as humiliating as usual. I slipped my index finger between my legs and stroked my moist center. My body craved release.

The phone rang and like a child caught stealing cookies, I snatched my hand above the sheet.

"Are we still on for lunch today?" Ursula's cheerful voice piped over the line.

"I hope so. I want to get out of the house."

"Just checking. Your mood last night was funky. I didn't know if you still wanted to get together."

"I guess I didn't do a good job of hiding my feelings, huh? Do you think Crystal knew it, too?"

"Not a chance. Don't worry about her. But the rest of us could tell something was wrong. Not only were you quiet but, you looked sad; like you lost your best friend. And you know I would never leave you."

"Ha. Ha," I said. "Will Carla be able to make it?" I turned off the television.

"I don't know. She's in her Sunday morning spinning class. I'll try her later. If you don't hear from me, then that means we're on."

"Same place as always?"

"Yes." She paused for a moment. "Were you and Walter getting busy?"

"I was, but not with him." My tone turned serious.

"Then don't let me disturb you. Go ahead and take care of yourself."

I hung up and climbed out of bed. My desire had faded.

Before going into the bathroom, I stood in the master alcove overlooking the garden. With my head pressed against the cool windowpane, I contemplated going to the country club and spending time with Walter. We used to golf together every weekend, but that was years ago. All the good stuff seemed so long ago.

I glimpsed my suitcases nestled in the corner of my closet. Packing was the first step, leaving was the second, and the hardest. I rubbed the rough fabric on the largest bag.

Walking away was something other people did, not me.

I closed the closet door and entered the bathroom.

The warm water from the shower pelted my shoulders, loosening the tightness. It didn't feel as good as what I'd planned for myself in bed, but it had to do for now.

Perhaps I could talk Walter into finishing what he'd started at the bar. We had been there before, stuck in a troubled place with no intimacy. He always snapped out of it. But this was different. This spell was rough to ignore. I felt like he wanted to be somewhere else, with someone else, doing something else.

I dried off and caught a glimpse of my body in the wide bathroom mirror. I froze at my image. My hips and thighs looked huge. I pivoted on my toes and looked over my shoulder at my backside. This view snarled at me. For ten minutes, I looked at my body from different angles. I sucked my stomach in, making it concave. I wrapped the towel over my breasts before turning away from the mirror.

I stepped on the scale and waited for the chime to tell me my weight was visible. After a deep breath I looked down, one hundred fifty three pounds, up two pounds from yesterday.

It had to be the alcohol and the excess salt from dinner, and the loaf of bread, and the gummy bears, and the fear living in my stomach.

My heady feeling vanished as depression showed up. My skin couldn't possibly stretch another inch.

I stepped off the scale, waited until the numbers cleared, then carefully positioned my feet back on the glass plate again. Making sure to place them in just the right places. Again, one hundred fifty-three pounds.

I plopped into the vanity chair, combed my short hair and applied makeup. After sorting through my closet, I found the Eileen Fisher pants that did an excellent job of hiding my pudginess. The slacks hung loose on my round butt, and my top fell over my hips. On a good day, I could have passed for pretty. Too bad I didn't have enough good days.

In the bedroom, I reached for the phone and did what I always do whenever I'm bummed. I called my mother.

"Hi, Sweetie. What's the matter?" Mom asked.

"I'm fine."

"You don't sound fine. What's wrong? Is it Walter? What did he do this time?"

"Why do you think Walter did something?"

"I'm smart enough to know something was going on between you two yesterday. And last week, he left us sitting in the restaurant without a call."

"I told you he had to work, Mom."

"He couldn't call and let us know?" Her voice held the same accusatory tone it held when I told her I was pregnant. "We waited almost an hour for him. I don't know how you put up with it."

"We're fine, Mom," I hoped she didn't hear my desperation.

"It don't look fine to me."

"He's under a lot of pressure at work. Anyway, you wanted to talk to me about Dad?"

"Well." She hesitated. "He hasn't been feeling good lately. I'm worried."

"What's wrong? Is he sick?" I sat on the bed to absorb the information. "What's he complaining about?" Her tone made me worry.

"You know your father doesn't complain. But he sleeps all the time, and during our morning walks, he sits on the bench and waits for me to make the circle around the track. He sweats a lot too, even when it's not hot."

"What does the doctor say?"

"That's just it, he won't go to the doctor. So, I want you to talk to him. He might listen to you."

"Mom, have you tried to talk to him?"

"I've talked 'til I'm blue in the face. He thinks I'm nagging."

"Will he listen to me? You know how Dad gets when you try to make him do something he doesn't want to do."

"Well, give it a try. Maybe if you volunteer to go with him. Maybe if Walter talked to him, you know, man to man. If he's not too busy." She sighed as if coming up with ideas drained her energy. "I don't know, but try something."

"Let's not get Walter involved, yet. Let me try. Should I talk to him now?"

"No, I don't want him to know I asked you to do this."

"I'll come by one night this week." I paused. "Or should I come today?"

"Not today, we're going out later. During the week is better." Her mood grew lighter. "Are you getting excited about the wedding?"

"Not yet. There's so much to do. I think we've taken care of everything, so I don't expect any surprises."

"Honey, life always gives you surprises."
Her comment struck me the way she knew it would.

After hanging up, I went downstairs and peeked in Walter's office for a note. Papers littered his desk. I sat in his soft leather chair and glanced at his neat handwriting scribbled on some of the pages. He spent so much time in here it smelled like his cologne.

Curiosity pushed me to open the top desk drawer and shuffle through the contents. I didn't know what I expected to find but if I found something of significance, I'd know.

The second drawer was full of pens and ink refills, all shapes and sizes. The bottom drawer contained junk; keys, scraps of paper with phone numbers, and several old wireless phone statements. Why would he save old phone bills? I leafed through the statements; one phone number showed up repeatedly each day. Some sales rep must have been causing Walter trouble.

I lost interest and shut the drawers. I tried to leave everything the way I found it, and padded into the kitchen. Snooping in his office wasn't one of my normal activities. He guarded his privacy like a centurion. But my mother's comment about surprises rattled me. Walter had had affairs before. I didn't want another surprise like that, ever.

I counted the number of secrets I kept from him. How much I weighed, but that didn't matter. Half the women I knew kept their weight a secret.

The packed bags in my closet were ready as soon as I got the courage.

And Marco.

Walter had no idea how many times I daydreamed about that tall, handsome, hunk. Walter probably thought I was incapable of thinking about anyone but him. He was my first real boyfriend and my only lover. The guy who stood me up for my high school prom didn't count.

Marco was only a fantasy. I wouldn't cheat. Just thinking about making love to Marco made me feel guilty. I would never do that to Walter, no matter how unhappy I was. I could imagine the shame in my father's eye if he found out his only child not only got pregnant out of wedlock, but was an adulteress, too.

I dialed Walter's cell phone. It kicked to voice mail without ringing. "Hey, I'm trying to catch up with you. I'm going to lunch with the girls this afternoon. See you this evening."

Next I tried his office phone. It went immediately to the company recorder.

I pulled a box of cereal from the pantry. Time to drop the two new pounds before they set up permanent residence on my hips. The box pictured a beautiful bowl of flakes loaded with blueberries.

My boring bowl barely had enough milk to cover the dull flakes. The crunch filled my ears, but did nothing to satisfy my stomach.

I grabbed my keys and headed out of the house. I needed to run some errands before meeting Carla and Ursula.

By the time I browsed Macy's shoe department and picked up my prescription to control my funky moods, it was almost one o'clock. Ursula and Carla were already seated by the window overlooking the Brandywine River when I walked in. I zigzagged my way to their table.

"*Ciao*, Tracy." I recognized the sultry voice even before I turned around to see Marco seated in the corner. His thick curly hair was the first thing I noticed about him. In my dreams, I was always running my fingers through his mane while he planted warm, wet kisses on my neck.

He broke into a broad smile. "*Buon pomeriggio. Come stai?*"

"I'm fine, Marco. How are you?" I stumbled over my feet as I made my way to his table. His eyebrows almost met between his eyes in an attractive way. He obviously lifted weights because his muscles bulged through his shirtsleeves and his waist narrowed above his hips.

He stood as I approached his table. If he'd stop flirting with me maybe I'd stop having wet dreams about him. I figured he was doing it for fun.

My intentions were a lot more sinister. He reached for my hands and kissed each one. His Italian charm made my insides flutter.

"Are you lunching alone?" He looked down at his table. "You can join me."

Ditching Carla and Ursula ran through my mind, but I knew better than to cross that line. As much as I'd love to have a long leisurely romp in bed with him, running from my problems wouldn't solve them.

"I'm meeting some friends. You know Ursula." I pointed to her across the room.

Disappointment slipped into his eyes. "You always have an excuse. I'm beginning to think you're avoiding me. Maybe some other time."

"For sure." My knees trembled. If he had any idea how many erotic dreams I had about him, he'd blush. "Maybe we can have lunch one day next week." The words tumbled from my mouth before I could censor them. I hadn't meant to say that.

"For sure." He held my gaze for what seemed like forever.

I walked across the room trying to hold my stomach in and hoping my rear end would turn him on a little.

"Well, someone seems to be in a better mood than yesterday." Ursula smirked.

"Yep, my mood is better now." I sat and reached for my napkin.

Ursula handed it to me before I could pick it up. "You need to wipe that drool off your lip." She pretended to dab my chin.

I snatched the napkin away and glanced over my shoulder to make sure Marco wasn't watching. He looked up and winked. My heart stumbled and for several seconds I felt like I was back in high school enjoying my first crush.

"You might as well go ahead and jump his bones, and get it out of your system." Carla's tone held a hint of I-dare-you, which mimicked the way she lived her life.

"If I wasn't married..." I shook the thought away. "I'm a married woman and I don't cheat. Besides he's… You know, I'm only into black guys."

"He's Italian, and you know lusting after him is just as bad as actually doing the deed. When you get to heaven you won't get any brownie points for only dreaming of making love to him." Carla sat back, looking satisfied with having planted the warning.

"Everyone is entitled to their fantasy. Marco's mine," I said.

"Mine too," Ursula chimed in.

"If Javier ever acts up, I'm getting on that boat, too." Carla glanced in his direction and used her napkin as a fan. "Anyway, how are you and Walter doing? Any better?"

"Well…" I didn't know where to begin. "Today has been a good day so far." It wasn't until I spoke those words that I realized I hadn't talked with my husband since last night. "I found a cute pair of kitten heels at Macy's, so I'm happy. Sorry I'm late."

"Don't worry about it. We haven't been here long and we're still waiting on our drinks," Carla said. "Let's enjoy lunch because I've got some news to share with you guys."

"What?" Ursula and I said in unison.

Carla's face lit up. She clapped her hands and sat on the edge of her seat. "Well…" She looked from Ursula back to me. "Javier and I are going to start a family. I want to have a baby." She almost sang the words. Her eyes bore the raw hunger of longing.

"Get outta here. You want a baby? You and Javier want a child?" I asked.

"Ah, I guess it was only a matter of time," Ursula said. "But what took you guys so long to decide? You're at the end of your baby-making years."

Carla hunched her shoulders. "I know, but we both really want a child."

"Wow." I reached for her hand and squeezed it.

"I know! It's unbelievable, isn't it? But we've been talking about it for a while and now it seems right. Maybe we'll have two."

"You're willing to stretch your tight stomach out of shape?" Ursula asked.

"I'm not worried about my body. I'll get back in shape." She ran her manicured tips through her long hair. "I'm so excited." She bounced in her seat like she couldn't sit still.

"Good for you." I patted her hand again then released it.

"I'll believe it when I see your stomach sticking out like a balloon," Ursula replied.

"We've already been trying for a few months. I'm surprised it hasn't happened yet."

"The way you and Javier go at it, there will be lots of little Valdezes running around in no time at all." I wanted to sound reassuring, but my voice came out too cheerful, like I was trying to convince her the world was flat and people didn't fall off the edge and get hurt.

The server returned with their drinks and took my drink order. From the corner of my eye I saw Marco eyeing me. I dropped my head before either of my friends noticed.

"I see you flirting with Marco," Ursula's eyes danced with mischief.

"Oh, don't start, Ursula. He was saying hello."

"Well, it sure was a friendly hello."

Every time Ursula saw me talking with Marco, she swore we were getting ready to have sex.

"I've told you, he likes you. Every time he looks at you, it's like he's imagining you with your clothes off."

"You're being silly. I'm married and he's separated. We're just friends." I glanced across the room and watched him take a bite of his burger.

"Marco's divorce is final. I think he may be seeing someone." Ursula sang the words, baiting me to take the hook.

I felt my cheeks flush. "Divorced doesn't mean he's ready to start dating."

The server set my drink on the table. "Are you ladies ready to place your orders?" she asked with her pencil poised over her pad.

"Give us a few minutes, please." I faced Ursula. "How do you know he's seeing someone?"

"Oh…" Ursula smirked. "*Now* you're interested. I keep up with the office chatter. If you could get away from your numbers long enough, you would know, too."

"Ursula, stop giving her such a hard time." Carla nudged Ursula on the arm. "You know Tracy is so faithful, so committed to her marriage, she can't even think another man might be interested in her," Carla teased. They both snickered.

When the waitress returned we all ordered salads.

"Have you ever flirted, Tracy?" Ursula asked.

"Okay you two, stop picking on me. I've flirted," I said. "But it's been a long time. I think…yes, I'm sure I've flirted."

"Don't you and Walter flirt?" Carla continued before I could answer. "Girl, Javier and I flirt all the time. Last week he called me at work, and while I viewed some proofs, we had phone sex."

Ursula and I burst into laughter.

"I'm not surprised," Ursula said. "You practically had an orgasm at the restaurant last night."

"Carla, I love your spontaneity. Walter would never do something like that. I can hardly remember the last time I had sex." I sipped my diet soda.

"Didn't you have an orgasm this morning?" Ursula grinned.

"No, I didn't. I was interrupted. Besides, masturbating doesn't count," I shot back at her. "Walter is so busy with work he comes home exhausted. And even if he weren't exhausted, there's no emotion in his touch."

"That's pitiful." Ursula shook her head.

Carla took over. "Take control. You gotta step it up. Set the mood." Her hands were animated. "I've never met a man so exhausted he'd rather sleep when you're in his face. Honey, all you have to do is strut buck-naked in front of him and, he'll forget about work or whatever is on his mind. Don't you own something sexy and frilly? Put it on and let it all hang out." Carla shimmied in her chair to demonstrate.

"Carla, everybody is not as aggressive as you," said Ursula.

"I'm not aggressive. I just know how to get what I want."

"Whew, girl you're too much for me." I sat back in my chair.

"Now it's time to pick on you, Miss Ursula." Carla turned to Ursula. "Are you going to tell us more about the mystery man you're seeing? The one you're keeping a secret? We don't even know his name."

"I'm not ready to talk about him yet. When it's right, I'll tell you guys. You know I tell you both everything!" Ursula blushed.

"Is he married?" Carla asked with her index finger pointed at Ursula. "You know how we feel about messing around with married men."

"No, he's not married. I'm not one of those women."

"I don't understand the secrecy," said Carla. "Is something wrong with him? Does he walk with a limp or have a third eye or something?"

"Very funny. No it's just…" She hesitated and hunched her shoulders. "The relationship is still new. When I know for sure it's going somewhere, I'll tell you all about him."

"That's never stopped you before," I said. "You usually parade your men past us like flags. A few months ago it was Sam, a few months before that it was Barry, and before him it was—"

"Okay, I got it," Ursula laughed. "But no matter how much you tease me, I'm not telling. Yet."

"And remember you were halfway down the aisle a few years ago with that guy… What was his name?" Carla looked at me for help.

"Oh, how can we forget the Denzel lookalike? What was his name?" I asked.

The server sat our meals in front of us, and for a moment we were quiet while we tasted our entrees.

"So what was going on between you and Walter at the graduation? Why were you so angry about the car?" Ursula shoved lettuce leaves into her mouth.

"It's not the car," I started. "I wish I knew what was going on. You know, every now and then Walter slips into one of those moods where he's quiet and distant. It takes a little prodding, but eventually he comes around. I'm waiting on him to come out of this latest mood."

They both looked at me and nodded.

"Why can't the man buy a car if he wants?" Ursula always took Walter's side.

"I don't mind if Walter buys a new car. But who goes out and buys a $70,000 car without mentioning it to his wife? He could have said, 'Oh honey, I'm thinking of buying a car today after work.'"

"She's got a point, Ursula."

"But it's not like a car is going to break your bank."

"When we were buying the house, I talked to Walter about every little change and upgrade, even the five hundred dollars for the security wiring. It's something we've always done. Now he's changing the rules mid-stream."

"I guess that's why I'm not in a permanent relationship. There are too many rules." Ursula put her fork down.

I shrugged, excused myself, and went to the ladies room. Maybe Ursula was right. Did we have too many rules? Inside the stall, I dialed Walter's BlackBerry. When the recorder came on, I punched out his office number. Then I called the country club and asked them to page Walter. I glanced at my watch, it was well after two now. If he played this morning, his game had to be over. Why hadn't he returned any of my calls? Before exiting the restroom I opened the prescription bottle tucked in my purse. At the sink I cupped water in my hands and swallowed a pill.

I walked to the table and tried to ignore the sour acid churning in my stomach. Ursula and Carla were whispering, probably about me. I know they thought I was weak and pathetic for putting up with so much stuff.

"You should try it," Carla said to Ursula.

I took my seat. "Try what?"

"I was telling Ursula about the spinning class I teach on Thursday evenings. I just put together a new jazz track, it's real nice."

"I should come too," I said. The numbers on the scale still stung. Instead of spending time trying to track down my husband, I could work on my wide hips and growing waist. "Will my hips get as slim as yours?"

"For sure they will. It's a good workout."

We paid the check and headed out. I glanced back to see if Marco was still there. He was gone. Now a woman with a young girl sat at the table. A vision of Crystal and me popped into my head. We used to go out for lunch after our hair appointments. That memory seemed so distant now it was hard to believe it belonged to me.

After hugging my friends in the parking lot, I pulled onto Main Street and found myself heading to the country club. Without planning, I crisscrossed through traffic until I pulled into the lush green grounds of the club. I drove up and down the neatly slanted rows of cars looking for his new Lexus. Even though I didn't see his car, I parked and went into the pro shop.

"Hi, what time is the Baptiste tee time? I hope I'm not late," I lied, and waited while he scrolled his computer screen to confirm Walter's appointment.

"Ma'am, his tee time was at eight this morning."

"Are you sure?" I feigned disappointment as I looked at my watch.

"Yes, I checked him in myself."

"Oh my goodness, my husband is going to be mad I missed it."

"Sorry, ma'am." I heard him respond, but I was already hurrying out of the clubhouse.

In the car, I dialed the house phone. Maybe he was sitting in the den watching television. After four rings, the recorder came on. I pulled out of the lot with every intention of going home and doing whatever I could to occupy my Sunday afternoon. Instead, I took the north interstate ramp to his offices. My stomach rebelled against my lunch, but I refused to turn back.

The white lines in the highway blurred. My fingers grew numb from gripping the steering wheel. I had no plan, but I wanted to find him.

Now.

Walter needed to find balance between his private life and his work life, to spend some time with me. We were supposed to work to live, not live to work. I wanted to cuddle in his arms like we used to do. I wished he looked at me with just a hint of lust like he did when we were in college and he convinced me to give him my virginity.

I pulled the car into a slot in the office garage, and walked across the street to his office building. Nodding to the security guard behind the desk, I signed my name in the visitor's log, and he handed me a pass that allowed me to go up to the ninth floor.

I rehearsed my speech as the elevator marked each floor with excruciating slowness. How to explain my surprise appearance? It wasn't often I went to Walter's office. Usually I came for a specific purpose, and even then he was always expecting me.

Before the elevator reached his floor, I reapplied my lipstick, and ran my hand over my pants to smooth out the large wrinkles. Maybe he would be so pleased to see me he would ravish me on the sofa in his office. After seeing Marco, I could use a tender touch to take the edge off.

The elevator doors opened onto the deserted floor. The offices were dark. Most of the overhead lighting was off. I expected some activity. I turned the corner and started down the hall. No light came from under his office door, but I continued. At his suite, I knocked and turned the knob.

The door was locked. His administrative assistant's desk was clean. I knocked again like an idiot, and tried the knob again. I needed solid confirmation that Walter wasn't behind the door. If he wasn't home, or at the country club, and he wasn't answering his phone he had to be here. He was always here.

My palms were sweating. Unsure what to do next, I stumbled back down the hall and pushed the elevator button for the lobby. After one last look down the corridor, I stepped into the waiting elevator.

I walked out of the building faster than I'd walked in. Outside, I almost ran to the car, gagging for air with each step. I put the windows down, hung my head through the opening and gulped. My head and heart thumped in unison.

I don't remember getting on the interstate or making any turns or stopping at any lights. I pulled into my driveway. My neighbor across the street played catch with his son. Next door, Ramsay placed lawn chairs into the trunk of his car. I hit the remote to open our garage door. I expected to see

Walter's car parked on his side of the garage. It wasn't. I pulled into the garage and sat for several seconds. I fingered the hem of my top before turning off the car.

Once inside I headed straight for the refrigerator. Leftover chicken along with macaroni and cheese and spinach called me. Forget the diet.

I ate the meat cold.

I ate the macaroni and cheese cold.

I ate the spinach cold.

I ate without sitting down. Without tasting. Without feeling.

While I gorged, I tried not to succumb to the twinge growing in my belly like tumbleweed.

Leaving my dirty dishes sitting on the counter, I pulled the prescription bottle from my purse, and took another pill.

Relief needed to catch up to me. Fast.

I picked up the phone to call the police, but dropped it back in the cradle. I was being silly. Anxious. What would I say? It's dark and my middle-aged husband isn't home yet?

I made my way upstairs. I had a bottle of merlot tucked under my arm and balanced a huge slice of cake with my other hand. I sat in the bedroom window seat overlooking the curved driveway and the tree-lined street.

Sometime after midnight, the empty wine bottle fell to my feet.

Chapter Nine - Tracy

When the sun broke over the horizon, I unfurled my stiff legs. The hard window seat was as unforgiving as the thumping in my head.

I smacked my dry lips and tried to swallow the cotton feeling in my mouth. It was easier to remain seated than to get steamrolled by life.

The bedroom grew lighter with each passing minute, and I continued to sit. Pushing the negative thoughts away, but dread curled around my neck like death. Usually he phoned to check in with me. At the very least, he returned my calls.

I stood on unsteady limbs. My lower back refused to let me straighten up. I raised my hands above my head and reached for the ceiling. My wrinkled pants clung to my damp legs. Everything on my body ached and my insides churned with nausea. I ran to the toilet just in time to empty my stomach.

After washing my face and teeth, I picked up the phone on the nightstand. The dial tone screamed in my ear. Our phones were working. I dialed his cell. The voice mail directed me to leave a message. Another message.

I dialed his office.

The same result as yesterday.

Directly to cover.

The red glow of the digital clock read 6:45, too early for his assistant to be in the office.

I found the anti-anxiety meds in the bottom of my purse, and swallowed two so fast they stuck in my throat like a hunk of meat before moving down. I pulled off my clothes, leaving them in a heap on the floor, then climbed into the shower. The hot spray fell over my head, down my face and body. I leaned my head against the cold marble and it numbed my forehead. The salty taste of tears lingered on my tongue. This kick in the stomach should have pushed my plan into motion. Fear of failing, of disappointing my parents, of making a mistake, rooted me in place. My body locked up. I stood in the shower until the water ran cold.

I picked a simple black dress from my closet, it mirrored my mood. I snatched it from the hanger and grabbed a pair of black pumps from the shoe rack. Without looking in the mirror I ran my fingers through my short curly hair before grabbing my purse, and running out the door. Staying in the house another moment, waiting on the unknown, was worse than the rumble raging in my stomach. It was better to escape the sadness.

My head railed against me as I maneuvered through the traffic and congestion to arrive in front of my office building. I needed to calm the constant thumping on my temples, but suspicion bombarded me.

He wouldn't betray me again.

He couldn't.

He promised.

I made my way to my office without greeting anyone and avoiding eye contact, I plopped my purse on the desk and flopped into the chair.

The message light on my phone caught my attention. I snatched the headset off the receiver. My heart pounded against my rib cage. The supply chain manager had left a long message about a cost sensitivity analysis. The second message was from the unit supervisor asking a series of mundane questions that I didn't listen to. I deleted both messages and hung up the phone.

Nothing from Walter.

I dialed his office, again.

Still no answer. I'd try his administrative assistant when she arrived at nine. Then I intended to call the police.

If life always gave surprises, that meant Walter could be lying in a ditch on the side of a road instead of between the thighs of some willing woman. Neither would be a major surprise.

I picked up the phone and dialed Carla. Of my two closest friends, she was the one who always took the pragmatic approach.

"He didn't come home last night." My voice was a hoarse whisper, shielding my heart from the truth. "I can't find him."

"Tracy? Tracy, I can barely hear you."

I took a deep breath and swallowed to regain my composure. Hysteria clamped its tentacles around my throat. The minute I sat behind my desk I lost the last bit of my resolve to be tough. A chill ran along my spine. I couldn't stop shivering.

"Carla…" My voice broke as sobs filled my chest. For several seconds, she allowed me to cry uninterrupted.

"Tracy, try to calm down. Has he been in an accident?" Carla's voice was measured with calm. She could have been talking to a child.

"No, I don't think he's been in an accident!" I resented her ability to overlook the obvious—my world was falling apart. "If your man doesn't come home at night what do you think it means? Besides, the police would have knocked on my door if there had been an accident."

"You said he's been working a lot lately. Maybe he was at work."

An unrecognizable sound escaped from my mouth. "Carla, I went to his office. And to the golf course. He wasn't at either place."

"Did you call his cell phone?"

"Duh!" I didn't want to be mean, but I couldn't stop myself.

"Okay, okay..." she said, slowly.

"I called his office, I called his cell phone. I called every device possible. He didn't answer any of them." Saying the words aloud gave birth to my greatest fear and the trembling started again. I pushed away from my desk and faced the window. Down on the street, cars moved through the intersection as if the world weren't tilting incorrectly on its axis threatening to shake us all off into outer space.

"Where are you right now?"

"In my office." I bit my lip to suppress a wail.

"Stay there, I'm coming over."

"No. Don't."

"I'm on my way." She hung up the phone before I could protest more. My knees shook. I backed the chair away from the window.

The strength it took to wipe my nose was almost too much to muster. An image of Walter with another woman flashed before me. My stomach lurched. I held my head over the trashcan until my stomach stopped retching. Afterwards, I rested my forehead on the edge of the desk and closed my eyes. The cool feel of the oak felt good against my burning flesh.

My legs continued to shake. If the building caught fire, I couldn't run around waving my arms like fire victims on television. I would have sat and burned in the flames. The thought of death brought relief. No decisions required.

Ursula came into my office and closed the door. The alarm in her eyes let me know she already knew.

"I just got off the phone with Carla. Why didn't you call me, I'm right upstairs?" She walked around my desk and enclosed me in her arms with a small squeeze. "Ugh, you threw up." She moved away from the trashcan and me.

"Yeah." I kicked the pail under the desk and lifted my head.

Other than the wide-eyed panic on Ursula's face, she looked great. Always in control. The consummate professional. Her makeup was perfect, even her sculpted eyebrows looked like a work of art. Did life ever catch her by surprise?

I wasn't ready to see my marriage through her cold analytical eyes. It was easy for her to look down her nose at me for putting up with Walter's antics because she didn't have to prove anything to her parents. She didn't need to prove to the world that she'd married the love of her life and intended to live happily-ever-after.

"Why didn't you call me?" she asked again.

"I don't know," I mumbled.

"You look awful." She sat forward on the edge of the chair.

"You think so?" Anger edged my voice.

She ignored my tone. "Don't assume the worst. Wait until you talk to him."

"Humph. Yes."

"Do you think he's having an affair?" The words inched out of her mouth as if they were afraid.

"He's done it before. I'm trying to save our marriage and he could be out there right now screwing some bimbo."

"Ah, Tracy, that was years ago. You guys moved beyond that and put your marriage back on track."

"Ursula, Walter cheated on me when we were in college, too. Remember the pretty majorette with the big breasts?"

"Lacy. He cheated on you with Lacy? Are you sure? Why didn't you ever tell me?"

"He swore it was a mistake. He was horny. He told me he would never do it again. That he loved me. I believed him. I had to believe him. I was pregnant. Then he screwed his secretary and I still needed to believe he loved me."

"Have you asked if he's having an affair?"

"Yes." I swiped my nose on the back of my hand.

Ursula pulled a tissue from the box on my desk and handed it to me.

"We've had this discussion more than once. Whenever I bring it up, he makes me look stupid. He says I'm insecure because I'm an only child, or I'm acting like his mother, that's why his father ran off." I dabbed my eyes with the tissue. "He denies it. Every time." I stopped rambling and asked, "What man admits to having an affair unless you catch him with his dick in another woman?" I was almost yelling.

"Well, I guess you're right about that." She nodded "But, honey, this is your marriage. So don't jump to conclusions. It could be a whole lot of things that kept him out last night."

"Ursula, you've been with enough men to know when something is different. Just like when you and Sam broke up. You saw it coming months before the end." I paused for a moment. "I can tell. I can tell by the way he doesn't touch me. I can tell by the way he kisses me—all lips and no tongue. I can tell by the way we don't talk and the way we do talk. You know, sometimes I even wonder if I want to stay with him. Walter is a bastard and being married to him is *sooo* much work."

"Confront him!"

"He'll deny it again." My shoulders slumped under the pressure of suspicion and doubt.

"Then…" Her cell phone vibrated and she reached for my hand. "Come on." She stood. "Carla is outside."

I took a deep breath. It felt so much better to sit in my office with my head on the desk. I cold pretend it was recess or nap-time.

"Tracy, come on," Ursula urged when I hesitated.

I pulled my purse onto my shoulder and walked behind her. Ursula's hand felt cool against mine. She held on like she thought I might flee in the opposite direction. I snatched my hand out of her grip. What if my employees saw me being led away from the building?

The humidity hit me with a jolt as we crossed the parking lot. I squinted against the blinding sun. Ursula never slowed her pace.

"Where are we going?" I climbed in the back seat of Carla's bright red, two door sports car.

Carla punched the accelerator and the car jerked forward out of the lot. She turned the air conditioning on high while maneuvering the steering wheel. Neither of them responded to my question. Carla veered north on Route 141, towards town.

"Where are we going?" I asked again.

"To his office," Carla yelled over the seat. "We're going to find your husband. We'll start with his assistant."

Her idea sounded better than any I'd come up with. My brain was paralyzed, circling around the same thought. *If he's cheating what will I do?*

"Wait a minute, Carla," I leaned forward. "I dialed his office number before I called you. He isn't there, and even if he decided to show up now, I'm not so sure I want to confront him there. Whatever is going on, me yelling at him isn't going to change anything. Besides, how do we know he hasn't been kidnapped or in an accident?"

Ursula threw me an incredulous smile over her shoulder, then faced Carla. "That's not what we agreed to on the phone," Ursula urged. "You and I don't need to get in the middle. Tracy has got to handle this, it's her marriage."

"Yes, that's what I'm doing, I'm helping her. And I'll punch the bastard if she wants me to."

"I want to punch him too, but what good is that going to do?" Ursula shot back.

"No. No." I rubbed my temples. "No. I've got to handle this. Ursula's right, I shouldn't involve you two." I fell against the back seat. "God, my head is killing me."

We rode in silence for what seemed like hours. Every idea swarming in my head involved mayhem and murder. I needed to turn back.

"I know you guys want to help, but not like this." I laid my head against the headrest. "If I go in there and act like a fool, what would Crystal think? She adores her father. I can't expose her to this right now with her wedding only a few weeks away. Gossip travels faster than lightning."

"Crystal will be fine. She'll understand," Carla yelled over the seat.

"I can't go to his office again." I stared at a gray smudge on the ceiling of the car. "I don't want his co-workers looking at me like I'm some pitiful puppy. I can't…"

"Well, what do you want to do, Tracy?" Ursula faced me. "We'll do whatever you want."

I took a deep breath and expelled it slowly. Tears slipped down my cheeks unchecked. I needed to confront Walter, but I had to do it in my own way, my own time. "I want to curl up in my bed and pull the blanket over my head. I want to sleep like Rip Van Winkle until this is over."

"Honey, we're not your fairy godmothers with magic wands. You're not in kindergarten so it's not nap-time. You can't go running home to Mommy. What do you want to do instead?" Carla managed her get-with-the-program tone without taking her eyes off the road. She was going to make an excellent mother.

"Thanks a lot, Carla, you're so damn supportive." I used the same sarcastic tone she had used. "I don't know what I'm going to do yet. Pull into the nearest strip mall. Let's…let's just stop and get some coffee or something."

"Are you sure?" Carla asked. "Because coffee won't make you feel better or resolve this bullshit."

"Yeah. Pull over."

Carla parked in the open space in front of a coffee shop. We sat in silence for a moment while I wiped my face. They both turned in their seat, focusing on me, but there wasn't anything they could do.

"Okay, get out," I said when neither of them made the first move.

The cool air of the coffee shop felt good. By the time we sat with our paper cups, I was breathing normally instead of like someone on the last mile of a marathon. I fished in my purse for the familiar plastic prescription bottle. I swallowed a pill with a big gulp of hot coffee.

"What are you taking?" Ursula asked.

"Huh? Oh, it's just a vitamin."

Ursula reached across the table and stroked my hand. The compassion in her eyes almost started me crying again. I blinked the tears away. I should have called her first. She had been coming to my rescue for as long as I could remember. As an only child, I needed a lot of rescuing. I couldn't stand the loneliness. My parents tried hard to keep me entertained, but they adored each other so much, I often felt like I was imposing on their time together.

"What are you going to do?" Carla's words were measured and even, as if the longer it took her to say them the more time she gave me to think.

"I-I don't know." I was being evasive. But I didn't have the answers. I didn't want to examine the alternatives. Maybe I'd go home, collect my bags from the closet, empty out the bank accounts, and disappear in the night. That sounded like a fine idea, except for one thing. My daughter.

"Do you think Walter is losing interest in me because I've gained weight?" It hurt me to ask, but I wanted the truth.

Carla dropped her head and shook it from side to side. "Tracy, you're not fat. And even if you got as big as a double-wide trailer, that wouldn't give your husband license to treat you bad, or have an affair."

"Carla's absolutely right. You're not fat. Just because you're not pencil thin anymore doesn't mean you're fat. You've got curves, nice curves. Don't blame yourself for Walter's shortcomings."

"Walter is an ass and he's always been an ass. Sorry, honey, but you know I have to tell it to you straight," Carla said.

"Yeah, well…I packed my bags several months ago."

"You did what?" Ursula pulled her chair closer to the table.

"Guys, I've been thinking about leaving Walter after the wedding. I didn't want to upset Crystal before her big day. But I wasn't expecting him to do this—"

"I don't believe it." Carla crossed her arms. "Why didn't you tell us before? Why are you so upset if you're planning to leave him, anyway?"

"He's my husband, Carla. Ending our marriage is…is something I don't want to do. My bags might be packed, but it's painful. I've got a house, a daughter and our lives are so, so—"

"Yeah, whatever." Ursula waved her hand, dismissing my comment. "My momma, God rest her soul, used to say 'if you make yourself a doormat, don't cry when people walk on you.' Take a day and enjoy your pity party, but sooner or later you've got to look Walter in the eye and demand some answers. If he's not dead, then he

has a lot of explaining to do. And when you're
ready to walk out the door, I'll be there for you."

"I can remember when Walter used to call
seven and eight times a day. And he didn't want
anything. He just wanted to talk—to hear my
voice."

"First, find out why he didn't come home
last night. That's the question to ask. If you don't
like the answer, there's no need to fight. Wait
until he goes to sleep, then cook up some hot grits
and pour them on his dick. If you go Al Greene on
his ass, I'll bet he gets the message." Ursula
looked satisfied with her resolution.

Carla lowered her voice and continued,
"Tracy, let me tell you from experience, because I
don't want what happened to me to happen to
you. Make sure your shit is in order. Before you
do anything, make sure you've got plenty of
money. Make sure you know where the accounts
are and how much is in them. If you can get your
hands on any of his account information, do that
too. If things get funky between you two…" She
sat back and exhaled. "It can be real nasty and
that's not the time to have to ask him about joint
assets."

I nodded. She was trying to be helpful, but
implying my marriage was to the point of
distributing assets increased the pressure on my
head.

"You can't make somebody love you," Ursula said. "So why try?"

"See there's your problem, Ursula, sometimes you can." Carla sipped her coffee. "You need to have a man who's worth fighting for or you don't have nothin'. Javier wasn't sure he wanted to get married, but I told him he had to make a decision or he was going to stop dipping his stick in this honey."

Their lips moved at a rapid pace as they discussed relationships. I zoned, unsure if any of their theories applied to me. They were the sisters I never had, but their lives were very different from mine. Neither had a child who needed to be protected. I never wanted Crystal to feel less than significant because of something between Walter and me. I knew how much it hurt to feel like an interruption.

Carla's two-year marriage to Javier hadn't experienced enough trouble to fill a thimble, and Ursula never stayed with anyone long enough to matter. Walter and I had a different relationship.

"Carla, how's Javier?" I took the focus off me. The level look Carla gave Ursula signaled she knew I was shifting the topic, but they allowed me this grace.

Ursula jumped in. "Javier has sexed her up so much she's like a crazy woman."

"You're jealous." Carla sipped her coffee.

"That's the same thing Walter said about me."

Carla gave me a quizzical look.

"Forget it, we were arguing…" I didn't finish.

"I told you guys we want to have a baby, so when you get to my age, you have to try all the time. We practice a lot."

"At the rate you guys are going, you'll be pregnant any minute now." My voice was flat with unconcern. "With twins."

"I hope. I thought it would have happened by now, but girl…" Carla fumbled with her napkin without lifting her head. Sadness shadowed her eyes. "Hey guys, Javier and I are picking out baby names. How do you like Ava?"

A voice in my head screamed to run out of the café, to get back on the interstate and run without looking back. I adored routine. There was harmony in consistency and now my life was upside down. The unknown hung over my head like a hatchet. Focusing on my friends as their lives marched along, seemed impossible. It hurt more than it helped.

"Suppose it's a boy?" I heard Ursula ask.

"We're not sure about boys' names yet. Maybe junior."

"Javier Valdez Jr. I don't like it, it doesn't flow," Ursula said.

Carla nudged Ursula. "You need to stop. There is nothing wrong with Javier's name," Carla said.

"I'm joking." Ursula stared at me and sipped her coffee.

"If I don't get pregnant soon, Javier and I are going to see a doctor."

"Be patient. As soon as you stop trying, you'll get pregnant," I reassured her.

"We're here to help Tracy," Ursula said shifting the conversation back to me. "What can we do for you?"

"I wish I knew." They were so sure Walter was a heel, but I wanted to believe in him. Acknowledging the last twenty-two years were a mistake sliced at my heart. He had a few good qualities, even if I hadn't seen them lately. Like the way he stroked my back after a stressful day, or his willingness to sit through romantic comedies even though he hated going to the movies. Maybe this morning I had simply panicked from the stress of planning Crystal's wedding.

"What about you? What's happening between you and the mystery man?" Carla asked Ursula.

"Yeah." I put my elbows up on the table and supported my chin with my palms. "Are you ready to tell us about him yet? Are you ready to tell us his name—and why all the secrecy?"

Ursula smiled. "Well…I don't know. You asked me this yesterday. Are you going to ask me every time you see me?"

"Yes. So you might as well tell it," Carla chided. "You tell everything else."

Ursula glanced out the window before shifting her gaze between us. "It's somebody I work with." She fingered her napkin without looking up.

"I don't work with you two," Carla said. "So you're going to have to give me more clues."

I wondered whom Ursula could be seeing at work. But my thoughts shifted back to Walter. I wanted to call him again.

Ursula hesitated for a long moment. "It's Anthony Russell." She looked at me.

"Okay, who's Anthony Russell?" Carla asked.

I blinked at Ursula several times. Anthony Russell was her boss. The man had enough charisma to be president of the United States. He was charming and educated, but not Ursula's type. He was shorter than the average guy, his belly hung over his belt—but only a little—and he was bald.

"You're kidding, right?" I sputtered and couldn't close my mouth.

"Who is Anthony Russell?" Carla smacked the table.

"Ursula?" I touched her hand, forcing her to look up at me. I was too caught up in the implications of Ursula's admission to stop and address Carla's questions.

"I'm serious." Ursula tried to hide a blush, but her eyes went all dreamy before she looked down again.

I measured my words. "Ursula, this could cost him his job. You know the company policy."

"Tracy, we're not five years old. *We've* thought it through. For now, we're going slowly and keeping it a secret. That's why I haven't told either of you anything until now. And promise you won't tell a soul."

"Oh no. Damn, girl." Carla gave Ursula an admiring stare. "You're talking about your boss. Get out of here! I didn't think you had that kind of nerve. I'm shocked. Is he any good in bed?"

"Shut-up, Carla."

"Ooh wee, I can tell by the way you smirked you know the answer to my question." Carla had the look of a dog satisfied that someone else was in the pen with her. "It's good to know you aren't always Miss Priss, you can get down and dirty too."

"Don't worry, Tracy," Ursula said. "You know me. I'm only in a relationship for a moment before I move on. Next week there may be nothing to talk about." Her words weren't convincing.

I took a deep breath. My chest constricted. "Hey guys, can we go now?"

"We can check hospitals and police stations if you want." Carla pushed a napkin into her empty cup.

I shook my head. "If it was that bad, the police would have found me by now. Let's get out of here. The walls are closing in on me."

I convinced Carla to take me back to my car. She was adamant I should catch him cold in his office and question him. I couldn't explain it to them, but I wanted him to have time to think about his response.

To give me a plausible answer.

One that I could believe.

Back at the office building Ursula and I got out of the car, and watched Carla zoom off. My head raced, wanting to be somewhere without my body.

"Are you going to be okay?" Ursula placed her hand on my arm to steady me.

"Ursula, I don't know how I'm doing. Right now I fee…I feel. I don't know. Maybe hollow. Am I going to be okay?" I held out my hands. "One day I'm going to be fine, but it won't be today."

She put her arms around me and allowed me to put my head on her shoulder. I looked up at the two-story office building but couldn't drag myself back inside. My legs were heavy. I couldn't concentrate on numbers or spreadsheets. Tears stung my eyes.

She released me.

"I'm going home and throwing something else into my suitcase."

"That a girl. Want me to drive you?"

"No. Go back to work. If I need you, I'll call you."

"Promise?"

I nodded.

Before walking away she gave me a long look. I sat in my car and watched Ursula enter the building. The car was hot. I turned it on, put the windows down, and let the air conditioning run for a moment. When the temperature in the car became bearable, I pulled my cell phone from my purse and dialed Walter's office.

His administrative assistant answered on the second ring.

"Hi Beverly. Is Walter there?"

"He's in a meeting, Tracy. I don't expect him back for some time, maybe later this afternoon. Can I give him a message?" I exhaled a deep breath.

He was fine.

He was at work.

He wasn't dead.

I heard her other line ringing as she shuffled papers.

Some part of me expected her to say she hadn't seen him today. But he was in the office. I almost began to probe about his calendar, but decided not to involve her.

"Just let him know I called." Before hanging up I said, "Hey Beverly, ask him to call me right away. Tell him to call me at home."

"Sure will, Tracy." She hung up.

I pulled out of the parking lot. The thought of waiting for him to come home was more depressing than the conversation we needed to have.

The rhythm of the tires on the road beat out a repetitive tune that lulled me into a trance. My heart thumped along with the sound. My eyelids grew heavy. I blinked several times to keep them open.

The car drifted into the right lane, almost side-swiping a large SUV. The driver made an angry gesture at me before pulling onto the shoulder to pass. I panicked and swerved back into my lane. My hands shook and my palms grew sweaty on the slick steering wheel.

The phone was ringing when I walked in the door. My hands were still shaking. I recognized Walter's number and picked it up.

"Are you coming straight home tonight?" I asked.

"Tray, you've been blowing up my phone to ask me when I'm coming home. Have you lost your mind? I'll be home at the regular time. Why?"

"You ungrateful son-of-a-bitch, I've been worried sick about you, and that's how you're going to respond to me?"

"I'm sorry," he said, but it lacked conviction.

"I can't talk now. I'll see you tonight." I hung up before I betrayed my feelings. There was so much more I wanted to say, but I had to say it when I could see his face to decipher his nonverbal cues. Over the phone, he could tell a lie.

This time I wouldn't be as forgiving. I sat down to calm my nerves.

I busied myself with everything I thought I needed to get done to calm my anger. I didn't want the phone to ring during the evening, so I called my father and told him I was coming by to see him in a few days. Then I called Crystal.

"I didn't talk with you yesterday, so I decided to give you a call and see how you're doing," I said.

"We're still on with the caterer later this week?" she asked.

"Yes, of course. We need to finalize everything."

"Are you okay? You sound funny."

"I'm fine," I tried to mask my feelings. Something I should have perfected since I had plenty of practice. "Did you and Max finish the menu and china selections yet?"

"Yes. Is Dad coming to the meeting too?"

"Yes, of course. He said he was."

"Mom, I've got to run, Max is here and we're on our way out the door. I'll see you and Dad on Thursday."

She hung up before I could say anything else. Tears sprang to my eyes before I placed the headset on the base. If only I could go back in time. To when Crystal was little and there was still hope for Walter and me. There was a lot of happiness in the house back then. Everything seemed surmountable by love.

Instead of being dragged down by the memory, I walked through the first floor. Every room reminded me of something we'd done in the past. Pictures of Crystal in Disney World and Girl Scout camp, pictures of me and Walter hosting our tenth wedding anniversary celebration at the country club.

I picked up the silver frame and traced our image. Nothing hinted to a collapse of our marriage. Walter's eyes danced with merriment. His wide smile seemed genuine. I ran my hand along his dimpled chin, longing to be held by someone who couldn't wait to gather me in his arms.

I plopped on the kitchen bar stool. Getting through Crystal's wedding was my first priority. No matter what, I would not ruin her chance to have a happy memory. It was only a few more weeks, but they stretched out in front of me like a desert. I took another pill with a swallow of wine. Before the familiar haze numbed my pain, I had a clear moment. I needed to check our accounts like Ursula suggested.

Chapter Ten – Walter

I put down the pen and rolled it across the mahogany desk. Contracts and proposals littered the corner, but the space in front of me was clear. My office, my sanctuary, couldn't insulate me from whatever Tracy was going to do or say when I got home. Prolonging the moment wouldn't make things any better.

The computer read 6:35 p.m. Time to go home. Tension ran from my shoulders, across my back, and down my spine. I needed five days of peace and quiet, but that wasn't about to happen. If I were a wise man, I would be preparing for the opposite. But contemplating the future was like staring at my belly-button. Useless.

I shut down my laptop, placed it in my briefcase and stared at the collection of awards and recognition lining the office wall. Here, I was a success.

In control.

Outside of this sanctuary, my skills weren't as sharp or Sasha wouldn't be knocked-up.

Still reeling from Sasha's baby news, the announcement of downsizing had greeted me during the corporate officers' call this morning. The financial future at Dynamic Enterprise looked bleak. After two years of diminishing markets, extreme cutbacks were announced just as Jay had predicted. I needed to layoff at least one sales rep in each of my six regions.

With everything going on, I couldn't process the idea of a baby. For the briefest of moments, I wondered if Sasha had gotten pregnant to make me commit to leave Tracy. I brushed away the thought.

I crossed my arms over my chest and rolled my shoulders to loosen the tension. Tonight I had to face Tracy. Certainly, my absence last night would be the topic of discussion. Compared to everything else chasing my heels, Tracy should be easy. Work was my trump card. She believed anything I told her about work.

Sasha and I had spent five days in Paris, dining at the finest restaurants and screwing like teenagers, and Tracy had thought it was a business trip.

Last night was the first time I spent the night with Sasha while Tracy knew I was in town. But, the elaborate story I'd concocted this morning and left on her office answering machine must have worked. This afternoon she sounded composed, even a little aloof. *Damn, I'm good.*

One crisis averted and a dozen more lurking on the horizon. I ran my hand along the cleft in my chin. A baby, how the hell was I going to handle this flub? The answers weren't coming as fast as the problems.

The floor was practically deserted. Most people split after putting in eight hours and not a moment more. The few stragglers left on the floor were those of us trying to keep the company afloat. The only plan we'd construed to save any measurable amount of money was shutting down several plants and laying people off. Just thinking about how this plan would impact the lives of the people I worked with daily sat on my chest like a sumo wrestler.

Before leaving the office, I thought about stopping to see Sasha. A part of me felt betrayed by her. The pregnancy was a trap. She needed something I couldn't give. She needed more than the empty promises I offered. Her eyes begged for a tangible life to hold on to at night when she was alone and lonely. Right now, with the business sinking, Crystal getting married and a baby on the way, I couldn't offer a starving man a piece of bread.

I closed the office door and headed to the car. Traffic on 95 South slowed. Enjoying the smell and feel of my new car made the purchase worthwhile. I imagined Tracy standing in the kitchen with her hands on her lush hips, her lips tight, and eyes narrowed, demanding to know where I was last night. If traffic could delay the confrontation, I was content to creep down the highway.

I used the voice command to call Sasha while I sat in traffic. "Hey," I said when she answered.

"Hey yourself. Heading home?" This was routine. I always called her before I walked in the door of my house. Calling from home was risky.

"Yep."

She hesitated for a moment. "I'm sorry about how I broke the news to you last night. I didn't know how else to say it. I imagined telling you in some romantic setting while candles glowed, but then I blurted it out. I wasn't trying to get pregnant. I know we didn't…" She stopped. "But you know…"

"I'm fine. W-we're fine," I stuttered.

She laughed softly. "Walter relax, it's a baby, not a bomb. We'll handle it. As soon as you tell Tracy you're leaving, we can start making plans and everything will be fine."

The pressure on my chest tightened, making me squint through the pain.

"Do you want to stop by for a quickie? I think being pregnant makes me horny. I'll get you out the door in an hour." Her voice softened.

"Aw Sasha, that's not fair. You know I can't."

"I know, but I don't like the way we left it this morning. We need to talk some more."

"We'll talk." I changed lanes.

"When are you coming back?"

"Let me see what kind of mess is waiting for me at home, and then I'll let you know."

"Home is here with me. You're going to a house," she cooed, her sexy voice filtering through the speakers.

I should have been resentful. She made my life twice as complicated, but I couldn't be angry with her. I'd used her to satisfy my sexual fantasy and now it was time to pay the price. I just didn't realize it would be so high.

"What are you wearing?" I needed to hear the sweet lilt of her voice a little longer. Nothing in Tracy's tone would be sweet when I walked through the door.

"Stop by and see for yourself."

"I can't. You know I can't."

"How much longer, Walter?" This was becoming her favorite question. The longing in her voice whined in my ear. I wanted to hold her and tell her everything would work out. But I couldn't be convincing.

"Soon Sasha, soon. I'll come by the store for lunch in a couple of days. How's that?"

"Can you come with me to my doctor's appointment this week?"

I swallowed hard against the lump in my throat. Determined not to let her down, I scrambled to say the right thing. "Sure, let me know what day

and I'll make the time." I tried to sound happy, but
with the shake-up going on at work I didn't want to
be out of the office. Sitting in a doctor's waiting
room didn't sound like a wonderful way to spend
the day even if nothing was going on.

"Thanks."

I knew she recognized this was a major step
for me. "I'll let you know when." Then she hung
up.

I pulled into the garage beside Tracy's
Cadillac. The pressure on my chest increased. I
turned off the ignition, gathered my keys, my
briefcase and my lies. After several minutes I forced
myself out of the car, squared my shoulders and
headed for the door of the house.

As soon as I opened the door the smell of
roasting meat filled my nose. The lights were dim.
It took my eyes a moment to get acclimated to the
darkness. The dining room table was set with a lace
tablecloth we had purchased in Belgium. A giant
candle thingy glowed from the center of the table.

If I didn't know better, I would have thought
Tracy was entertaining a lover. But Tracy was loyal
to me and would never think about treating me as
badly as I treated her. In all the years we'd been
married, she never even looked at another man. The
extra weight she'd put on was like an added
insurance policy for me. Even though she was still

very attractive, she didn't think so, so I didn't have to worry.

I dropped my briefcase on the kitchen floor and headed for the bedroom to find her. This was not the scene I expected when I got home. I was exhausted and wanted to sit like a vegetable and watch ESPN.

"Walter?" Tracy called.

I walked into the dimly lit family room. Jazz played from the Bose system. Tracy sat on the leather couch with an expression on her face that I couldn't read. She didn't look like a woman ready to fly into a rage. The message I left must have worked better than I had imagined. I should have tried it months ago.

"What the fuck is going on, Tracy?" Those weren't the words I expected to exit my mouth, but I was drained and wanted to be left alone.

I wasn't prepared to spend a romantic evening with her. Not after everything that had transpired in the last twenty-four hours. I didn't have the required stamina.

"I was going to ask you the same question. Minus the profanity of course." She patted the sofa next to her and offered me a glass of wine that had been sitting on the coffee table.

I continued to stand in the middle of the room and watched while she took a long swallow from her glass.

From the lacy gown she wore, the food cooking, the dim lights, I knew what she had planned, and my heart twisted in my chest. All I wanted to do was go to bed without hurting her again. I felt like a jackass. I should have been cooking her dinner and serving her wine. I wished I could be the man she saw when she looked at me. And, even with her full breasts, curvy hips and skin so lush it invited me to touch, I couldn't perform.

I was willing to betray Tracy, but I couldn't betray Sasha. Not on the same day—that was Sasha's rule. Somehow Sasha could accept the fact that I made love to Tracy as long as I never made love to the both of them on the same day. And this morning, before leaving for work, Sasha had wrapped her lean legs around me and I surrendered, so happy she wasn't upset by my reaction to the news.

I crossed the room, accepted the glass of wine from Tracy, and sat on the sofa beside her. "I'm so exhausted." I sipped the Merlot and began my Oscar-winning performance.

"Like hell you are. Before you go to sleep, maybe you need to tell me where you were all day and night." She stared at me, her eyes were as cold as the polar ice cap and about as welcoming, too.

She was looking for some telltale sign I was lying, so I focused on the part of my story that was true. "Don't start any shit with me, Tracy. I left you a message." I averted my eyes and rubbed the cleft in my chin.

"The hell you did. I checked the messages as soon as I got home today and the phone hasn't rung once since I've been here. There weren't any messages on the recorder and I checked. I called you nine hundred times on every phone listed to you."

"You didn't get the one I left for you at work?"

"At—you left a message for me at work? Why the hell would you leave one there? I don't work on Sundays." Her eyes narrowed. "Come on Walter, even you, the master prevaricator, can do better than that."

"Why would I lie to you? You know what I've been going through at work," I kept my voice level. "I left a message as soon as I could this morning."

"Umm humm," she said. But I knew she didn't believe me.

"Dammit Tracy, you know what a mess the company is in. We are meeting night and day to figure out how we can…how to save jobs." I raised my voice. "Every time something comes up, I can't stand up and say wait a minute, I need to call my wife and get permission first." I set the glass on the table so hard wine spilled. "I'm under enough pressure trying to prove myself as the only black

VP. I have to demonstrate leadership and guidance—how would it look if the CEO calls an immediate meeting and I can't show up until I clear it with my wife?"

"All day, Walter. All day long and you couldn't tell me where you were? You couldn't reach me? I went to your office and no one was there." Tears gathered in her eyes. "I drove down. There wasn't any meeting going on. You must think I'm some kind of idiot."

"The meeting was in the board room on the tenth floor. I got a message to you as soon as I could. I didn't want to call you here at home during the night and wake you up, so the first opportunity I had this morning, I left a message for you where I thought you could get it. In your office." I picked up the phone from the base and shoved it into her hand. "Check it now, dammit! Check it!" My excuse was flimsy thin, but I was pulling it off. A bead of sweat rolled down my chest.

She didn't take her eyes off of me while she dialed the number. The cold stare was eerie. I picked up my glass, and took a sip of wine, hoping to disguise my nervousness. I crossed my legs while she punched in the codes.

She listened.

I watched.

Disappointment washed over me for the pain I was causing her. At least a small portion of my story was true.

She placed the headset on the couch between us. "Well," she started, then stopped. In a more gentle voice she said, "I was so upset this morning, I left the office before nine and never went back.

Tears streamed down her cheeks. Her lips puckered. "You are such a bastard. The last few years everything in this marriage has revolved around you and what you wanted or needed. You can't begin to imagine what the last twenty-four hours have been like for me. All because your company is having a crisis. Well, Walter, I'm having a crisis too." Her hands went to her hair and she ran her fingers through her short curls.

I gathered her in my arms, pushing my nose against the tender part of her neck. She smelled like lavender. I ran my hand across her back and down to her butt. The thin fabric did nothing to shield her soft flesh from my touch.

My body warmed up. Even the discomfort in my chest melted away as she wrapped her arms around me, teasing tension out of my shoulders with her fingertip.

With my lips pressed against her ear, I whispered. "I'm sorry. I didn't mean for you to worry," I kissed her several times before moving to her neck. "I called you as soon as I could. We were in a strategy session. No phones, no computers. I was probably the only one standing in the bathroom stall leaving a message for his wife. All the other wives understand. You've got to trust me, Tracy. We've been down this road before and you said that was behind us." I tried to soften the look in my eyes to get her to give a little, too.

When I released her, we sat in silence listening to the music. I pulled her back against the cushions and rubbed her thigh to placate her. Inching closer to the thick patch of hair between her legs.

Without saying a word she loosened my tie. No matter how much she wanted to, I wouldn't make love to Tracy tonight.

"Tray, I've been in a seventeen hour meeting that started yesterday afternoon. The only thing they fed us was dry sandwiches and weak coffee. I'm starving and so exhausted I barely made it home this evening. Please, let's have dinner first."

She looked disappointed. "I cooked *my* favorites, tonight." She uncoiled her legs and stood up. "Lamb chops, roasted potatoes and broccoli. I even made dessert—walnut cake."

"Can I have some of your favorites?" I followed her into the kitchen. She tugged on the camisole to pull it lower over her hips. She was so conscious of hiding what she believed didn't look good. But the view was perfect. I loved her curves.

Dinner was delicious. Tracy hated to cook, but she worked wonders in the kitchen. I even went back for seconds and polished the succulent lamb bones. I smacked my lips, quite pleased with being able to deceive my wife.

"Where did you think I was?" I asked between bites.

"I don't know what I thought." She hunched her shoulders.

"Yeah, you do," I chuckled with a mouth full of food, but I didn't dare say it.

She laughed. "Yes, that's what I thought." She placed her elbow on the table and placed her chin in her palm. "Maybe we need to set up some kind of signal for when this stuff happens."

"Like what?"

"I don't know. But—"

"It's going to be pretty bad, Tracy. I'm talking about a massive layoff."

"How many?"

"We're going to close the plants in Rhode Island and Florida. Most of those people will lose their jobs. A few will be transferred to other plant sites. My staff will be cut in half and—"

She reached across the table and ran her hand along my cheek. "Are you going to be okay?"

"I'll be fine, but I don't trust Joe. Remember the promotion he promised me that I haven't seen yet?"

"Do you think you could lose your job?" Worry flickered in her eyes.

"Don't stress. We'll be fine." I bit into my lamb chop and chewed slowly. "There will be many nights when I'll work late or sleep on the couch in my office. You've got to hang in there with me. It's going to be hard enough. I expect the sales people will need me even more as they try to find new jobs or apply for unemployment, or cry in their soup. Some of them will be upset. But you can't start thinking the worst of me just because I don't call when you expect or I don't show up for a few dinners." Some of this was true. The rest gave me an excuse to be absent from home more often and it was coming so easy, it made me giddy.

"Yeah, okay, I'll chill out, but after this is all over, maybe we can plan a trip or something. We've got an anniversary coming up. Maybe we can go away and do something together."

"Yeah. Sure we can." I agreed even though I had no intention of going away anytime soon. I needed to deal with Sasha and work. With all the havoc facing me, vacationing never entered my thoughts. But I pretended.

"How about we leave the dishes until the morning?" Tracy said when I couldn't eat another morsel. She rubbed my crotch with her toes. Only she could manage to be so gentle and arouse me at the same time.

I enjoyed the evening more than I thought I could. Being with Tracy, I didn't have to worry about holding my stomach in, or if I held my erection long enough to satisfy her. With her, I could be lazy. The thought of not worrying about performing made my penis stiffen. One glance at my watch told me I still had to wait.

"Let's hand wash the dishes like we used to do before we had all these fancy appliances."

Her face lit up. "Are you serious? You're going to wash dishes?"

"After that meal, I'd do anything for you." I grabbed her ass.

I drew water in the sink and she cleared the table. After we finished she asked, "Are you ready to complete what you started on the sofa? I think you owe me a little sumthin-sumthin." She brushed her hips against me before kneading my shaft through my pants.

My promise to Sasha paled as Tracy snuggled against my chest. For the first time in weeks I wanted to make love to my wife and nothing could keep me from it. Tracy's soft curves were like a siren, revving up every cell in my body. My loins warmed.

I climbed the stairs behind Tracy, dropping my shirt, my tie and belt in the hall leading to our bedroom. By the time I reached the bedroom door, only my silk boxers remained in place.

In the middle of our bedroom she turned to face me. Her soft eyes danced with excitement. She was so easy to please and tonight I wanted to make her happy.

She removed my boxers and I removed her gown.

I groped her large breasts, one in each hand. She released a low growl that meant she liked what I was doing.

"I've waited for you for weeks." She pushed up on her toes and kissed me.

Instead of responding, I backed her to the edge of the bed and captured her tongue. I didn't want to talk. I wanted to be inside of her. I climbed on top, pushed her legs apart with my knees and drove deep inside of her. She was warm and wet. Each thrust into her wet center was deeper than the last as I buried my guilt.

Chapter Eleven – Tracy

Without turning on the light in the darkened bedroom, Walter nestled his nose against my neck. His heavy breathing sounded like a wild animal stalking our room. He skipped the foreplay and went straight to the main attraction. His hurried actions reminded me of our rushed love-making in my dorm room before my roommate returned and interrupted us. My thoughts slipped back to his weak excuse for his absence, refusing to accept his explanation.

If he put half as much energy in our marriage as he did in his work, our relationship wouldn't be near death.

I ground my hips against him, trying to slow him down. This precious moment needed to last long enough to make me believe in him, again. The passion between us exceeded anything I could remember for months.

Walter pumped against me as if he'd forgotten the fine art of shared orgasm. His eyes were squeezed so tight, tiny lines formed around them.

Was Walter enjoying me or the act? I turned my head away and envisioned Marco. Marco looked like the kind of man who knew how to treat a woman. He looked like the kind of man who built pedestals for his woman. He looked like the kind of man who could hold me close and be proud to call me his woman.

I doubt Walter even realized I was under him. He grunted and panted like his was a solo mission to reach ecstasy. But no matter how much noise he made, or how hard he pushed, he never lit my flame.

He pumped faster.

His body grew rigid in my arms.

I wrapped my legs around his back, whispered a few ahs and threw in a few ohs. Walter was so self-absorbed, he probably didn't even hear me fake my way to ecstasy.

When his body went still with his orgasm, I contracted my muscles, and threw in a few quivers before pretending to fall limp.

Walter had given me five full minutes before collapsing. Maybe I didn't love him the way I used to. Or maybe I expected too much. Thinking about Marco while Walter tried so hard wasn't fair. Walter was under a lot of pressure at work.

"After Crystal's wedding, everything is going to be better." I ran my fingers across his chest. "Weddings always stress people out."

"It's not supposed to. Crystal and Max should be the ones stressed." Walter rolled off of me and onto his back, and clasped his fingers behind his head. "I think you just need to learn to relax. You're way too uptight, Tray."

"Oh, so I'm the problem," I drew away from him. As usual, he managed to make me the crazy one.

"No, I didn't mean that. You think everything should be perfect. Even people. And nothing is perfect. Ever."

I grabbed the extra pillow and held it against my body. Walter had to be wrong. Even if perfection wasn't something to expect every day, I didn't think I was asking for too much. I felt like someone had raked their nails against the insides of my stomach.

I tightened my hold on the pillow, pulling it tight enough to push down the panic.

The next morning, Walter was gone by the time my alarm clock rang. The bedroom was dark, except for the hint of sunrise peeking through the slats in the blinds. I tried to ignore everything he'd said last night. He had his reality and I had mine. Before I left the house, I peeked at my packed bag. Knowing they were still waiting for me helped just a little.

I skulked into my office and dropped my bag on the desk. After yesterday, I felt like a kook. I couldn't picture that woman who called her friends in tears, or the one escorted out of the building. The whole scene reminded me of a soap opera drama. I winced as the image clarified in my head. I saw myself the way Carla and Ursula must have seen me.

The list of activities I needed to finish before the end of the day was as long as my arm. But I sat at the desk, and crossed my legs like a woman with nothing but time. My leg swung back and forth in a steady cadence while I scrutinized the events of last night, without the romantic lighting or the sweet taste of merlot on my tongue. Fear clogged my throat. We had to make our marriage work, the thought of divorce made it almost impossible for me to breathe. Life without Walter did not exist in the creases of my mind. He was persuasive. The ultimate salesman and I wondered if I had just bought another one of his show stopping performances.

I decided not to push the thought too far away, but to keep an earnest eye open for another sign. My heart was still scorched from the pain of his last affair with his assistant Tonya. The skinny little hussy quit when I found out about their midday tryst on his office sofa. She was young, pretty and had stroked his massive ego by performing fellatio and typing memos all in the same day, like it was a skill taught in college.

Walter swore his loyalty to me and told me she meant nothing. He even sought counseling. Crystal was only fifteen. I wasn't ready to let my marriage disintegrate. Instead, I found a way to believe his apology.

I sighed, then picked up the phone to hear Walter's message again. Listening in earnest this time for any nuances I might have missed.

Some telltale background noises like heavy breathing or soft music. I repeated the message two times but heard the same thing I heard last night—only his voice.

I intended to start on the pile of work on my desk, but called my dad first.

In my most chipper voice I could fake, I greeted him as soon as he picked up the phone.

"Girl, I'm fine, just fine," he said in his easy manner.

My father trusted me, so I had to be honest with him. "I'm worried about you, Dad, about your health."

"Oh, now your mom's got you all worked up. I'm feeling fine. Everybody slows down when they get my age. You wait and see," he chuckled.

"Just the same, I want you to see a doctor."

"Aww…"

"Please don't be upset with me, but I'll make an appointment for tomorrow."

"Um…" he snorted. "Can't go tomorrow, I'm meeting Ray and some others. We're playing poker."

"I haven't even told you what time the appointment is yet."

"Doesn't matter. Can't make it."

"Dad—"

"Tracy, maybe another day." He paused for a moment as if he wanted to find a more appropriate time. "I'll go after the wedding, but only if you promise to buy me lunch too."

"Why? Why do you want to wait until after the wedding?"

"'Cause I'm grown." He laughed. "And I want to eat at that place you always take your mother to on Chestnut Street."

I grinned. "Okay, I'll make the appointment for the week after the wedding. And you promise to go with me without being difficult?"

"Can't promise I won't be difficult, but if the Lord's willing, I'll go."

"Okay, Dad. Now make sure you remind Mom that a car will pick you both up the evening before the wedding. That way you won't have to drive."

"How sweet, honey. You know we're looking forward to this. You and Walter aren't sparing any expense, are you?"

"We only get to do this once, so why not?"

"Is Walter's crazy mother coming up? I don't want to spend too much time around that poisonous woman. It's a wonder he turned out so good with a crazy mother like her."

"You have to ignore Evelyn. She's had a difficult life, that's all."

"Yeah, I'll bet it was difficult. You can't spew that much poison and be Miss Happy-Go-Lucky. She won't be staying with you guys, will she? 'Cause if she is—"

"Don't start. You and Mom are staying here. Evelyn and Walter's brothers are staying at a hotel. And you'll be on your best behavior around her, won't you?"

"Aren't I always on my best behavior?" he asked. "Just ask your mom, she'll tell you."

"You always are. I love you," I said.

I sat back in my chair and laced my fingers. Suppose my father was really sick? He was my constant, I still leaned on him. Before that thought could burrow too deep, I shook it away, turned on the computer, and pulled up the spreadsheets to review the financial closing.

"*Buon giorno,* good looking. How was your lunch with your friends?" I looked up to find Marco standing in my door in a custom-made suit that made him look like Adonis. I opened my mouth, but my brain faltered and no words came out. He took a seat and gave me a look that almost brought me to orgasm. A smile like that from Walter and my life would have been blissful. If

Marco knew how many times I made love to Walter with him on my mind, he might have bolted out of my office.

"I stopped by to see you yesterday, but you were gone. You must have banker's hours."

I gave him my full attention. "I had to leave early yesterday. Something came up."

"How was your lunch?" he asked again. His dark eyes penetrating mine.

I looked away and forced my legs together.

"Whenever the three of us get together we have a good time." I ignored the warmth spreading up my spine.

Part of the tattoo on his hand peeked from beneath the cuff of his shirt. "How did you handle Crystal's graduation?"

"Let's say I was happy and sad." I pouted, a lame attempt to look youthful.

"You know you're cute when you pout?"

I pushed a curl behind my ear. Good it was working. "That's the nicest thing I've heard in a long time."

"Come on, I'm sure Walter compliments you all the time. You just take them for granted."

The fact that he knew my husband's name touched my heart. All those stories I shared with him were boring as hell—and he was listening.

"Believe me, Walter doesn't have time to compliment me. If he did, I would remember."

He leaned across my desk, his eyes darkened. "How about lunch with me today? You promised." His request left no room for me to say no. After last night, I would have accepted an invitation to a snail race.

"Okay." The perkiness in my voice surprised me. I don't know why I accepted so quickly. My head was yelling no, but I ignored it. Was I that desperate for male attention? I leaned back in my chair to put some breathing space between us.

"Good, I'll drive. I'll stop by to pick you up at 11:30. And, just in case Walter didn't tell you today, you look gorgeous. *A piu tardi.*" He winked.

"Yeah, see ya," I said before he walked out.

As soon as he turned the corner I exhaled through my mouth. Lunch with a colleague was not a big deal. Lunch with Marco was a very big deal. If Walter or Crystal saw me, there was no way I could tell them it was business. One look and anyone could tell my heart was cheating.

I pulled out the mirror I kept in my bottom desk drawer and checked my face. Was he kidding? Gorgeous? Wow, it had been some time since anyone called me that. I smiled at my reflection, then tucked the mirror away.

Good married women don't lunch with men they want to screw. If I had a cheating heart, Marco would be the one. If I counted the erotic images I had about him, I already had one foot in hell. The seductive wink he gave me would keep me company for several weeks.

Ursula walked into my office and closed the door. "Okay, okay, I can't wait any longer. What happened last night? What did you do?" She sat in the chair vacated by Marco. "What did he say?"

"Ursula, slow down." She was shooting questions at me so fast I didn't know where to start. "Should we get Carla on the line so I don't have to repeat this a second time?"

"Whatever." She waved her hand. "That's up to you. But whatever you do, hurry up, I can't wait any longer. I started to call your house last night but…but I thought Walter might answer. God knows I didn't want to talk to him."

I dialed Carla and put her on the speakerphone. "Carla, can you hear me?"

"Yeah. I was getting ready to call you. What happened? What did he say? Why did it take you so long to call me?" Carla fired off questions without taking a breath.

"Ursula is here in my office. I might as well tell you both at the same time."

"Tell it, girl," Carla said.

"Okay, okay. Instead of losing my temper and yelling at him—"

"How could you not yell after all that shit?" Carla interrupted.

"I decided not to yell." I sat back in my chair and watched Ursula screw up her face as if I'd given her lemons to suck on. "Instead, I cooked a nice dinner and waited for him to come home."

"Did you ask him where he was?" Carla asked.

"Where the hell was he all night?" Ursula asked almost simultaneously.

"Of course, that was the first thing I asked. Do you think I'm an idiot? He left a message for me yesterday morning, but I never came back to the office to get it. He said he was pulled into an all-nighter and couldn't get any messages out until early in the morning. He said he couldn't get up and say he needed to call his wife." I swallowed the lump in my throat. I repeated Walter's exact words. I hunched my shoulders like a third-grader. "We talked and had a bottle of wine, then—"

"Yeah, we get the picture now." Ursula rolled her eyes. "You did what you always do."

"What does that mean?"

"He says sorry. He whispers in your ear. You part your legs." Ursula shook her head.

"When Walter messes up, he'll do a royal job of it. After Crystal's wedding, I'll think things over, again." There was calmness in my chest that hadn't been there before. I liked this plan.

"Are you okay?" Carla asked.

"Yeah, I'm okay. The clock is ticking on our marriage, anyway."

"Girl, you know we're here for you no matter what. His story sounds pretty weak. Do you believe him?" Carla asked.

"Leave it alone," Ursula's tone was heavy with warning.

"I'm just asking. I'm not sure Javier could tell me some lame story like that. Shoot, you can always come up with a reason to leave the room long enough to make a quick call. Say you gotta go to the bathroom. Even corporate executives have to take a pee."

"Carla, his story held together good enough. If something is going on, Walter will hang himself. He did before and he'll do it again. I'm so numb I really don't care what he said."

For a moment the three of us sat in uncomfortable silence. Carla broke the tension. "You're a better woman than me because I would have smacked him just for being him."

"Why don't you keep on trying to make that baby and stay outta other people's business?" Ursula asked.

"I don't want to bring you guys down." Carla's voice dropped to a whisper. "I came on my period this morning."

"Oh Carla. I'm so sorry. Give it time. It'll happen." I hoped it didn't sound like a platitude.

"I was so sure this was it. My period was a week late this time."

"Be patient. It'll happen," I repeated.

"Yeah, okay. My problem is I'm not twenty-five years old. My doctor said the odds of a woman over forty getting pregnant are low."

"There are plenty of women your age who have babies," I said.

"Tracy, please don't feed me your 'everything is going to be okay' bullshit. Suppose I've missed my opportunity? What if I never get pregnant?"

I glanced across my desk, hoping Ursula would have something to say. She was focused on her hands in her lap. I didn't know how to respond. Carla could be right.

"Anyway, Javier and I are going to the doctor this week to get the results from the test. And…and then…maybe. I've got to go now."

"Was she crying?" I asked Ursula when the line went dead.

"I think so. What was that about? She acts like she can't keep trying."

"She wants babies. She's always had her nieces and nephews running in and out of her house. Now she's craving her own. Everybody needs someone to love and someone to love them." I paused for a moment. "I understand that. I'll call her later. You need to stop being so hard on her, Ursula. The two of you are always going at each other."

"What'd I do? What'd I say?"

"Just go easy."

"All right," she said reluctantly. "But she always has something to say. She has a comment to make about everything. Do you know anyone with more mouth?"

"Yes. You. Still…this is something she wants and we need to support her."

"Okay. I'll be nicer." She stood. "For a little while."

"How's Anthony? I mean, how are the two of you?"

"Tracy, please don't start." She held up her hand. "It's good. It's scary good." She smiled. "I like him. I want it to work. I'm tired of always having to go places alone, or waiting until you and Carla can clear your calendars to do things with me." She paused. "I love him Tracy. You know what?" She looked at me with her big brown eyes. "I'd marry him if he never bathed and was the funkiest man on earth. I don't want to be alone anymore."

"Would you marry him because you love him or because you don't want to be alone?"

"Both are good reasons, don't you think?"

"Maybe, maybe not. But what do I know? My marriage might be in the toilet. Maybe you should ask Carla, she's happily married and getting plenty of sex."

In all the years I've known Ursula, I'd never seen her so vulnerable. She usually changed men like I changed my lipstick color. I thought she'd stay single forever.

"If he never took a bath?" I teased. "Are you sure? And did you just say love? You love Anthony?"

"Very funny. I do." She sat back down in the chair. "I think he wants to marry me."

"Whoa, Ursula. Marry? Are you guys moving that fast, or have you managed to keep it from me that long?"

"I've kept it from you for a while." She laughed.

"So everybody is keeping secrets, I guess. Carla's only now telling us she wants babies."

"Yeah, so what's yours?" She didn't wait for an answer. "Are you having an affair with

Marco? I saw him coming out of your office with a big smile on his face.”

“Ha. Ha. I can only handle one man at a time and I’m not doing that very well right now. But…” I lowered my voice.

“Ah ha, that’s what I thought.” She snapped her fingers.

“Maybe it’s time I switched up and gave Marco a try.” We both laughed.

“Yeah, give him a try and let Walter know. Nothing brings a man back in line faster than knowing somebody else is eyeing his woman.”

“Yeah, but—”

“Oh yeah, that’s right. You’re Miss Goody-Two-Shoes. You wouldn’t cheat no matter how miserable you are.” She paused then added. “No one likes a martyr, Tracy.”

A stab of guilt pierced my heart. After the emptiness of our lovemaking the night before, I wondered if Ursula was right.

“Girl, you better take care of yourself. I won’t tell anyone.” She stood again.

Marco walked in my office just as she was about to leave. “Hey Marco,” Ursula said.

“Ursula. Want to join Tracy and me for lunch?” He waved his hand to include Ursula in the lunch date.

Ursula shot me a glance. "No, I can't. Three's a crowd. But you guys enjoy yourselves." She gave me a wink that only I could see before slipping out the door.

"Ready?" His warm baritone tickled my ears.

My heartbeat sped up. I reached in the drawer, extracted my purse, and stood. "I am."

Chapter Twelve - Tracy

Marco led the way out of the building. The hall just narrowly accommodated the two of us, side-by-side.

"So we're really doing this?" Marco beamed a brilliant smile as we exited the building.

"What? Having lunch? Of course." I hoped my reply sounded breezy, like this happened to me every day.

"I can't believe I was actually able to pull you away." He opened the door and allowed me to exit first.

The sun slipped behind a wispy cloud as we stepped outside. The bright blue sky sparkled like glass. His eyes traveled the length of my legs as I pulled them into his car. He lifted his chin and his fiery gaze flickered with desire. My breathing accelerated before I could look away.

He closed my door, circled the car, and slid into his side.

"I can't seem to get this seatbelt to work." I tugged on the strap without success.

"Let me help you. It sticks sometimes." He leaned across my body to pull the belt.

God, he smelled good. The warmth of his presence penetrated my pores. He had to hear my heart thundering in my chest. I wanted to touch the tiny pulse beating in his neck, but the belt popped free and he sat up straight. I swallowed the taste of desire lining my mouth. Going to lunch with Marco was like fanning the flames of a forest fire. With my marriage crumbling, I should have stayed away from temptation.

At the deli, we stood in line, inching our way to the cash register with the other customers. Marco's hand brushed mine as we stepped up to the counter to place our order. My heart raced like a schoolgirl. This was silly. I was married for God's sake.

He ordered a huge sandwich of different deli meats and imported cheeses. After my two-day gorge fest, I ordered a garden salad with low fat dressing. He placed an oatmeal raisin cookie on the counter.

"They will bring our lunch over as soon as it's prepared. In the meantime, do you want to share the cookie?" he said. He led the way to a table in the corner and waited until I was seated before sitting.

"Are you always this polite?"

He shrugged his shoulders. "It's something I do when I'm with a beautiful woman."

"It's nice." My cheeks grew warm.

Marco broke the cookie in half and held the other half across the table for me. "Peace offering."

"Why do you think we're not at peace?"

"You've been avoiding me."

"I've been busy with the graduation and the wedding," I lied. But looking temptation in the face over lunch would not have been helpful.

"Too busy for a friend?" His eyes danced with mischief.

Marco had a hook in my heart. All he had to do was reel me in.

"Never that busy. I'm sorry."

"No apology necessary, just share the cookie with me."

"No, I shouldn't." I shook my head. "I'm trying to be good. I'm eating like an adult for the rest of this week."

"Nobody can resist a warm oatmeal cookie."

A cookie I could resist, he was a lot harder. His sharp good looks satisfied all my senses at once.

He waved the cookie again. More than I wanted that cookie, I wanted to run my finger along the center of his hand to see if it was as hot as I imagined.

"If I gain a pound can I blame you?" I broke off a piece.

"Yes, you can blame me." He sounded sincere. "But you look fine." His smile was crooked.

"I hear your divorce is final and you're now seeing someone." The warm cookie melted on my tongue. I gobbled it down hoping he wouldn't notice.

"How did you hear that?" His eyes widened without blinking.

"Office gossip, you know."

"Humph! I am interested in someone." He leaned his elbow on the table, his face inches from mine. "My marriage was over long before we admitted it. When she finally got up the courage to call it quits, I was relieved. I was tired of praying things would get better." His candor surprised me. "She and my daughter moved back to Houston. That's the hardest part. Not seeing Briana every day. Not watching her grow up." He shoved the last of the cookie in his mouth without telling me who he was seeing.

I'd find another way to pry the info from him.

"When Crystal was in grade school she came running home one day, her eyes brimming with tears. She wanted to know if Walter and I were getting a divorce. I asked her what gave her that idea, she told me she heard us arguing the night before, and all parents get a divorce when they argue. I made a vow to myself to stop arguing within earshot of her. It took me an hour to convince her things were okay. Finally, she stopped crying and her little body collapsed against me. She hugged my thighs so tight I had to pry her loose.”

“I couldn’t make that promise to Briana. The tension in our marriage was doing more harm than good.”

I patted his hand. Had Crystal grown up with any ill effects from all the angst in our marriage?

“It seems like you’ve done an excellent job with her. She’s finished college, getting married, she sounds happy.”

The warmth of his hand penetrated my flesh. If he’d placed it between my legs, my heart would have sung. I resisted the urge to run my finger along his skin. He didn’t pull away. I couldn’t justify touching him too long. The last thing I needed today was to complicate my already-strained marriage or blur the lines. Before drawing my hand away, I squeezed his fingers.

“It’s okay, Tracy. My parents and brother live there too, so I get to see her a lot. Besides she’s near cousins and grandparents.”

The server approached our table with a tray in each hand. She placed the salad in front of me and his huge sandwich in front of him.

“Anyway.” He took a big bite out of his sandwich before continuing. “Enough about me, now let’s talk about you.”

"There isn't much to say. Crystal's wedding is in a few weeks and I feel like I'm running a race. Walter's moodiness has kicked up another notch. Besides being super grouchy and irritable, a few nights ago he didn't come home." I stopped abruptly, not believing I had shared family secrets. But it felt good talking about this stuff.

Marco's eyes grew large and focused on me. "Why not?" He put his sandwich down.

"Work. An all-night meeting he couldn't call to tell me about."

"You sound like you don't believe him."

"Should I?"

"That's something you've got to answer. I will say when my marriage was happy I came home or called home every night no matter what. When it was falling apart, I had lots of reasons for staying out."

I chewed a mouthful of lettuce. "That's what I thought, too."

"I've probably said too much."

"No. No, you didn't. You didn't say anything I haven't already said to myself. But you already know how hard it can be when two people who are supposed to be pulling together end up tearing each other apart."

He took a bite without averting his eyes. "Don't ignore your instincts. They've probably been talking to you for months, you just haven't been paying attention."

"My instincts are mute. I don't hear a thing."

"Keep listening. Your intuition will grow louder when it matters." The intensity of his stare made it impossible to look away.

The knots in my stomach multiplied.

I placed my fork over the remaining salad as the server removed our plates. "That sounds like good advice."

"We've already had dessert and as much as I'm enjoying your company, I don't want to keep you away from the office too long. It might give you an excuse not to have lunch with me again."

I could have looked at him for the rest of the afternoon. The concern in his voice drew me in and had me talking about things I'd never said. His extraordinarily good looks didn't hurt much either.

Marco placed money on top of the check and stood up. "We need to do this more often," he said as we walked out.

"I needed to get away from the numbers for a while."

He opened the car door for me.

"Oh!" He sounded offended. "You went to lunch with me to get away from your spreadsheets."

I wanted to hop in his lap and kiss his exquisite lips. "Aw, Marco." I pushed his arm. His warm, tight flesh felt good. My fingers should have burned from the betrayal, instead my heart raced. "You know I didn't mean it that way. I always enjoy your company."

"Yeah. Yeah. Yeah. I think you used me."

"But it felt good, didn't it?" I teased as he pulled into a parking space in front of our office building.

"Real good." He turned the car off and turned toward me. "One thing my divorce has taught me—I need to be honest with myself, and others." The timbre of his voice changed, gone was the joking quality from earlier. "So I need to tell you that I'm attracted to you. You're the woman at work that I'm interested in. I know you're married and how important your family is to you. But I think you're a fantastic woman, perfect in every way. I don't expect you'll come running into my arms, but if Walter trips up, I'm here."

My heart stumbled. I swallowed. "I-I..." I swallowed again. "Marco, I don't know what to say."

"I don't expect you to say anything. I don't expect you to do anything. I just wanted you to know that I think I'm falling in love with you."

"What? I can't."

"You can't what? I'm not asking you to do anything." He touched my shoulder.

"I-I've…never had an affair. I've never even thought about cheating on Walter. Well, that's not quite true. I've had some very vivid fantasies, but that's all they were."

"I'm not asking you to have an affair with me or to leave Walter. I love you because I know you wouldn't do either of those things."

The unmistakable desire that blazed in his dark eyes made it hard to breathe.

I got out of the car before he could open my door.

"One day I might ask you to tell me about your fantasies," he said as he caught up with me.

"Oh no." I smiled. *They're all about you and they're X-rated.* "You'll need a note from your parents before we have that conversation," I said with a straight face as we walked back to the building.

He laughed and wrapped his arm around my shoulder. I hadn't heard Walter laugh in months. Marco's jocularity lifted my spirits. His arm around my shoulder felt right and wrong simultaneously. I fell into his rock solid chest with ease. His arm around me felt better than my hand over his. Guilt enveloped my whole body.

"The next lunch is on me," I said, hoping to put us back on neutral ground.

"If I waited on you to take me to lunch, I'd starve to death."

"We'll go later this week. I promise. I'll set it up."

He dropped me off at my office. "I hope my confession didn't upset you. It's part of my new philosophy, to tell the truth and to be honest."

"I'm fine. I might adopt your new philosophy too."

He held my cheeks between his palms for a moment, then disappeared down the hall.

I placed my purse on my desk. I was rolling in waves of emotions. I wanted to dance around the office like a schoolgirl, but I could see the disapproving glare of my father. Was I cheating on Walter? Every touch was innocent, every word I spoke was appropriate, but my heart and my head were all on a different script. His confession muddled my emotions.

The afternoon passed in a blur. I couldn't stop thinking about lunch. I glanced at my watch. It was almost six. I pushed the notebook into my drawer, saved the spreadsheet, and shut down my computer.

I reached for my cell phone and called Walter. "Are you leaving the office soon?" I asked when he answered.

"Yes, I'll meet you at the caterer at 6:30."

"Just checking. We're going out to dinner afterward."

"I guess you don't cook anymore," he snorted.

"Who do you think cooked the meal you licked from your fingers last night, your fairy godmother?" I took a deep breath. Walter's snide comments stung.

"Tracy, calm down. We can go out. I was only saying," he stammered. "Okay, whatever you want. I'll go."

"We won't have many more nights with our daughter before she becomes Max's wife. I want to treasure all the time that we get. You understand, don't you?"

"I guess so. But she's only getting married. She's not going into hiding."

"When she's married, our relationship will change. She won't be able to run off and go shopping with me at the drop of a hat. Or drop by and talk all night while you're working late. It'll be different."

"You'll be fine. You're tough, you always have been."

"I may not be as tough as you think. Bye Walter." I hung up the phone without waiting for him to respond. I reached in my purse, grabbed a pill and swallowed it without water. From the drawer I pulled out my personal file. The cluttered folder contained savings account numbers and our financial information. But after ruffling through the stack, I couldn't find the latest statement. The office clock read 6:15 already. I had just enough time to get to the caterer's.

I pushed the paperwork into my briefcase and vowed to work on it later. By the time I walked out of the office, the pill had mellowed my mood.

Crystal sat in her car talking on her cell phone as I pulled into the parking lot. I gave her a chance to finish her conversation before getting out of the car. No matter what happened the rest of the evening, Walter's words wouldn't turn me into a prickly bickering princess. My heart raced with expectations as I remembered my wonderful lunch with Marco and the way he held me for that brief moment. I hadn't felt this giddy since my wedding day. I closed my eyes and exhaled. Only Walter was supposed to make me feel that good.

"Hey baby." I kissed Crystal on the cheek, but avoided her eyes when she got out of the car.

"Mom, you look fantastic." She stared at me. "You're almost glowing. What's going on?"

Could she tell I was hiding something? I swallowed. "It was just another day. Nothing special. Are you ready to do this?"

"I'm ready."

Soft classical music played in the posh showroom. After our first visit we knew why Jean-Paul was so expensive. But our only daughter deserved the elegant affair Walter and I didn't have. Our shotgun wedding couldn't compare to what we planned for Crystal. Walter was so afraid my father would shoot him for getting me pregnant that he stuttered all through his vows.

I wanted to take off my shoes and sink my feet in the deep pile carpeting. Original Wyeth paintings adorned the walls, and the receptionist sat behind a mahogany desk that was as wide as a king-size bed. The waiting room was decorated with Queen Anne chairs in a deep burgundy broche that matched the carpet and the thick velvet drapes. The room felt heavy and dark, but I was comfortable here.

"Have a seat please, ladies, Jean-Paul will be with you in a few minutes. May I get you something to drink?"

"Wine," we responded at the same time.

This was our fourth visit to Jean-Paul Fairfield Events and we loved the wine. Besides, as much as we were paying for the wedding, we should have stopped by at lunchtime and chit-chatted with Jean-Paul while sipping his expensive vintage.

"You can tell we both had a rough day," Crystal laughed. "You want to tell me about your day or should I go first?"

"You go first," I said. "You're not even working yet, so how bad could your day be?"

"Looking for a job is hard work." She crossed her slender legs. "When was the last time you had to tell somebody how wonderful you are and why their business would fall apart without you?"

The receptionist handed us the wine flutes and disappeared into the back.

"Okay, you got me there."

We clicked our glasses together. I took a long swallow of the white wine to calm my nerves.

"What time is Dad getting here?"

"He promised to get here by 6:30." I looked at my watch. "So, I guess he's going to be late."

"Is Granny Baptiste staying overnight for the wedding?"

"Honey, you know Mom-Baptiste doesn't talk to me unless she absolutely has to. She and your uncles are staying at the hotel." I laughed.

"Aw Mom, you can put up with her for one night, can't you?"

"Honey, talk to me when you have a mother-in-law." I sipped my wine.

"I like Max's mother, she's always very nice."

"Yes, but Mom-Baptiste isn't nice to anyone, not even her own sons."

The receptionist sauntered back into the room in her skin-tight pencil skirt and silk blouse unbuttoned at the right level to reveal ample cleavage. "Jean-Paul is ready for you now." She led us down the mirrored hall. I watched her five-inch heels. With that tight skirt, I expected her to lose her balance when she walked.

When we walked in, Jean-Paul stood up and shook our hands. Our thick file was open on top of his desk. The wedding was costing a small fortune and the file proved it.

"Okay, where are we?" Jean-Paul flexed his fingers before sorting through several pages.

Crystal sat on the edge of her chair with her list in her hand. "We've decided on the china and crystal patterns. We're going with the Antique Scroll pattern for the china and the Connoisseur Gold Collection Glassware."

I sat back in my chair, crossed my legs, and finished my wine. Marco's comments played across my mind non-stop. I decided to take him out to lunch again on Thursday or Friday, the whole time imaging his large hand stroking my back or holding me.

Walter breezed into the shop in his pinstriped Brooks Brothers suit, crisp white starched shirt and expensive Bally shoes.

"Hey, sorry I'm late. I got tied up at the office and traffic was a bear." He kissed Crystal on the cheek and gave me a weak smile, that didn't even measure up to the greeting I'd received from Jean-Paul.

Walter waved his hand for us to continue the discussion.

"Do you think we have covered everything?" Jean-Paul asked.

"Oh… there is one more thing I want." Crystal looked over at her father. An addition to the mounting bill hung from her lips.

"What do you want now, Crystal? I know this is going to cost me." Walter crossed his legs, but smiled.

"I want the chocolate fondue fountain." She clasped her hands together pretending to pray.

Walter looked at Jean-Paul. "What's that cost?"

I could have sworn Jean-Paul's pupils turned into dollar signs. "I'll have to check. Give me a minute." He scurried from the room.

"You're going to let me have it, Dad?" Crystal sounded elated.

"Let's see how much it costs first." He grinned.

Crystal jumped out of her seat and planted kisses on her father's cheek. "Thank you, thank you, thank you." She swirled around the room and kissed me too, before taking her seat. Walter never denied Crystal anything. Even at five, when she demanded a television in her room, Walter brought one home the very next day.

Jean-Paul walked back in the room with three pieces of papers in his hand. Everything in his place seemed to cost one thousand dollars per page. I braced for his pronouncement and Walter's rejection.

"We can do milk chocolate, dark chocolate, and white chocolate, with fresh fruits and an assortment of cakes in a porcelain swan fountain for three thousand five hundred dollars."

"That's what I want. Doesn't it sound delicious?" Crystal's eager eyes pleaded with us.

"Crystal, you'll be ripping and running so much that day you won't even taste the chocolate fountain." I laughed at her innocence and excitement.

"Yes, I will. You know I can't resist chocolate. Even when I'm wearing white." She looked at her father with her huge, brown doe eyes.

I was ready to write the check for her, myself.

"Okay Jean-Paul, that's it." Walter pulled out his black American Express card and held it over the edge of the vintage desk.

"Victoria will have a final invoice for you at the front desk. It's going to be a glorious wedding. Money well spent." Jean-Paul stood and shook our hands before escorting us to the front desk. "I'll see you at the church on the 15th. The big day."

Walter made the final payment, then held the door as we stepped outside into the humid evening night air. In the distance, a night bird chirped—an odd sound. How could he be so happy when the rocks in my stomach continued to shift because we were losing our baby girl?

"I'm so tickled," Crystal said. "Where are we going for dinner tonight?"

"We'll go to The Savoy. Isn't that your favorite restaurant, Crystal?" I asked.

"It most certainly is. Let's ride in one car, that way we get to spend more time together. I'm in no hurry to get home tonight because Max is working late."

The low hum of activity greeted us as we walked into the dimly lit restaurant. We were seated in a booth near the back.

"I'd like a bottle of Dom Perignon, we're celebrating tonight," Walter said as the server filled our water glasses.

We placed our orders for dinner while Crystal chattered non-stop about the wedding.

"Have you been able to find out yet where Max is taking you for the honeymoon?" Walter asked.

"Ah, yes, we're going to Hawaii. Can you believe it? But please don't tell anyone. He wants us to keep that to ourselves." She squirmed in her seat. "But here is the best part…we leave Saturday night, right from the reception. We go first to San Francisco, where we will spend two nights. And Mom, you know while we're there, I've got to go back to that Macy's in Nob Hill with that massive shoe department." She swooned in her chair.

"That was a fabulous trip. I still can't get over the height of those trees in Muir Woods. But you're right, that shoe department was the best. I think I bought three pairs on that trip."

"No, the best part was the wineries. Nothing beats a whole day of wine tasting," Walter piped in.

"Then we're flying into Honolulu for three days, the Big Island for three days, and then Maui for four days," Crystal continued.

I took a relaxing breath, my first one of the day. Contentment coursed through my veins. I listened to Walter and Crystal chat like two old friends. I closed my eyes to freeze this moment in my memory. Maybe Marco was right; maybe I was highly sensitive because so much was happening all at once.

"I don't have to wait a week or two or a year for my honeymoon. It starts right after the reception. Isn't Max great?" Crystal reached across the table and laid her cool hand on top of mine.

"Okay, I guess," Walter teased. "He'd better take care of my daughter. As much as we're spending on the wedding, he'd better plan something spectacular for the honeymoon."

"Daddy…don't start." Crystal shook her finger at him.

"You deserve the best. He needs to know that from the beginning." Walter picked up his glass and took a long swallow. "He's off to a good start."

We finished our entrees. My pants grew so tight I wanted to come out of them. I needed to slip into something with rubber in the waist. A nice pair of sweatpants would have felt just right.

"Would you care to see our dessert menu?" the server asked.

"I can't eat another thing. I can't gain an ounce or my dress won't fit," Crystal said.

"Same here," I said, even though I wanted to order something rich, thick and sweet.

"Since no one is ordering dessert, I'll have a cappuccino." Walter sat back and placed his arm over the chair.

"I have something I want to tell you guys." Crystal's eyes shot from me over to Walter.

"Oh no. How much is this going to cost?" Walter slid down in his chair.

"Oh, Walter, stop it!"

"Okay…" Crystal hesitated. "It's like this. Max accepted a position at a law firm in New York City. He starts in mid-July."

It felt like someone had poured ice water down my back. I shivered and sat ram-rod straight, afraid to breathe. The entire restaurant grew silent. I saw lips moving but I couldn't hear a sound. I dug my nails into the palms of my hand. Crystal and her father sat face to face, making happy gestures, but I couldn't make out their comments. A bell rang in my head and grew in intensity.

"New York, Crystal?" My voice came back in a tenor that sounded foreign to me.

"Yes, Mom. Now don't start getting all sentimental and stuff. It's only a two-hour drive. You and Dad go to New York several times a year anyway. Now you'll have a place to stay. Plus, this is an excellent firm. There's a chance Max could make partner. I've got some interviews scheduled with a couple of investment firms right after the honeymoon. So everything is going good." Crystal talked fast when she wanted me to agree with her.

"Hey, that's wonderful. You'll love living in New York. There's so much going on and so much to do." Walter leaned over and hugged her.

"Last week we looked at apartments. We found this really nice loft in Morningside Heights overlooking the Hudson River. It has two bedrooms and it's huge by New York standards." Crystal looked at me. "Mom, you're too quiet."

My heart slowed to a problematic beat. "I'm a little surprised. I didn't know Max was looking for a job in New York." My voice sounded distorted and heavy.

"He's been sending his résumés out all over the place, and so have I. Aren't you happy for us?"

Her giddy excitement twisted my stomach.

Tears gathered in the corners of my eyes. In a tight voice, I said, "Yes baby, I'm very happy for you. Very happy."

"Crystal, you know how your Mom is. She'll be weepy for a day or two but she'll get over it. This is great."

The waiter set the cappuccino in front of Walter. After adding a teaspoon of sugar, he sipped it.

I shot him a cold stare. He had no idea how I was going to put one foot in front of the other and keep moving forward, and neither did I.

"I'm a little shocked, that's all. I had no idea you guys were considering moving away. I'm going to be fine. I'll just come up to visit you every weekend while your father is at work." I tried to smile, but my lips couldn't cooperate.

During the drive back to the caterer's office to pick up our cars, I sat in the front seat with my arms crossed over my stomach, watching life whiz by at a dizzying speed. My body screamed for the anxiety pills buried in my purse. I clamped my hands together and regulated my breathing until I got back to my car.

Walter cruised through the streets of Wilmington, catching every red light. I chewed my bottom lip as he expounded on all the wonderful museums and theaters in New York. The placating sound of his voice felt like daggers in my ears.

When he pulled into the parking lot, I released my breath.

"Mom, see you at the soiree." Crystal leaned across the seat and kissed me on the cheek. "You know we'll be okay, stop looking so sad."

"I'll be fine," I whispered, not trusting my voice.

"Don't forget, Dad, you can't come to the soirée."

"You can always come home, Walter. But you might want to stay out of the way," I said to him as I got out of the car.

Crystal planted a kiss on his cheek. She looked at me for a long moment then jumped in her car. Walter backed out of the parking lot before I could even get into my car. I watched their tail-lights pull out of the lot. My hands shook as I fumbled for the pills in the bottom of my purse. Unbelievable sadness clutched me. After shaking a pill out of the bottle, I threw it in my mouth and swallowed it without water, the bitter residue exploded in my mouth.

I drove home with only the sound of the wind rushing through the window. Visions of my past life flashed before me like a silent movie. Happy times with Crystal and Walter, the house bursting with smiles and laughter, teenage girls lounging around the pool, birthday parties, sleepovers, camping in the back yard. It all faded into a solid gray haze with an empty house, a distant husband, and years of nothing stretching ahead of me.

Marco's comment about how his marriage was over, long before they acknowledged the end made me wonder if Walter and I were in the same state of denial.

I walked in the house and opened the refrigerator. I grabbed a bottle of wine and filled a water glass. Leaning against the kitchen counter, I twirled the wine and contemplated my life. Maybe taking Carla's spinning class could shift my state of mind. At least it would get me out of the house.

When the glass was empty, I set it next to the sink and swiped tears before they landed on my cheeks. On my way up the stairs I could hear Walter in his office, pounding out a message on his keyboard and talking on the phone. I started to tell him goodnight but it didn't seem important, or necessary, and I didn't care if his night was good or bad.

After washing my face and brushing my teeth, I climbed between the sheets. I picked up the phone and dialed Ursula's number. When she answered I said, "Can I have an affair with Marco?"

"Yes. Want me to call him for you?"

"I'm serious."

"I know you are. You've been lusting after him for years, but if you're asking the question, something else must be wrong. So what's the matter? What did the bastard do this time?"

"Walter didn't do anything specific but everything in general. He's in his own world and I'm alone in mine."

"Marco is the person you want in your world?"

"He's a good choice. He meets all the qualifications."

"Then give it a try. If you get caught, tell Walter it's payback."

"What should I tell my father? I could go to hell for having these thoughts." I chuckled and wondered what Walter would do if he caught me having an affair.

"You can always repent at the last minute. Are you going to be okay tonight?"

"Yeah. I'll be fine," I managed.

"Hey, Tracy, can we talk tomorrow? Anthony just walked in."

"Crystal is moving to New York," I blurted.

"Oh no, Tracy. Are you falling apart? Want me to come over?"

"No." I couldn't stop the cascade of tears. Ursula made cooing sounds but she didn't have what I needed. "Go to Anthony," I finally said, and hung up.

Chapter Thirteen – Walter

Every seat around the large oval table was filled. This meeting was merely a formality. I'd completed my list of employees to be terminated, weeks ago. Now I only wanted to validate my assumptions. So far my instincts were right.

"What do you think, Walter?" Thompson's questions drew my attention back. He'd been posturing all morning, trying to secure his position. But he needed to sit down and shut up so I could end the meeting.

I rolled my thumb over the crystal of my watch, keeping my eye on the second hand. "This meeting has already run longer than I had scheduled. I have an appointment, so we're going to have to reconvene later today." I stood up and placed my palms on the table.

Thompson held his pencil up in the air to get my attention. "Excuse me, Walter, we need to get our numbers and names submitted to Personnel first thing tomorrow morning."

"I'm aware of that. So this afternoon, when we get back together, each one of you needs to come into the meeting with a list of under-performing employees. I'm not going to help you put together that list. Look at the employee performance reviews for the last year and compile your list. Those will be the names submitted for termination unless there are extenuating circumstances we need to discuss as a group." I surveyed the room. "Are there any questions?"

Thompson looked dumbfounded. "I think we're making some progress here. I'd hate to stop now. Can you postpone your meeting?" His cold stare caught me. He wanted my job. I relished the idea of being *his* boss.

"We'll meet back here at four. Be prepared." I picked up my papers without addressing his question. "If you have something on your calendars this afternoon, I suggest you clear it." I barreled out of the room. Sasha's doctor's appointment was in twenty minutes and the last thing I needed was to hear her whine because I was late.

I stopped at Beverly's desk. "I'll be out of the office until four. Please reserve the same conference room for the team and make sure everyone is back here by then. If I get any calls, tell them I'm tied up and will return their call later this evening."

"Okay. Anything else?" She scribbled a note on her pad.

"Yes, call Ms. Samuels and let her know I'm on my way."

Beverly raised her head and glared at me. Her pencil poised in midair.

"Did you hear me?"

"Yes, I'll make that call." She turned back to the computer and began punching the keys.

Without saying anything else I made my way out of the store. The Black Book was only two blocks from my office so I pulled up in front of Sasha's store with ten minutes to spare.

I turned off the car and rushed inside. Thankfully, Sasha didn't expect me to attend every doctor's appointment, but she thought these appointments were special.

A few customers milled around, browsing.

"Walter, we're going to be late." Sasha's thin voice and dark eyes meant trouble.

"Are you okay?" I pulled Sasha closer and slipped my tongue into her mouth. She was slow to respond.

"Your secretary called. As usual, she was curt." Her tone launched my warning radar.

"You know I've spoken with Beverly before. She's very loyal to Tracy."

"Can you speak with her again? I don't want to be treated like a…like—"

"Honey, what does it matter? It won't be much longer." I placed my hand around her waist and pulled her closer. Her stomach was no longer flat, now there was a roundness that hinted at her condition. Her breasts had increased two sizes and I found it all appealing.

"Maybe before returning to the office we can stop by your house." I stuck my tongue in her ear.

"I've been having morning sickness, the store was hectic this morning, and you're ten minutes late. Should I go on, or do you get the picture?" She pulled her purse onto her shoulder. "We'd better leave, now. We don't have much time." She yelled instructions over her shoulder to Jeanette, her helper, before walking out the door.

"Are you okay?" I asked when we were on our way.

She turned to face me. "I feel like I'm going through this alone. I'm sick all by myself. I'm having cravings all by myself. I shopping for baby stuff all by myself. I don't want to go through this pregnancy all by myself."

"Sasha, what do you want me to do? I said from the beginning nothing changes until after the wedding."

"I guess I thought you'd come up with something by now. It's been weeks. With the pregnancy, I thought you'd make a change. I didn't trick you into this. It's what happens when consenting adults have unprotected sex."

"I know it wasn't a trick, but I wish—"

"Don't say it, Walter. Please don't say you wish I weren't pregnant. It'll change everything."

I heard anger bubbling like an angry cauldron. "You've only made a partial commitment to me. Are you really going to leave Tracy, or is that what you tell me to keep this thing between us going?" She used her finger to point at herself and me.

I'm sure she meant to ask if I wanted to keep screwing her and I did. I relished the look on my brothers faces when I told them about my twenty-something girlfriend. Even though they were being faithful husbands now, neither of them ever had an affair with a woman as young as Sasha. I saw the admiration in their eyes; it was the only time I felt equal to them.

"Don't start with this again, Sasha. By now you ought to know how much you mean to me. Dammit. But I have no intention of turning Crystal's world upside down right now. Not before her wedding. So don't ask me to do that."

She huffed, faced forward, and crossed her arms over her stomach.

I could understand her doubt, but leaving a marriage is not like putting on clean underwear. My life with Tracy was so intertwined with material things, memories and people. "I told you before, that after the wedding I'm telling Tracy I'm leaving. Nothing can change that."

We got into the car.

"I've heard that before," she hissed before buckling her seatbelt.

"You have to be patient. We've had this discussion."

"We're having it again. When? When are you leaving her?"

"After the wedding." I gripped the steering wheel with both hands.

"Walter, I mean it, are you really leaving? Are you going to leave the big house, the fancy parties, and your well-connected friends, and come to live with me and the baby? What does *after the wedding* mean? The day after, the week after or the year after?"

"What's this about, Sasha? What's wrong?"

"You keep saying you're leaving, but you keep finding reasons to stay. Tracy is having a hard time, wait until Crystal finishes school, and wait until after Crystal's wedding. There's always a reason, another delay. I don't want to wait another month. I won't." She turned back to me. "If you want, I'll tell Tracy about us and I'll tell her your marriage is over."

"No. That's not an option. I told you I'd talk to Tracy. It's only a few more days, Sasha."

"We'll see." She sat back in the seat with a defiant thump.

"I've made a full commitment to you. I'm paying your mortgage. I bought you a car. I give you money every month to help with the expenses. You know the pressure I'm under at work. And the wedding is days away. Once this stuff is all behind me…we…I…can tell Tracy I want a divorce." I banged my hand against the steering wheel. "Stop acting like a brat. You knew what you were getting into."

I glanced at her from the corner of my eye. She looked young and vulnerable. I wanted to believe her insecurities were borne out of her youth, but I was beginning to think it was a character weakness. From the very beginning of our relationship she had challenged me to demonstrate my feelings for her. With increasing frequency she laid out ultimatums to see how well I performed.

I pulled into the doctor's office parking lot and turned off the engine. Her short dress exposed her thighs. I stroked her knee then ran my hand under her hem. A weak smile danced on her lips. I pulled her into my arms and held her tight.

"Damn, those pregnancy hormones," I whispered in her ear.

She giggled and wrapped her arms around my neck. "Okay, Walter. I believe you." Her eyes lightened.

I got out of the car and opened her door. She gave me a clear shot of her hot pink panties as she stepped out of the car.

"Jesus, Sasha, did you have to do that? Now I'll be thinking about you all afternoon."

"That's exactly why I did it." She tossed her curly mane over her shoulder.

"What about my idea of swinging by the house for a quickie?"

"I think you still love your wife." She maneuvered her body closer and grabbed my crotch.

"What? Why Sasha? Look, let's get back in the car and finish this conversation. People will be staring at us."

"No, let's just go inside. We'll be late." She turned on her high-heeled sandals and marched towards the building. I fell in behind her, my eyes on her shapely bare legs. The hassle she gave me was worth it, I thought as I stepped up beside her to hold her hand.

While she signed in at the receptionist desk, I sat in a waiting room chair as far away from the other pot-bellied patients as possible. Women in various stages of pregnancy lined the room. Some of them were alone, others were with husbands or the guys unlucky enough to knock them up. I fit into that unlucky category. Because, even with the shapely legs, great food, and wonderful sex, I was hiking up the rough side of a mountain.

I crossed my legs and sat up straight to alleviate the pressure on my chest, and waited for this appointment to be over. Staying at the personnel meeting would have been a lot less painful than this.

Before Sasha could finish at the receptionist desk the door that led to the examination rooms opened. My eyes locked on Carla the second she crossed the threshold with Javier schlepping behind her.

I jumped up. My heart smacked against my rib cage.

"Walter, what are you doing here?" Carla's obnoxious voice filled the room. She sauntered towards me, her hips swaying in a way that was sexy only to Javier. "Is everything okay with Tracy?" She placed her blood-red fingernails on her hips.

I trained my glance on Carla and Javier, refusing to look at Sasha standing behind them.

"Everything is fine." My voice sounded far too chipper for the environment.

"I didn't know Tracy came to Dr. Johnson. Where is she?" Carla was so loud, everyone turned to stare. She peered around the room like she expected Tracy to suddenly appear, then her gaze landed on Sasha. My heart refused to beat until

Carla snapped her attention back to me. Sasha took a nearby seat and watched us.

"She's not here. One of the admin assistants got sick in the office and this is her doctor," My knees shook. I thought Sasha would come our way.

"Hmmm." Carla placed her index finger on her cheek and didn't try to hide her suspicion or contempt.

"Hey, Walter man." Javier extended his hand for me to shake. "Look Carla, we have to go, I've got to get back to work." Javier did a two-step toward the door.

"Okay darling." She patted his hand. "Tell Tracy I'll call her later. I'm so excited about the little soiree we godmothers are throwing for Crystal tonight. You won't be hanging around, will you?" She ran her hand through her tresses.

Javier shuffled from one foot to the next.

"I don't plan to be there. I'll be working late," I said.

"Yeah, just make sure. Because there won't be any men there, hanging around eating up all our goodies and trying to rule the night."

"I have no intention of doing any of that."

Javier grabbed her hand and pulled her toward the exit. I plopped into my chair and exhaled.

"Are you sure everything is okay, Walter? You look funny." Carla asked over her shoulder.

"Carla, he's fine, let's go." Javier grabbed her hand and pulled her out of the room.

Sasha frowned at me for a full minute before crossing the room and sitting beside me. "She will probably call Tracy from the lobby."

A stream of sweat rolled down my back. The pressure on my chest increased, making it harder to catch my breath. A massive heart attack would have solved all my problems. Every one of them.

"You're busted now, aren't you?" Sasha positioned her purse in her lap.

I couldn't respond. My heart was beating a million times a minute. Instead, I turned my attention to the television positioned in the corner near the ceiling.

"What are you going to do?"

I shrugged. "Can you be quiet for a moment and let me think?"

She leaned over her chair and drew close to my ear. "I'm not going to live like this much longer. I'm tired of hiding, Walter."

I clamped my jaw and shifted my position in the chair away from her. Sasha didn't say anything else. She flipped through a parenting magazine while she waited, but only glanced at the pictures and articles before turning to the next page.

"Ms. Samuels, you can come back now." Sasha cut her eyes at me as I followed her into the examination room. She undressed, following the instructions the nurse gave her, the whole time giving me a cold stare as if I were one of American's Most Wanted.

"What could I say, Sasha, my pregnant mistress is here for an appointment?"

She hunched her shoulders. "That would have been fine. Just drop the mistress part. I hope I'm more to you than that." She flashed the ring I'd given her.

The doctor came in and closed the door. He didn't look old enough to be out of medical school. His buzz-cut and clean face reminded me of a first year intern.

"So, Mr. Samuels, are you hoping for a boy or a girl?" He tugged on latex gloves and wheeled his chair toward the examination table. He motioned Sasha to place her feet in the stirrups.

"It's Baptiste, and a boy would be nice."

Sasha stared at me, disapproval burned in her eyes. The doctor looked from Sasha and back to me. "Next month we'll do an ultrasound and tell you for sure. Can you wait that long?"

"We'll manage," I responded.

The doctor prodded and poked Sasha. "Based on the information you've given us and the exam, you are about six months along. Everything appears to be fine. Keep taking your prenatal vitamins and I'll see you in a month." He gave me a quick once-over before clicking his pen and rushing out the door.

Sasha slid off the table, her bottom lip tucked under her teeth. She turned her back to me while dressing, which meant I was being given the silent treatment. At least it had a good view.

We pulled out of the parking lot and Sasha's mouth was still twisted into a frown. "Why was it important for you to make sure the doctor knew your name?"

"Do you think I should have let him think I was Mr. Samuels? Did he think I was your father or your husband? Either way, he needed to know."

"What does it matter what he thought?"

"It mattered to me. Just like the run-in with Carla meant something to you." I glanced over at her. "Why are you crying?"

"How the hell do I know? I'm pregnant, be thankful I'm not homicidal." She fished a tissue out of her purse and swiped her nose.

The tears were a device and nobody used it better than Sasha. She could start bawling at the sight of road kill. I was smart enough to know I was being manipulated, but too exhausted to fight back. Maybe it was my fault she was in this situation.

"I have an idea." I made a sharp left turn away from the bookstore. "I think I know just the thing to bring that perfect smile back to your beautiful face."

"Oh yeah. What?"

I pulled to a stop in front of Goldstein's Fine Jewelry.

"You think jewelry will make everything better?" The twinkle in her eyes betrayed her tone.

"I do." I held her face between my hands and stared into her innocent eyes. Her cheeks glistened with tears. I must have been crazy trying to please two women. I kissed her delicate lips. Her mouth was salty. Afterwards, I walked around to her side of the car and held her hand to escort her into the store.

She walked along the glass showcases. Her slow thorough examination of the trinkets reminded me of my mother. It wasn't until I was in college that I realized my mother manipulated me by slowing her pace. Sasha moved with excruciating slowness. I allowed her this victory.

I stood aside and let her browse in peace. How our relationship got so far mystified me. I thought it was just fun-crazy sex. But the deception morphed and grew into an apocalyptic affair. I couldn't love Sasha like I loved Tracy. She shouldn't expect me to. But the baby...

I rubbed my chest. The pain was intense.

"Sasha, I need to get back to work." I walked up behind her. "I'm sure you see something in here that you like."

She pointed to a two-carat diamond tennis bracelet. Her eyes sparkled along with the gemstones and her sweet smile returned. "It almost matches the necklace you gave me for Christmas." She ran her hand along the fine gold chain around her neck.

"Let me see that bracelet, please."

The salesman unlocked the case and placed the bracelet on a velvet pouch. Sasha turned the bracelet over again and again, allowing the sunlight to catch the facets of the stones. She was like a child with a new bauble. If it kept her quiet for a while, it was worth the money.

"Is that what you want, honey?" I ran my hand around her waist.

"Yes, isn't it gorgeous? I love it."

"We'll take the bracelet. You don't need to wrap it. I think she's going to wear it home," I said.

I paid for the bracelet and hurried Sasha back to the car.

She cozied up to me. "Do you still want to make a stop at the house before going back to work?"

"I can't now. I've got a meeting. I'll be there tonight and you can make up to me." Sex and gifts solved all her problems.

"I'll be waiting." She licked her lips, taunting me with seduction.

Before she got out of the car at the bookstore, I held her arm. "Sasha, you've got to be patient. Everything will be fine. Trust me."

Chapter Fourteen - Tracy

The sight of my parent's semi-detached Fairmount Park house made me exhale. Beautiful Bur Oak trees lined both sides of the street, forming a lush green canopy across the road. Thoughts of the street where I grew up gave me a warm feeling.

As little girls, Ursula and I ran along the street collecting acorns that fell from the huge trees. We scooped up the nuts in empty mayonnaise jars and counted our loot at night. Every day we rushed from one end of the street to the other to see who could collect the most acorns before Halloween, when the yellow-green canopy of leaves fell from the trees and covered the lawns with a crunchy carpet.

My mother stood in the door waiting on me, so I stopped reminiscing and got out of the car.

"Hey Mom." I kissed and hugged her.

"Girl, what has taken you so long to come home? What has got you so busy?"

I followed her into the kitchen. No matter how many years I'd been away, she still called this my home.

"You're not working today?"

"No, I'm off all week taking care of some final wedding details."

The rich aroma of coffee greeted me as I walked into the bright yellow kitchen. I pulled my favorite oversized mug from the cabinet and poured a cup. After adding cream and sugar, I sat at the table with my mother. "You know, this wedding is keeping me really busy. I'm sorry I haven't been here sooner." I sipped coffee and tried to give my mother a look that would make her feel sorry for me. "Where's Dad?"

"He's still sleeping. He'll be stirring soon."

"It's nine, he's usually up with the sun."

"I told you, he hasn't been himself lately."

"Can you believe he said he'd let me take him to the doctor after the wedding? But only if I take him to lunch afterwards," I chuckled.

"It's a good thing the wedding is soon. I can't wait much longer." She stood and poured another cup of coffee. "You want more?" She held the pot to me.

I nodded.

"It's his way of controlling his life," I said.

"He hasn't gotten any better. He's falling asleep right after dinner, and sometimes he sweats profusely while he's just watching television. I guess a few more days won't matter." She paused for a moment. "Everything will be okay," she finished slowly. Her look said she wasn't pleased with the way I was handling this matter, but I didn't feel like I had much choice. My love for my parents was unrelenting, but sometimes I felt like I was always letting them down.

"How's my granddaughter? I'll bet she's so excited an elephant couldn't hold her down."

"She's moving to New York." The words caught in my throat.

"New York?" She set her cup on the table. "Why?"

"Max has been offered a job with a law firm. They've already found a place to live, and now Crystal is submitting her resume around town to find a job, too." I tried to mask my unhappiness.

"Don't look so sad. It's not the end of the world." She gave me a smile. "When you and Walter decided to live in Delaware, I thought I would die, but I made out okay and you will too. Look at it this way—at least now you get a nice place to visit."

"You always try to find the bright side to everything, don't you?"

"Might as well."

My father walked into the kitchen. "Good morning ladies." The sharp crease in his khaki pants and his fresh shirt made him look like he was on his way to do something important.

"You sure are dressed up. Where are you going?" I kissed him on the cheek.

"I like to dress up for your mother. Besides, I heard you down here, too."

"I like it when you get all dolled up for me, honey." My mother stood and kissed my father on the lips before opening the refrigerator. She removed eggs and bacon.

"It's about time you got out of bed sleepyhead. I thought I was going to have to come up there and drag you down here." I poked my father's arm.

"I'm retired now, I can sleep as long as I want and get up whenever I want.

"I've made you an appointment with the doctor on Monday morning after the wedding. And before you ask, yes, I'm treating you to lunch."

He clicked his tongue as he looked at me over his coffee cup.

My energetic parents were in their late sixties. But I saw a difference in my father. His sunken eyes sported bags and his darker coloring had a grayish undertone I hadn't noticed before. Even though he had only descended one flight of stairs to get to the kitchen, a thin sheen of sweat peppered his skin. My mother was right to worry about him.

"Dad, are you feeling okay?" I leaned closer to him as if a better look would give me a diagnosis.

"There you go, sounding like your mother. If the two of you don't stop nagging me, I'm going to cut off your allowances. Now that's enough from both of you, questioning me every time I sneeze or have to sit down. I'm an old man, what do you expect? This is what old men do."

"Okay…okay, Dad. I'll be quiet, but you promised—"

"Yeah, yeah, yeah, Tracy." He waved my comment away. "And nothing else about how I'm feeling until next week." He punctuated his words with a final look.

I knew that look. I'd seen it before whenever he didn't approve of something.

The only sound for several minutes was the clicking of the knives and forks against the plates and the cups hitting the saucers as we sipped coffee. It was then that I understood my mother's worry. My father wasn't being stubborn, he was in denial. What if something was really wrong with him? I put the thought away and picked up my cup.

My mother got up from the table and began clearing the breakfast dishes. "What time should I get to your place tonight?"

"Ursula and Carla are calling all the shots. I don't have to do a thing. All we need to do is be there at seven. Do you want me to come back here to pick you up?"

"No, no. I'll drive. I might leave after a short while. This is for you young people anyway. And I don't want to leave your father alone too long."

"Frances, go on down there and have a good time. I'm old enough to stay home by myself. Be there for Crystal. She didn't put the cart before the horse. That's something to be proud of." My father laughed but we both knew he wasn't joking.

It had only taken him twenty minutes.

I should have been used to the jab, but this time stung as much as all the rest.

I kissed my parents, promising to come for more frequent visits. Before starting the car, I pulled my prescription pills from my purse. With the bottle tucked in my palm, relief pulsed through me. I didn't need the tiny white pills, but it was good knowing I could stop the unhappiness within minutes. I twisted the lid and extracted solace with my index finger.

***

On the way home, I stopped by my office to retrieve the banking information. It would have been easier to check from home, but Crystal had taken over the house to prepare for the soirée and I needed to stay out of the way. Besides, I didn't want to be distracted again.

The joint account Walter and I shared popped up on the screen. I scrolled down the page to identify several of the transactions. The check to the caterer had already cleared the account. Jean-Paul wasted no time collecting his funds. I scanned the page, another large withdrawal for five thousand dollars trumpeted for my attention. It had cleared the day before the check to the caterer. I wrote down the transaction number.

I reached into the credenza to find the phone number of the bank. After several prompts, I spoke to a live person.

"Yes, I'd like some information on one of my accounts." I provided her with the security details she requested.

"Got it. What are you looking for?" she asked.

"There was a large withdrawal made from my account last week. I want to know who it was made out to." I tapped my pen on the desk while she pulled up my data.

"Check number 5672 was made out to a Sasha Samuels."

"Is that S-a-s-h-a?" I asked.

She confirmed the information and disconnected the call. I scribbled the name onto a note pad, thinking I would recognize it if I saw it in print. Maybe she had something to do with Crystal's wedding—the photographer, the florist, or one of the planners. We had written so many checks for the wedding, I was losing track. There was something familiar about the name, but I couldn't remember what it was.

Marco stood in my door. "I thought I saw your car in the parking lot."

I couldn't help but smile at the sight of him.

"I just stopped by to pick up some stuff I forgot."

He walked into my office and stood at the edge of the desk. "Wow! You look nice."

"Thanks. You look pretty hot yourself." My seductive tone sounded like I was channeling Sharon Stone in her infamous leg crossing scene.

He inched closer to my desk, giving me the perfect view of his thick lashes and dark eyes. "Have lunch with me."

"I…I…"

"Come on, you have to eat," he said with a crooked smile that I was beginning to look forward to seeing. "I'll drive."

I came within inches of saying no. My father's words, Crystal's move, all pushed my sensibilities to the recesses of my mind. For an instant, I wanted to be selfish, to put what I wanted above anybody else.

"Okay." I gathered the papers and my purse and followed him out of the building before I changed my mind. I scanned the street when Marco pulled from the lot. As long as the conversation stayed off of us, then lunch was just lunch.

"So, do you think Bill from accounting knows he's wearing his toupee backwards?" I asked.

"You think that's a hairpiece?"

"The man didn't have hair last week, now he's got a full head. Don't tell me you didn't notice." I covered my mouth.

"Truthfully, I didn't." His hearty laugh tickled my ears.

Office politics kept us chatting until we pulled into the restaurant parking lot. With words, I could defend my behavior to the Pope. If he saw my heart, I would be preached into hellfire and damnation.

There were only a few patrons in the restaurant, which allowed us our choice of seats. I picked a small table by the window. It was the furthest from the door.

"This place is more upscale than the deli I selected." Marco fingered the linen tablecloths and napkins. "I was afraid if I picked this fancy last week, you'd go running in the opposite direction."

"I'm not that bad, am I?"

He flashed a broad smile. "Pretty much."

"I didn't run when you told me how you felt."

He leaned across the table, his face inches away from me. "No, but you wanted to. It's a good thing I had the car locked."

"How is it you're so easy to talk to?"

"I've had a lot of practice." He pushed his face closer to me, his features softened. "You look like something's bothering you today. Want to talk about it?"

I ran my hands along my lap. "I'm fine."

"If you keep fidgeting with your dress, it's going to be a rag by the time we finish lunch."

I looked up long enough to see a furrow between his brows.

"Tell me something. If you're unhappy, why do you stay?" His eyes challenged me to tell the truth.

I pushed a curl behind my ear and focused on his face. "It's not so bad. We have a nice house. We take nice trips, and there's Crystal. Besides, my parents never thought it would work."

He nodded but there was no pity in his eyes. "So you're staying in an unhappy marriage to prove your parents wrong?"

I cleared my throat. "I don't expect you to understand. I'm not sure I do."

He reached across the table and cradled my hands. I'd love to fall into his arms every night, wake up to his touch every morning. But my marriage came first. It always had. But now…

Chapter Fifteen – Tracy

After lunch with Marco I should have felt ecstatic. Instead, I was coming up short and couldn't explain why. I sat behind my desk waiting on the phantoms clawing at my stomach to settle down. The message light was blinking. I ignored it for several seconds, not wanting the real world to interrupt.

"Tracy, call me when you get a chance," Carla sounded rushed. "I have something to tell you."

I deleted the message and pulled out the pad with Sasha Samuels' name. Maybe Crystal knew if she was one of the vendors we were using for the wedding. As I picked up the phone to call Crystal, Ursula walked into my office.

"I saw you coming back in with Marco. You two looked pretty cozy." She sat and crossed her legs. "I thought you were on vacation this week." Her high pitched voice was filled with suspicion.

"I am. But I came in to get some stuff and he—"

"Yeah, yeah, Tracy's human." She threw her hands in the air. "After what you've been telling me about Walter, I'm not surprised. You two make a good-looking couple. I think he's got a thing for you."

"I haven't done anything that can't be printed on the front page of the paper." I paused. "But I feel guilty because I certainly want to." I know I had a silly dreamy look on my face, but I couldn't mask my emotions. Whatever whacky thing was going wrong in my head and heart causing these feelings would straighten out soon. I was sure of it.

"All I can say is, think about it before you do. If Walter finds out, he won't be nearly as forgiving as you were."

I shook my head. Ursula was right. I wouldn't cheat on Walter. And I wouldn't leave him. But I wondered how many sacrifices I had to make. Did I have to live my life regretting the choices I'd made? I was only enjoying my daydreams for as long as I could. "Anyway, I need to get out of here and run some errands before the soirée tonight."

"Look, before you go, I need to tell you something." She paused.

"Oh shit, Ursula, I don't like the sound of this."

"I'm leaving the company."

"What? Why?" My hand flitted around the desk not certain where to land. Ursula had been in shouting distance of me since grade school. Growing up, we lived a few doors from each other. We went to Spellman together. We started working at the company within weeks of each other—her first, then me. She was an extension of me. The sister I wanted but never had.

"Tracy, I'm in love with Anthony and—don't lecture me okay? I'm going to take a job in Philadelphia."

"In Philly? Why?"

"Anthony and I are getting very serious. We think this is the best thing. He helped me find the job."

"Why doesn't he take a job in Philadelphia so you can stay here?"

"Don't do this." Ursula shook her head. "We talked about it and he was willing to leave. We were both looking for jobs. I found this one first. Plus it pays more and offers more opportunities. I'm not moving away, I just won't be working upstairs from you. That's all."

"You sure you want to do this?" I reached for her hand. "Are you really sure?" I knew she wouldn't change her mind.

"I'm sure. It's a bigger company. I'll be Director of Finance with an opportunity to make Vice President. That's if Anthony and I don't decide to start a family." She looked at me with a twinkle in her eye.

"Not you, too. You're older than me, you can't be serious. You don't even like kids."

"I'm just kidding," she laughed. "You know I don't want children. Being a godmother is good enough for me. I adore Crystal."

I sat back in my chair and took a breath. "Is he going to marry you?" I tried to negotiate with her, equating marriage with love. My marriage didn't have any resemblance to love lately.

"Maybe you ought to ask if I'm going to marry him." Ursula placed her hands on her hips and looked indignant.

"Are you?"

"He's asked and I've said yes." She laid her left hand on my desk, flashing a huge diamond ring.

"Oh Ursula, get outta here! When did this happen?" I dashed around the desk and swept her into my arms.

"Last night. We're thinking about getting married next year."

"I thought you were never getting married."

"I know, but—"

"How many carats is that ring and who helps you carry it around?"

"It's three carats. Isn't it exquisite?" She wiggled her freshly manicured fingers.

"Ursula, it is absolutely fabulous. And even though I'm upset that you're leaving me here all alone, I really am happy for you. I really am." My voice sounded genuine, but Ursula couldn't see the havoc tearing at my insides. The fortress of friends and family that held me up was slowly crashing into rubble.

"You won't be alone, *you'll* have Marco," she giggled.

"Oh girl." I poked her. "But you know…"

"Yeah, yeah, I know, you're married."

We sat in my office talking about her relationship with Anthony. She couldn't stop gushing about all the wonderful things they did together, how he was willing to do anything she wanted. How they stayed at her house eating microwave popcorn while they watched *Schindler's List*. She'd asked Carla and me to watch it with her years ago, but we always had an excuse. She was bursting with happiness. She reminded me of me when I started dating Walter. We could have rolled the clock back twenty years to when Ursula and I sat in our cramped dorm room. I was the one gushing about Walter while she had her nose wrinkled with questions.

She stood to leave. "See you in a few hours. Don't be late." She hugged me. "Stop looking so sad. I'm only getting married, not moving to Hong Kong."

"Yeah, but everything is changing. Changing so fast."

I couldn't budge from the chair. After she left, I continued to sit opposite my desk with my hands folded in my lap, staring. As long as I sat there, time stood still. Crystal was my little girl, Walter loved me, my parents weren't getting older, and my best friend lived close. I could slow time just for a moment if I didn't budge from my seat, setting the world back in motion.

By the time I had roused myself, then bought gifts for Ursula and Carla and had them wrapped, I was almost late for my hair appointment.

When I arrived home Carla and Ursula were already there along with a caterer. The living room was transformed into a spa with a massage table. The smell of eucalyptus scented candles and oil permeated the air and smooth jazz filtered through the stereo. The family room was turned into a salon with a manicure and pedicure station. Water bubbled in the foot tub. A multitude of nail colors lined the mantel.

The savory smell of delicious food filled the house. I drifted into the kitchen to see what activity was going on in there. The kitchen island was laid out with seared foie gras. I immediately loaded some on a cracker and popped it into my mouth. The delicate pate melted on my tongue. Poached Maine lobsters, tempura soft shell crab, and braised short ribs looked just as tempting on the far counter, but I resisted the urge to gorge until the party was in full swing.

With the precision of a welder, the chef ignited a torch and began caramelizing the tops of individual chocolate crème brûlée. They smelled so decadent, I had to push myself out of the kitchen. Leave it to my two best friends to create such an elaborate soiree.

I heard Ursula and Carla squealing in the dining room.

"Hey, you guys." I breezed into the room and kissed each of them on the cheek. The two small pills that I popped on the way home had me feeling good. "Everything looks great." I surveyed the room. "What are you two so excited about?"

"Did you see that ring on Ursula's finger?" The excitement in Carla's voice matched the look in her eyes, all glossy and happy. "It is huge! It is absolutely huge!" She held up Ursula's hand for me to see.

"I know. It is, isn't it?"

The three of us were quiet for a nanosecond. Then we hugged each other again. We all had tears in our eyes.

"Ahhhhh." Ursula jumped around the room in her four-inch heels and pencil skirt. "I'm getting married and I'm so happy. I can't believe this."

Carla and I stood back and let her have her moment. I said a silent prayer that the joy she felt in that moment lasted her a lifetime. Someone deserved to be head-over-heels happy.

"Okay. Okay." She shook her arms and jumped from one foot to the next. "Tonight is about

Crystal and I will not steal her joy. So don't say anything to her about this. She'll be so excited about everything, she'll probably never notice the ring." She looked to Carla and me for confirmation.

We nodded.

"Oh good, 'cause I can't stand to take it off, even for a night." She stomped her feet in quick succession as she pumped her fist in the air, like she was doing an African tap dance.

When she finally settled down, I said, "Everything looks so nice, you guys really outdid yourselves. The food in the kitchen smells so good I want to start sampling now."

"Don't you dare! Crystal called, she's on her way. Toni, Keisha and Donna Lee are already upstairs changing into their pajamas." Carla shook her hips. "How do you like mine?" She did a graceful pirouette so we could see her lacy outfit with her trademark plunging neckline that exposed her generous cleavage.

"Honey, your boobs are huge, look at you popping out of that top. You sure you aren't lactating already?" Ursula teased.

Carla dropped her head. Pain filled her eyes.

"Carla I was only kidding," Ursula said.

"Look, I might as well tell you this now. Today the doctor said my ovaries don't release an egg every month." She caught her breath. Making the statement must have been painful. "The likelihood that I'll get pregnant is slim. That's how she said it—slim."

"Oh, Carla. Be strong honey," I whispered in her ear. "She said slim chance. That means it *could* happen."

"Tracy, I'm not gonna sit around and pine for something that might not happen. There are thousands of children out there waiting on a Mommy and a Daddy. I'm sad that Javier and I might not have our own child," she drew a deep breath, "but we will keep on screwing like crazy and keep on trying to have our own. But we'll adopt if we have to. It's okay, really it is." She shook her head. "I'm okay." She wiped her nose on the back of her hand then smiled a sad grin. "Javier and I talked about what we'll do next, and we're okay. Really I am. If we have to adopt we will," she said with forced cheerfulness.

"Carla, I wouldn't have teased you if I'd known," Ursula said.

She waved her hand to indicate she was finished with this topic for now. "Hey, somebody get me a tissue. Can't you see the snot running from my nose?" She laughed.

I handed her the box.

"Did Walter tell you I saw him this morning?"

"No, we only talked for a few minutes this evening. Where?"

"At Dr. Johnson's office, this morning."

"Who is Dr. Johnson?"

"My ob-gyn. Javier and I go every week for testing and prodding and poking and torture. This morning, Walter was sitting in the waiting room just as pretty as you please. He said one of the secretaries got sick and he had to take her to the doctor." Carla positioned her hands on her hip like I was supposed to have the right answer.

Fear inched down my spine until it settled in my gut, while my right eye twitched. I fought to keep my face neutral. Something stunk, but I didn't know what.

Not one inch of me would allow this evening to turn into another soapy scene like the one I had dragged the three of us through a few weeks before. Walter wasn't the type of person to do a good deed unless it benefited him. Maybe he was trying to impress his boss by trying to appear sympathetic.

I almost laughed at the thought. In the most chipper voice I typically used for a Sunday morning welcome, I said, "I hope everything turned out okay."

The two of them gave me doubtful looks that I ignored.

"I better get upstairs and change so we can get this *soirée* started."

"Did you tell Carla about your special lunch today?" Ursula insinuated.

"A special lunch?"

"I had lunch with Marco. That's all there is to it."

"He hinted he more than just liked Tracy."

"You're playing with fire, honey." Carla wagged her finger at me.

"I'm not playing anything with Marco. He's just a co-worker. Nothing more. Since Ursula is in love, she enjoys wrapping her magic wand around everything within reach." I strutted across the room and said over my shoulder, "I'm going to change."

Upstairs, Crystal's bedroom door was closed. Since she went away to school, we usually left it open, but I could hear girlfriends in there chatting. I should have stuck my head in the door and greeted them, but I needed to be alone.

I closed the master bedroom doors, went directly into the bathroom, and pushed those doors, too. I wanted to be as far away from everyone as possible. I picked up the phone and dialed Walter's office.

No answer.

I sat on the vanity chair with the phone in my hand. If I waited long enough, the curtain would part and reveal Walter's secrets. If I waited long enough, whatever was dragging me down would

give up and let me breathe. If I waited long enough,
I'd be numb enough to walk away.

Chapter Sixteen – Walter

I drummed my pen on the desk. For the moment, the fire burning my ass wasn't extinguished, it had just moved up to the middle of my chest and continued to simmer. There wasn't a single soul I could share my mess with. Even Jay wouldn't believe this big pile of shit I was in now.

I was back in the office just in time for the afternoon meeting. My team sat around the table in the same formation from earlier.

"Why the grim expressions, gentlemen? This is why we get paid the big bucks. We have to make the difficult decisions." I placed my palms on the table. "So let's get started."

With a lime green marker, Thompson wrote the names of the under-performing employees on a large white-board. By six-thirty we were able to construct the list of one hundred and fifty employees worldwide to let go.

Afterwards, the room was silent as we eyeballed the final list. Some of the names were people I'd befriended over the years.

"I don't know how we're going to break this to the employees. Can you imagine the chaos?" one manager spoke up.

"I know we should be relieved this part of the process is over. But this is only the beginning," I said.

"Now that we've cut our staffs what about our jobs? We all know the senior VPs are going through this same exercise. How many of us are going to lose our jobs?" Thompson placed the lime marker on the table. His eyes met mine.

"We've got a lot of meetings planned. As soon as I know something, I'll let you know. Try to stay focused. We'll make this as painless as possible." I looked around the room hoping my speech was convincing. "It's late. Let's call it a day. Thanks everyone."

I strolled out of the conference room behind everyone else. I was pretty confident my job was secure. Nobody worked harder or made more sacrifices. My wreck of a life was an example of the sacrifices I made for the company.

I cleared the papers off my desk, shoving them into the top drawer. My phone vibrated.

"Did you change your mind about coming over tonight? I'm sorry I was such a bear today. It's just hard, you know—"

"I'm leaving the office in a few minutes. My meeting ran longer because…" Sasha's sigh cut me short. She didn't want to hear about my problems and I didn't want to share them with her. That *was* something I talked to Tracy about. "I'll be there shortly. Just be ready for me."

"Oh, you can count on me." She used her voice like a weapon.

Before I could get out of the office, the senior vice president walked in. Joe Johnson was still in his suit and tie, and wore his authority like amour. We all tried to emulate the tall, lean man. We dressed like him. Came in early like him, worked late like him and some of us even talked like him.

Even though I tried to be a clone, too, I hated him. I didn't trust him.

"You're around mighty late tonight, Joe. You must have had a day similar to mine," I said as he sat down.

"I imagine. How did your meetings go today?" Joe crossed his legs and even though he tried to look casual, his stiff back said otherwise.

"We have a list. We'll turn it in tomorrow morning. It was painful, but we got it done."

"Good." He drummed his fingers on the table. "Walter, I want to warn you some vice presidents will be offered packages. Your name is being batted about." He avoided direct eye contact with me.

My chest constricted. I hid my discomfort as best I could. I placed my hand on the top of my desk to steady myself. "What…when? When? Joe, you've gotta be kidding me. I've been working my ass off around here. My performance has been stellar. You've said so yourself. Batted about…what does bat about really mean?"

"We're still reviewing the list and won't have a final decision until the end of the week. I'm doing everything I can for you, but I wanted to give you a heads-up."

"Does this have anything to do with the incident a few weeks ago?" The words clogged in my throat, sounding more desperate than I wanted.

Joe re-crossed his legs and cleared his throat. I knew the answer even before he spoke.

"There are several factors that we're taking into consideration." He continued to look down at his expensive shoes.

"Is there anything I can do to improve my chances?"

"Sit tight and focus on bringing in the second quarter earnings."

"With my direction, my team has exceeded their profit objectives in the last six quarters. I've made this team what it is. How can you even consider letting me go?"

"We're thinking about taking the company in a new direction." He stood and shoved his hands in his pocket, still without making eye contact with me.

"Good night, Joe."

"You too." He eased out the door as quietly as he had entered.

I grabbed my briefcase, threw my laptop inside on top of the mounds of paper and slammed it shut. "Bastard," I muttered. "This company would have tanked years ago without me."

I sped down the interstate with the music blaring to drown out the pain in my chest and the pressure building in my head. Darting from lane to lane. I even flashed my lights on a late model station wagon driven by a gray-haired couple holding up traffic in the left lane.

I pulled into Sasha's driveway and sat in the car for several minutes taking deep breaths. Through the windshield, the little house that used to bring me so much joy didn't look the same. Tonight the light calming sensation that usually comes over me when I pulled in the drive was noticeably absent.

Other than the constant pain burning in my chest, nothing else registered. I was a man on a constant mission for satisfaction even though I knew it didn't exist.

The implications of Joe's words flashed in my head. What would happen if I were forced to take an exit package? An attractive financial package would mean nothing. I was only forty-two years old—too young to go fishing every day. Now I had another child to put through college.

Shit.

I was going to be sixty years old when the baby was ready to start college. I'd be an old man attending a high school graduation; everyone would think I was the grandfather.

I hung my head.

Who was going to pull my balls out of the fire this time?

I climbed out of the car, straightened my back, and headed inside. Sasha walked out of the kitchen wearing a pair of tiny shorts and a fitted top. Her breasts pushed at the fabric. The sight was almost enough to make me forget all the other stuff. I could be happy, for a while, between the beautiful mounds.

"Are you hungry?" She leaned against the door frame.

"Yeah, but not for food." I kissed her mouth.

"That's what I figured. After a long day at work, you're always horny. Do you want dinner first or me first?" She put the spoon down.

"I'll need my stamina, let's eat, then I'll do you."

She pushed her lips into a perfect pout. "I've never come in second before."

"It's been a trying day."

She placed the plates on the table. "I'm having tea for dinner, but there's some wine in the chiller if you want."

I need the whole bottle after the day I've had."

"Let's enjoy dinner without talking about work."

Relief ran through my veins. I didn't have to relive the lousy details again.

"Are you okay after that little run-in?" she asked between bites of grilled chicken.

"Carla caught me by surprise. I didn't know what to say to her."

"That was obvious. That was really a lame excuse you gave her. Of all the doctors in town, what's the likelihood that I'd have the same doctor as your wife's best friend?" Sasha looked at me as if she expected me to provide the statistical odds. "By my next appointment, Tracy will know about me, so you won't have to keep making excuses." Sasha spoke the words like rapid gunfire, making sure she hit her mark.

Trouble brewed behind her pretty brown eyes. She wanted me to co-sign her statement, tell her what she wanted to hear. I nodded instead.

"Crystal's bridal shower thingy is tonight. I need to stay out of the way. I won't be missed."

Her eyes lit up. She got up from the table and came to sit on my lap.

Ahh. That makes you happy, huh? I put down my fork and cupped her breast.

"I'm always happy when I don't have to share you with Tracy." She grabbed my chin between her fingers and kissed me hard on the lips. I dropped my hand inside the band of her shorts. "Why are you wearing panties?"

"You think I walk around with nothing on under my clothes all the time?"

"A man can hope."

"Later. I'll take them off and you can put them in your pocket and take them with you. How's that?"

"How about you take everything off right now?"

She slipped her tongue in my mouth. The forceful drill of her tongue warmed my whole body. "God, you're good at getting my attention."

When she moved to stand up, I held her in place. "Are we okay?"

"We're okay if you make an honest woman out of me."

"You're an honest woman and I love you. Everything is going to turn out just fine." The hole I dug got bigger and bigger but I couldn't stop. I had to tell her what she wanted to hear.

She stroked my penis through my pants. Her long, even caresses made my breath catch. I found her soft mouth and assaulted her tongue. The sweet taste enveloped me. The more she gave me, the more I wanted. She was like an addiction, a habit I didn't want to break. In a perfect world, I would screw her every day before going home to Tracy and acting like a sensible adult male.

"You and I could go on like this forever, screwing in the afternoon, flying around taking expensive vacations, and hiding out in my house. But now things are different."

"What do you need, Sasha? A father for the baby or someone to share your life?" I pulled her closer and tried to kiss her.

She wrenched out of my grip and shook her finger at me. "Don't spin this around and make me the bad guy. I love you, you know what I want." She rolled off my lap, her feet hitting the floor like a cat landing on all fours.

In the middle of the kitchen she took off her pants and whirled her seductive hips. "So come upstairs and give it to me." She laughed, back to her youthful playful self.

"I'll be right up."

She turned to go upstairs, then stopped. "Hey, Walter, thanks for the bracelet." She held out her arm towards me. It sparkled on her wrist.

Alone in the kitchen, I pulled my phone off my hip and called Tracy. Joe's comments still burned in my head. The thought of losing my livelihood was incomprehensible. I could find another place to work, but at my age, the thought of peddling my skills was frightening.

I dialed Tracy. "Is it okay if I sleep in the office tonight?" I asked, wanting to sound as if I was making a great sacrifice for the benefit of my family.

"Sure, Walter. Why don't you stay there?" She sounded guarded.

"I'm not feeling so good. I feel tight, so I'm going to just stay at the office and relax."

"Are you okay? What's tight?"

"It was a rough day. After spending all day cutting my staff, Joe told me my job may be in jeopardy. And you know I don't trust that weasel. But I'm fine, don't start worrying about me."

"If you're in the office, why did you call me on your cell phone?"

I had to think fast.

"Damn, Tracy, I had to step out of the office long enough to get something to eat. I thought we had this shit all figured out. Did you hear a damn thing I told you the other night? So why are you giving me the drill? I just told you how hard my day was, now you're grinding my nuts."

"Walter, chill. Every time I ask a question, it's not a drill. If you don't have anything to hide, quit acting like it. You know you can always come home. Ursula and Carla were just kidding about you not showing up. I'm sure you can slip upstairs without being seen."

"I'll stay here. Have a good time."

"I tried to call you earlier."

"What's up?" I closed my eyes. Carla must have told her about our run-in.

"Just checking in before things got too hectic around here. We can talk later."

I hung up and exhaled. This was getting harder. Tracy was getting more suspicious, always looking for something. With me, there was always something for her to see. I put the last of the dishes in the dishwasher, then turned the lights off and hurried upstairs.

Sasha was in the shower. I shucked my clothes, dropping them on the chair. The steam in the bathroom was thick, but I could see Sasha rubbing soap on her stomach. I climbed in the stall behind her. Her warm body was covered in rosy smelling bubbles and her eyes were closed. I cupped her stomach with my palms. It was only beginning to protrude. I pulled her into my arms and held her tight. She ran her hands along my back and the pressure in my chest eased a little.

I traced my finger between her breasts, her silky skin pebbled up with goose bumps. I cupped her firm, round buttocks. She released a deep moan and pressed against me. With a firm grip on my penis she stroked it. The smooth rhythm was like a potion, helping me to forget and relax at the same time. My body warmed under the hot spray of water. She had me right where she wanted me and I couldn't resist.

"If you want to get clean, you shouldn't do that," I said.

"Getting clean is the least of my concerns." She stood on her tiptoes and placed her lips against mine for several seconds before slipping her tongue into my mouth. The kiss was slow and gentle. Water cascaded over her shoulder as she increased the intensity of her strokes. Getting clean was the last thing I wanted, too.

I turned off the water and grabbed her plump breasts, rolling my tongue over each darkened nipple until they hardened. She gasped when I flicked her breast with my tongue, and moved up her torso. I planted a kiss in the small of her neck because it turned her on as much as it did me.

After grabbing a towel to pat her dry, I picked her up and carried her to the bedroom.

"Walter, I'm still wet and so are you." Her voice was a faint whisper between short breaths.

"It doesn't matter. I want you." I sat on the bed, allowing her to straddle my lap. If everything had to be so different, then this moment had to be pure and satisfying. I captured her mouth and slowly slipped my tongue in, drawing out the pleasure for as long as I could. Even though my breathing was faster than my heartbeat, I let our tongues dance the slow waltz.

I slipped my finger between her legs and kneaded her moist folds. Her eyes glowed with desire, but she didn't rush me. Allowing me to take my time. I lifted her just enough to enter her. Her muscles tightened around me like molten heat. Inside her, the world was beautiful.

The colors were stunning.

The sound was mellow.

Life was easy.

I tried to keep up with her rotating hips. The pores on my scalp prickled, as the sensation slowly rolled down my back. I closed out the world and focused on the heat surrounding my penis.

Her hands raced across my back, blazing a trail of fire, consuming me with desire or pure lust. I didn't care which.

She found my tongue and pulled it into her mouth. I lived for this ecstasy. I was willing to sacrifice everything, for moments like this. Sasha's young, firm thighs caressed me and promised an even more glorious tomorrow.

She tightened her legs around my waist, drawing me into the depth of her beauty. My chest constricted, but that didn't slow me. All I could think about was releasing the pain that was building in my body. Her body shuddered and my absolution immediately followed. I fell against the bed, drawing her down on top of me. The tightening in my chest was severe, but I didn't want to move.

Sweat rolled from my forehead like rain and I couldn't control my breathing.

"Are you okay?" She stared down at me, her eyes large with concern.

I tried to answer but the pain constricted my words.

"Did you hear me? You couldn't fall asleep that fast." She nudged me.

Again I tried to tell her I was fine, I only needed to rest, but my voice wouldn't come. My body shot full of pain, like splintering glass.

"Walter!" Her voice grew louder. "Walter, are you okay?"

Still my mouth wouldn't work. She pushed off of me. "Walter, honey, what's wrong?" Panic laced her voice.

I faced the ceiling, gripping my chest and grunting in agony. She looked down on me. Tears from the corners of her eyes fell on my face. My body wouldn't cooperate. I wanted to fold my arms around her and hold her. To tell her not to cry but nothing worked the way I wanted. If I moved my hands from my chest, my heart would rip through the flesh.

She picked up the phone and spoke to an operator. I wanted to tell her not to do that. Tracy didn't know I was here and if I needed to go to the hospital, it had to be from my office. But Sasha wasn't looking at me.

I tried to shake my head.

Couldn't.

What would Tracy think if she saw me now?

What about Crystal? I struggled to get up. I needed to dress. Pain pinned me to the bed like nails on a cross. I gasped for air.

I rolled my eyes towards the heap of clothes on the chair. I wanted my pants. I didn't want anyone to see me naked.

On the bed.

Like this.

Sasha grabbed my face between her palms.

"You better not die on me, Walter." She was screeching, her face contorted with fear. Tears spilled from her eyes and landed on my nose. She ran out of the room. I'm sure I had the ability to move, but I couldn't tell my body what to do.

Sasha came back into the bedroom tugging on her pants. Her areolas were darker than normal and standing up, I wanted to tell her how much I liked that, but the words were trapped in my head.

Except for the fear in her eyes, she was beautiful. She looked down on me. Tears flowed freely. Before I could tell her not to worry the doorbell rang and she ran from the room. I focused my attention on my hand, on my index finger. All I needed was to move it an inch, just enough to cover my penis. Nothing. My body was stiff. The pain took my breath, silencing my voice and my movement.

Suppose this didn't pass. What if I was trapped in my body forever? How would I explain this to Tracy? How would I tell her I was sorry? How would I ask her to forgive me and love me?

I didn't want to sleep. I strained to keep my eyes open. But the room grew dark. Behind my eyelids I saw a bright orange glow like a pile of burning leaves. Gradually the color darkened like someone had pulled down a shade.

Chapter Seventeen – Walter

Euphoria surrounded me, so it had to be a dream. My favorite one. A vision of me sitting in the back seat of a car, happily waving goodbye to my mother's stone-faced expression, came into focus. Seeing her stand so stoically on the front porch, her arms pinned at her side, filled me with elation as the car pulled away.

I struggled to open my eyes. Not quite ready to relinquish the peacefulness.

After several attempts, I parted my eyelids a fraction of an inch. The blinding light made me squint. I could hear people talking and lots of unfamiliar noises that seemed to rise and fall at regular intervals. The bed was much harder, smaller, and positioned at an odd angle. I was in the hospital. There was a clip on my index finger like a clothespin and an I.V. in my arm.

I exhaled a deep breath. At least I wasn't naked anymore. A faded blue and white paisley hospital gown thin enough to see through swaddled me. I tried to turn away from the light, to find a more soothing place to focus my attention. In the corner, Sasha was slumped in a chair beside the bed. Her head was thrown back and her legs dangled over the arm.

I tried to pull myself up in the bed without waking her, but an agonizing bolt of heat blazed across my chest making it impossible. She woke up, rubbed her eyes, and stretched. Her full round belly peeked from under her top. Tracy had worked so hard to disguise hers behind big tops and loose pants. Sasha flaunted her stomach like she flaunted the diamond on her finger and her new bracelet. I preferred Tracy's way better, which labeled me an old man. The finger clip and the monitor beeping reinforced my opinion.

"Hey." Sasha came to stand beside the bed. Even though she sounded chipper, her face looked distressed. "How do ya feel?"

"What happened?" My voice sounded deeper, or maybe I was talking too loud. Sasha rubbed my arm, the one free of hospital contraptions.

"The nurse said the doctor would be back in a minute. No one will talk to me about what happened."

"What did they tell you?"

"No one will talk to me because I'm not your wife." She drew out the words as if to emphasis her unfair treatment.

But I wasn't in a mood to pamper her back to euphoria. I needed some answers.

Without the benefit of softening my voice to coddle her, I said, "How long have I been in the hospital, Sasha? Has anyone called Tracy?"

She gave me a quizzical look and studied my face. "Walter, you came here last night. You don't remember?"

I was talking to a stranger. Sasha didn't seem to understand the importance of my questions. Her youthfulness prevented her from seeing how this situation could collapse my world and hers, as well. I tried to talk with authority, but wearing a gown with my butt exposed didn't make it easy.

"Sasha, how long have I been here and what is wrong with me?"

"Walter, you're scaring me? Don't you remember?" Tears gathered in her eyes.

"Dammit, Sasha how long?"

"Last night. We've been here a few hours. It's seven o'clock in the morning."

Only a few hours. I expelled a long, slow breath. Some comfort washed over me knowing I didn't have to fashion another excuse for Tracy. I was so tired. I wanted to sleep for the rest of the day. I shifted my weight and tried again to sit up.

"I'm fine, I'm feeling fine, Sasha"

She fingered the edge of my gown. Her bottom lip trembled, either with fear or she was about to cry. Would she leave me now that she knew I was defective?

A doctor walked into the room, flipping through documents on a clipboard.

"Good morning, Mr. Baptiste. How are you feeling?" He never looked at me. I ignored his jocularity.

He made notes on some of the pages and nodded, giving me the impression he wanted to be somewhere else. Like the golf course.

"Well the good news first, you're alive. The bad news is we aren't sure what caused your attack."

I closed my eyes and swallowed. Not once did I imagine I was lying in this hospital bed because of something serious. When had I reached the age of having attacks? I was too young to have a heart condition or any other major health problems. I grimaced at the thought.

"What happened? Why?"

"The test isn't definitive. You're not overweight. Your blood pressure is normal. You're not a smoker. So we need to run more tests. We'll keep you another day and check you out. Have you recently experienced personal loss or some significant life change?"

I looked at Sasha, who stood beside the bed wringing her hands. I reached for her hands to hold them still.

"No, we're going through some turmoil at work, but I'm handling that quite well." I shifted my weight again. "Look, doctor, I can't stay here overnight. Is there some other way we can get these tests taken care of? Can't I just go somewhere and have the test taken?"

The doctor ignored my question. He scribbled notes on the clipboard. "Something triggered the attack. Have you started any new medications lately?"

"No."

"Heart disorders sometimes run in families. Is there a family history?"

"No." I couldn't mask my impatience.

"How about stimulants? Has there been an increased use of caffeine?"

"No. None of those things."

"Like I said, we'll run some tests."

"Doctor…by the way what is your name?"

"Delaroy, Dr. Delaroy."

"Look, Dr. Delaroy, I cannot stay another night. Please write me out a prescription for something and I'll see my family doctor to get the tests you suggest."

"Walter, don't you think you should listen to the doctor?"

"Look, both of you, I can't stay another night. I'll see a doctor tomorrow."

"Fine. I'll write it all up in your release papers. You'll have to sign a document releasing the hospital from any liability if something happens to you."

"Just bring me the papers and let me get out of here. I need to leave."

"The nurse will be here in a minute with the papers, and then you can go home." He looked at Sasha. "When you see your dad overdoing it, you have to remind him to slow down, to take it easy." He walked out of the room.

"Did that asshole say *Dad*?" I swung my legs over the edge of the bed.

Sasha patted my hand to dismiss the comment. "Forget about it." Her smile was anemic.

"Please tell me you brought some clothes for me to wear home. I want to put on real clothes."

"In this locker." She pulled out the suit and shirt I'd worn to work the day before. I dressed as quickly as possible, feeling like a thief. The icy fingertip of my mother pressed on my chest.

Chapter Eighteen – Walter

I felt like I had been paroled from prison as Sasha and I stepped out into the oppressive June heat. I stopped to look up at the sky. I inhaled what seemed to be the freshest air in the world before grabbing Sasha's hand. We walked to her car. The pain in my chest subsided a little.

At Sasha's house, I showered and changed clothes. Before joining Sasha in the kitchen, I perched on the edge of the bed. The mussed sheets felt warm to my palm. Life threatened to swallow me whole without providing an escape. Even though I didn't love Tracy with that burning passion that I once had, life with her was simple and uncomplicated. With her, I wasn't always expected to perform, I didn't have to try so hard, or suck in my gut whenever she was in the room. The thought of raising another child scared the shit out of me. Instead of directing my path, I always seemed to be following someone else's direction. No matter how hard I tried, I couldn't get my footing right. My mother's words echoed in my head as I rubbed my hands over the sheet. *Don't be foolish, boy.*

"Fuck," I uttered to myself as I finished dressing and went downstairs.

"You feel okay?" Sasha's eyes were red, like she'd been crying.

"I'm fine. Don't worry about me." I sat down to the plate of eggs and bacon she placed on the table. I pushed the eggs away but ate the bacon. "Once the wedding is over and the layoffs at work are done, I'll be able to relax. Maybe we'll go on a trip just before the baby comes," I said with a mouth full of bacon.

"Uh-huh." She gave me a weary smile.

"What?"

"Stop making promises, Walter. Right now, I only want one thing. One thing in the whole world and that's you. Permanently." She sat across from me and held my hand.

"I know. Soon. We're this close." I measured with my thumb and index finger. "Look you must be tired. Why don't you call Ella and let her take care of the store today."

"That's a good idea. I am exhausted." She pushed away from the table. Her stomach looked twice as large as it did last week. The sight of it made me rub my chest.

"You know I'm going to be out of pocket for a few days. With the wedding and all. Call me if it's an emergency. I'll try to call you every day. But I won't be able to come by." I stared into her eyes. "You understand, don't you?"

"As long as it gets us closer to being together forever, I can handle it. It's only for two or three more days, right?"

"Right." I was getting so good at lying I was beginning to believe myself. In two or three days something magical was bound to happen.

She waved good-bye to me as I pulled out of the driveway.

Beverly was already at her desk when I walked in the office. "Your wife called, she wants to talk with you as soon as you get in. She said to call her at home."

"What did you tell her?"

She arched her eyebrows. "I told her I'd give you the message." She handed me the message and turned around to her computer.

"Thanks, Beverly," I said.

She didn't look up.

I placed my briefcase on the desk and turned my computer on before dialing Tracy's number. I'd checked my messages and knew I was in for a lot of questions. "What's up?"

"Good morning, Walter. How are ya?"

"I'm stiff from sleeping here on the couch, but I'm fine."

"What kind of excuses are you going to give me about not answering your phones last night when I called?" There was no anger in her voice.

"I told you I was going to be working. Why did you call?" I had enough edge in my voice to let her know I didn't feel like being cross-examined.

"Walter, where were you last night?"

"Right here asleep on the couch. Why didn't you come down here again looking for me? Or maybe you could have sent that loud mouth bunch of friends of yours to hunt me down."

"Why didn't you answer your phone?" She asked again in the same even tone. "Even if you were screwing somebody, can't you stop long enough to answer the phone?"

"Tracy, I was exhausted, I put the phones on vibrate so I could get some sleep. Why did you call?" My irritation grew.

"Carla told me she saw you at the doctor's office. What was that about?"

I knew that loud mouth was going to tell Tracy before I could blink. With everything thing going on I didn't know what to say, so I decided to give a very casual reply. "Yeah, and what else did she tell you? Did she tell you what I was wearing? Every fricking time I turn around you're questioning me or tracking me down. Damn woman, you're worse than my mother."

"What was that about, Walter? Why were you there?"

"I was there with one of the administrative assistants."

"Walter, you never do anything so altruistic, so why were you there? Is this assistant, your lover? Is that who keeps you so busy you can't answer your phone, or return your calls, or come home at a decent time, or make love to me?"

"Whoa, boy. Here we go."

"Yeah, here we go. You won't go with me to a doctor, so why did you do it for someone—"

"Listen Tracy, she got sick at work, she couldn't drive. What should I have done? Tell her to crawl on her hands and knees to get to the doctor? You need to stop being so damn suspicious all the time."

"You need to stop giving me reasons to be suspicious all the time. Oh yeah, and do you remember writing a check for the wedding for five thousand dollars? The name doesn't sound familiar to me. It was someone named Sara or Sasha Somebody."

I hoped she didn't hear me suck in a gallon of air. "I-I think…I'm not sure. It sounds familiar, maybe for the extra chairs or something. I'll look into it." I smacked my forehead, how could I be so stupid? Was the stress getting to me? That payment should have come out of my personal account.

"I've got the piece of paper somewhere with the name on it." I heard papers shuffle in the background. "I'll find—"

"Don't worry about it, I'll check it out. You go ahead and do whatever you and Crystal have planned for today. I'll even make it home early tonight so we can celebrate her last night as a single woman, together." I switched to presentation mode, using my authoritative voice so she'd stop delving into the black hole I'd created.

"Crystal might not be here. She's doing something tonight with her girlfriends. I think she's staying with one of them tonight."

"You're stuck with me tonight." I forced a chuckle.

"Yeah, who the hell did I piss off?" Her voice was flat.

"That's cold, Tracy," I teased. "It'll be our special night. I'll even give you a foot massage."

"You're on, buddy. And it better be longer than two minutes. Oh yeah, my parents arrived this afternoon so they could be here for the wedding breakfast."

"My mom gets in tomorrow. Are we ready for her?"

"Are we ever ready for Nellie?" She disconnected the call.

"Shit, shit, shit." I slapped my forehead. How the hell was I going to explain this one? The easiest thing to do was to pack up my stuff, move to a new town, change my name and disappear into a crowd.

I realized I was still wearing the hospital bracelet. I twirled it around my wrist several times. How careless, if someone at work, or Tracy, saw it, I couldn't even begin to explain this incident. I shook my head before cutting it off and burying it under some papers in my trash.

The phone jarred me away from the list of management cuts.

"Have you called the doctor yet?" asked Sasha, breathing hard.

"No, I've been pretty busy here today. I'll make the call in a day or two."

"Why don't you let Beverly make the appointment for you?"

"Because I don't want everyone knowing my business. I'll handle it. Stop worrying."

"If you could have seen your face last night you wouldn't be so flippant with me. I thought you were dying." She didn't pause long enough for me to respond. "I miss you already."

I needed some time alone, to slow down long enough to think. I sighed.

"I heard you sighing, Walter. I guess you think I'm being a pain, don't you?"

"No, no, it's…it's been a hectic day and I'm a little exhausted. The wedding is on Saturday and then you and I can start making plans."

"Do you mean it, Walter? Are you talking long term plans? Like marriage, or just getting you moved into this house?"

When did Sasha start pulling in the opposite direction of Tracy? Seldom did either of them ask me what I really wanted.

"Sasha, please don't do that. I was there last night." I shifted the phone to the opposite ear.

"You were kinda here. Mostly you were in the hospital."

"I've got to go now."

"Will you call me tonight or Saturday morning?"

"I'll call you every chance I get," I promised.

"You know I love you baby? I just want us to be a family, to be together."

I hung up, put my pen down, and stretched out in the chair. My chest was tight, I struggled to breathe. Something had to change, and soon. I closed my eyes to concentrate on my breathing. The last thing I needed was to end up back in the hospital.

The relationship with Sasha was good. My marriage, on the other hand was comfortable. I could relax in it and I didn't have to work so hard. I didn't have to worry about making Tracy happy anymore, I could fall asleep in front of the television.

I turned back to my desk. Reading contracts, verifying sales volumes and productivity numbers felt like mindless activity compared to what waited for me at home. When I could no longer delay life, I packed up my stuff and headed out the door.

Tracy sat in the family room watching a game show on television, a glass of wine in her hand.

"Hey, baby." I gave her a dry kiss on the cheek before sitting on the opposite end of the couch.

"Walter." Tracy turned off the television.

"How was the—what do you call the thingy you all had last night for the wedding party?"

"The soiree was very nice. I think Crystal and the girls had a good time. Everybody did."

"Including you?"

"Nope." She lifted her wine glass to her lips. "I spent the whole night trying to figure out what you're up to now. I know you think I'm stupid and naïve. You might even think I'm fat and unlovable, but I'm not a fool." That same calm resolve from earlier laced her voice.

I put my head in the palm of my hands and didn't respond. She was going to be jawing for a while and I didn't have the strength to argue with her. The pain from the last twenty-four hours was taking its toll on me and all I really wanted was to crawl into bed and get a good night's sleep.

"But keep doing whatever it is you're doing, because your rooster will come home to roost. I'll not forgive you if you rake me over the coals like you did before. I think I deserve better than that. Every day I give our marriage 110%. Even when I don't have the strength to take care of myself, I take care of you."

"Tracy, you're always bitching about one thing or another," I yelled at her.

"Shhh! Keep your voice down, my parents are asleep in the guest room. I don't think you need to wake them up with your nonsense."

"You're exhausting. I was working. I fell asleep. The story doesn't get any deeper than that."

"I don't want to exhaust you, Walter." She brought her glass to her lips and emptied it. "Let's just forget it. For now."

I stood up and headed for the kitchen. "What's for dinner?"

"There are leftovers from yesterday. And I braised some short ribs and made garlic mashed potatoes. Everything is still in the warming drawer." She followed me into the kitchen.

"Did you find out about the check?" Tracy pulled down plates from the cabinet.

Shit, I was hoping she would let that go. "Ah, yeah, I gave it to Beverly to follow up on. You know how Beverly can dog something, I'm sure she'll track it down."

"You shouldn't ask her to check personal stuff, I can do it."

"Tracy, you've got enough stuff to do with the wedding, your parents, and everything. Beverly doesn't mind."

She sat next to me at the island and fixed my plate.

"Are you going to eat with me?"

"I ate with my parents earlier tonight. But I want to keep you company. We haven't spent much time together lately. You seem like a stranger to me." Her creamy complexion glowed under the soft light.

"I know. We need to make time for just us. We'll do that after the wedding. I promise." I handed out promises like gold coins.

"We have guests arriving tomorrow. I'm pleading with you to try to be amenable until after the wedding."

I put my fork down and stared at her. She had a small wisp of hair curled on her forehead. Her pants hugged her thighs and butt in just the right way to accentuate her womanliness. Even though she was angry enough to bite my face off, there was tenderness in her eyes that I had forgotten.

She was waiting for me to commit to something and I was remembering the first time we made love. It was in her dorm room, on a twin bed. We spent most of the night just talking, and as the sun rose, I couldn't resist kissing her any longer. When she parted her lips and accepted my tongue, it was in her eyes that I saw the beginning of my life and how I wanted to live it.

"I'll be so sweet you won't even know me. Maybe I'll be so sweet, I can get extra lucky tonight."

She lifted an eyebrow. "You want to get lucky, huh?"

"Maybe if I try real hard, you'll give in." I could never leave Tracy, but what would I tell Sasha?

Chapter Nineteen – Tracy

Walter nudged me awake. "What are you smiling about?"

"Umm, I just had the best dream." I stretched my arms above my head. "Carla was pregnant with twins and asked me to be the godmother. Instead of Ursula quitting the firm, she married Anthony. They moved into the house next door to me in the cul-de-sac. And Max accepted a position in a prestigious law firm in Wilmington and moved into the house on the opposite side."

"I like the Crystal and Max part, but I don't think I'd want to live next door to one of your best friends. I already see them enough."

"It was my best dream, not yours." I propped up on the pillow.

"Where was I? You mentioned everyone but me."

I gave him a blank stare. "I don't know. I don't remember seeing you in it." I pushed off the bed and made my way to my closet. "Anyway, what time are your mother and brothers coming today?"

"Oh shit. I forgot." He ran his hand down his face dragging his skin. "I'm not ready to deal with my mother. How long is she staying up here?"

"I don't know. She's your mother. Don't you know? I've been too busy to coordinate your family's arrival and departure. I thought you were handling those details."

"Tracy, you know I can't handle my mother, you've got to keep her away from me."

"Walter, you haven't seen your mother in several years. She's getting old. Why do you let her get to you like that?"

Walter sat in the chair and studied his hands.

"I'll try to be the buffer. But don't expect much. As the mother of the bride, I'll be busy weeping. My main goal this weekend is to make sure Crystal has the day she's always imagined." I glanced at the clock. "The non-stop activity begins at nine when the caterers arrive to cook the buffet breakfast. So we better get moving."

"Thank you, Tracy, you're the best." He pecked me on the cheek.

"Yeah, whenever you get your way, I'm the best." I pulled on my robe and hurried down the stairs. I heard my mother talking to someone in the kitchen. "Good morning, Mom."

"Morning sweetie."

"Are you talking to yourself?"

"You know I am. Ain't nobody else in here." She opened and closed cabinet doors. "Where do you keep your coffee? I need to brew some to get your father moving this morning or he'll never be ready in time."

"The caterers should be here any minute." I pulled the coffeemaker out of the cabinet. "I'll make the coffee. Sit and keep me company."

I measured out the coffee and water. My mother watched, but something other than coffee was on her mind.

"Go ahead and say it, Mom."

"How are you and Walter really doing?"

"We're fine. He's working really hard and we're both a little stressed…you know with the wedding and everything." Without looking at her, I pulled napkins from the pantry.

"Tracy." She got up from the table and stood next to me. "I've known you longer than you've known yourself. Something ain't right here."

"Let's talk about it later, okay? The caterers are at the door." I left her to answer the front door, happy to escape the conversation for at least several days. By the time I escorted the catering team into the kitchen, my mother was pouring coffee into the cups.
"Bernice and Brenda, you remember my mother, Frances." I breezed through the introductions then made my way to the stairs.

"I'll go check on Walter and put on some clothes. The other guests will be arriving soon."

"We know where everything is. We'll start the prep," Bernice yelled up the stairs after me.

Walter stood in his closet already dressed in a pair of khaki slacks and a pullover shirt. He stuck his hands in his pocket.

"You look like you're feeling better."

"I'll be feeling even better as soon as my mother is in the car and on her way back to Raleigh.

"B and B are here. Can you go downstairs in case they have any questions? I'll be down as soon as I get dressed."

"Got it." He wrapped his arms around me and kissed the top of my head. I held his gaze for several seconds, looking into the eyes of the man who I should have known better than anyone. But I didn't know if I should be happy or sad at what I saw. It was like looking into the eyes of a stranger. I stood in the middle of the room like a star-struck teenager. Walter hadn't been pleasant in so long, the gesture that hundreds of thousands of couples did daily seemed foreign. Experience said whatever made him attentive would leave him and the inconsiderate boob would return. Unlike Marco, Walter's thoughts centered on his wants and needs. In the little time I'd spent with Marco, he always put me first. When I talked I actually thought he listened to me.

I threw my robe across the bed and ran into my closet. Just looking at my bags extinguished any stupid pleasure I thought I felt from Walter's display. In a few days I was supposed to walk into my new life. My knees began to tremble. The idea was so scary I had to grip the door handle for support.

I fingered the beautiful floor-length azure chiffon dress I planned to wear to the wedding. Crystal and I had spent weeks visiting different boutiques before giving up on that hapless pursuit. So she'd helped me select the fabric and the design for this dress. At my final fitting, we both had tears in our eyes when she zipped the dress.

"Mom, you are so beautiful," she said, and the look in her eyes made me think she was telling the truth. The other two outfits I managed to design on my own. Crystal was so busy with the bridesmaids and the wedding, I felt guilty pulling her away.

This morning I dressed in a white silk and nylon tunic adorned in gold threading. The top hung just at my hips, and the wide-leg pants were just right without looking ridiculous. I slipped on a pair of Stuart Weitzman gold metallic sandals before draping a towel over my shoulders and applying a little blush and lipstick. My hair was nearly dry, so I ran my fingers through it to loosen the curls before heading downstairs.

The chatter came from in the family room, so I went straight to the voices. Crystal and Max were seated on the loveseat; she in his lap and his arms encircling her. Several groomsmen and bridesmaids were lounging around the room.

"Hey, Ms. T.," Max yelled as I walked in the room. Crystal jumped off his lap and threw her arms around my neck.

"Hey, Mom." Crystal looked like she could float away. Maybe that's why Max kept his hand around her waist.

"Isn't it supposed to be bad luck for you two to see each other before the wedding?" I wiggled in on the loveseat beside them.

A chorus of "I told you so's" filled the room.

"We're not superstitious." Max grinned. "We don't plan to see each other before the wedding, but the wedding isn't until six this evening.

My mother joined us from the kitchen. "I think it's the wedding dress he's not supposed to see her in before the wedding."

"Something sure smells good," Carla said as she and Javier came into the family room. "We're not too late for the food, are we?"

"You two shouldn't be together, should you?" Javier pointed to Max and Crystal. Laughter broke out in the room and I nodded in agreement.

"Hey, where's Walter?" I asked.

"Here I am. Who's looking for me?" Walter walked in the room and for a short minute I forgot our troubles and was struck by how handsome he was. Seeing him and Crystal in the room together and how much they resembled each other made me smile.

"Where have you been?" I asked, and it sounded more like an accusation than I intended.

He sat on the arm of the loveseat closest to me. "I was in my office making a few phone calls. Before I could moan my complaint, he said, "It's not what you think, it wasn't about work. I'm planning a little something and I had to make some calls."

"Mmm hmm," I said. He bent and kissed my cheek. Across the room Carla raised an eyebrow and smiled.

"Everybody, breakfast is ready, and if ya'll don't come on and get it, I'm going to start without you." My father stood in the doorway looking a little less vibrant than the week before.

"I'm ready, Granddaddy." Crystal jumped off Max's lap and looped her arm through my father's and together they walked into the kitchen.

The kitchen island was loaded with fluffy scrambled eggs, steaming hot grits, pancakes, crispy scrapple, and lots of other stuff. I was happy to see Crystal hadn't lost her appetite. Once the photographer showed up and she started preparing for the wedding, I was sure she would be too excited to eat.

"I'm sorry I'm late," Ursula called out as she walked into the room with Anthony at her side. "We got a little caught up this morning, if you know what I mean," she whispered in my ear.

"That's too much information this morning," I said to her. "Hey Anthony, get in line and help yourself. You might need the stamina," I said to him.

He had an electrifying smile. It was easy to see why Ursula loved him. She stood behind him. They helped each other fill their plates, touching each other every few seconds. Ursula hadn't looked this happy since college when she dated the second string quarterback and picked out the names of their four future children.

I felt like a voyeur, watching everyone else's happiness, wishing it were mine. I pushed that thought to the overstuffed compartment in my mind where all the other matters waited to be dealt with. I even tried to push thoughts of Marco away. Thinking about him only complicated an already muddled life.

We all sat around the kitchen and dining room tables, sandwiching chairs as close as possible to make room for everyone. My food grew cold, but I continued to listen to the conversations and laughter. Walter sat next to me, gobbling his food like a man eating his last meal.

Midway through the meal, the caterers walked in with a tray of Moet Mimosa balanced on a silver tray. Together, they went around the rooms, placing a goblet in front of everyone. Crystal raised her glass and nodded just for me from the end of the table.

"Before you sip your mimosa, I'd like to say something." Walter stood with his glass in his hand. Fear shook my heart. What would come out of his mouth? Walter shied away from the limelight, and getting him to say something aloud at family outings was like seeing snow in July. I glanced at Crystal to see if she knew what was going on. She hunched her shoulders.

Walter waved his hands for everyone in the kitchen to join us in the dining room. My parents stood side-by-side at the end of the table. The look on my father's face said he'd rather finish his breakfast.

"Later today things will get real busy and I might not have this opportunity. But as I look around this room, some of the most important people in our lives are here, so this makes it a good place to say what I have to say." Walter turned to me and my face froze.

"The wedding and reception will be about Crystal and Max and I wish them all the happiness in the world, but this morning I want to take a moment to thank the woman who has made all this possible. The woman I have loved since the day I met her." He lifted his glass a little higher, "To my darling, beautiful and sexy wife, Tracy."

I took in his performance from my seat. My breathing came in short spurts. I expected him to say it was all a joke. Walter bent and kissed me on the mouth, sticking his tongue in my mouth in front of everyone in the room.

When he straightened, I tried to look normal. This announcement shouldn't have made me nervous, or my stomach sour, but I settled into his compliment like I should have.

"She has been under a lot of stress lately. I've been working late. She and Crystal have done most of the wedding planning without me. So just to thank her for always being understanding and loving, I'm taking her on a third, fourth, or who knows what, but we're going on another honeymoon next week, too. A little get away to Nassau. To you baby." He raised his glass to everyone in the room, then to me. Through the glass in my hand I could see his blurred handsomeness.

"Walter. Why?" I stuttered. "What made you decide to do this?" This was so unlike the Walter I've known lately that I could not fathom what would have brought him to this loving gesture. Had he seen my packed bags and was trying to preempt my actions?

"Ah Tracy, didn't your mom tell you not to look a gift horse in the mouth?" he said, grinning.

"Yeah, but…"

"Tracy, we deserve a little fun. Some rest."

"Here, here." Crystal raised her glass, ending our discussion.

I sipped my mimosa. Walter wrapped his arm around my waist and lifted me from the chair. Carla and Ursula whispered their congratulations in my ear, but my mother's skeptical look said everything I couldn't voice.

"Hey Mom, it looks like we're both going away. Way to go, Dad." Crystal nudged her father and gave him a thumbs-up.

Maybe I was blocking my own happiness, looking around every corner, suspecting the boogey man to snatch away my joy. I warmed to the idea. The handsome man with his hand around my waist was the man I remembered. Everything he said could be true, but I was too blinded with a silly flirtation to trust Walter. Guilt crawled up my spine. Allowing my feelings for Marco to step beyond friendship was unforgivable.

I was afraid to speak and reveal my ambivalence. Spending several days away with Walter would have been my dream come true.

Months ago.

But now it felt as if Walter had tossed me a wooden token. I couldn't muster much excitement.

Instead, a dull finger strummed the strings of my heart with no enthusiasm.

A mirage of Marco and me frolicking on a beach danced across my mind. I blinked the image away and dropped my head.

Everyone looked at me, expecting me to say something kind and loving. I cleared my throat. "Wow! Walter this is great. We need a getaway. Thank you, honey." Why wasn't I more excited? Wasn't that the gesture I wanted?

"The photographer will be here shortly. We better get ready, because everything we do will be captured for eternity," I said.

"Yeah. Mom is right. I asked him to snap pictures of everything, so get ready," Crystal put the last forkful of food in her mouth.

Max and his parents, along with the ushers and groomsmen, left for the hotel. Crystal and her girls headed upstairs, giggling and crowing about events that only they understood. Walter and I sat at the table with my mother and father.

"What time will Aunt Edna and Uncle Bill get here?" I stirred my coffee.

"They got a late start. They're going straight to the church and you should be happy. You know the way they carry on, arguing all the time. It's best if they take that mess right on to the church where they have to be quiet."

"Frances is right, the last time they came up for Thanksgiving, they upset the whole dinner arguing about who controlled the remote and how much weight Bill had put on. I had indigestion for the rest of the evening." My father shook his head.

"But they are my godparents," I laughed. "I wanted to get pictures of them."

"Get 'em at the church. Take my word for it, that's best for all of us."

"Dad, you look tired, maybe you need to get a nap before—"

"Yeah." He stood up. "I think I'll get forty winks, that way I can dance the night away with my granddaughter." He stood, but leaned on the chair before heading upstairs.

Before my mother followed him out of the kitchen, she gave me a look. "See what I mean?"

"I have an appointment on Monday. Stop worrying, Mom."

The doorbell chimed, stopping her reply. She twisted her mouth into a disappointed line and walked out.

"That must be the photographer." Walter got up from the table. "Let's get this show on the road."

From where I sat in the kitchen I could hear the heated conversation and guessed that instead of the photographer arriving, Walter's mother had landed on her broom. I sighed and made my way to the front door.

"You know your brother drives like a maniac, I don't know why you didn't just send me a ticket and let me fly up here last night." Mrs. Baptiste set her purse on the table in the foyer. "You're stingy, Walter, always have been."

"Well, he got you here safe, didn't he? Come on in and stop complaining." Walter closed the door and rubbed his chest.

"You are a mean self-centered ass. You only think about yourself. Always have. After all I sacrificed for you and your brothers, I deserve better treatment than this. I pray for your narcissistic soul. Out of all my boys, you are my biggest disappointment because you could be so much better."

I tried to rescue him from his mother's bite. "Good morning, Mrs. Baptiste. We just finished breakfast but I'm sure we've got plenty here for you guys." I tried to sound chipper.

"See Warren, if we had left when I told you, we could have gotten here so we could have a decent meal. Now we're stuck with leftovers," she yelled at her son before following me into the kitchen.

"Tracy, it's a wonder you're still with him. You must be a saint." His mother rolled her eyes before plopping into the chair with a huff.

"I'm sure we can ask the caterer to fix you a nice hot meal. Please get comfortable, I'll talk to them." I indicated a seat at the table, then disappeared into the kitchen, happy to be away from the fire-breathing dragon.

Walter slipped into the kitchen behind me, looking like a little boy caught shoplifting candy.

"I hope you made a reservation for your family at the hotel. Please don't give her another reason to be angry," I whispered to Walter.

"Yeah, I did. Now let's get them fed and out of here as quickly as possible." He gripped the counter so tight the veins in his hand bulged.

Chapter Twenty – Tracy

Before Walter and I escorted Crystal down the aisle, I grabbed a tissue from the coordinator to wipe the tears from my eyes.

"Are you going to be okay?" Crystal asked me. She wore a simple but elegant Rivini gown—her strapless, satin A-line dress was tiered and fit like the design was made especially for her. She looked like a princess as she stood between her father and me.

"Yeah, I'm okay. These are happy tears."

"Come on Tracy, you can do this." Walter wrapped me in his arms. "We've been getting ready for this day for over a year."

"Yes." I faked confidence. "Yes, I can. Let's get this show on the road." I signaled the coordinator to start the music. We took Crystal's arms after positioning ourselves in front of the vestibule doors. Before we proceeded down the aisle, I gave her hand a strong squeeze.

Throughout the ceremony, Walter kept his arm around me, comforting and shoring me up. Tears gathered in the corners of my eyes at the impeding emptiness in my life. Beside me, my father reached for my left hand and held it between his massive warm palms. He beamed with happiness. Maybe this was the thing that would allow him to forgive me. After twenty-one years, I detected a smidgen of forward movement.

"Your mother cried when you got married, too, but she stopped long enough to smile for the pictures. Are you going to cry through the pictures, too?" He leaned over and whispered in my ear.

"No, Dad." I kissed him on the cheek. "Are we okay?"

"We're fine, baby. You've made your parents proud. We couldn't have asked for a better daughter." He kissed my nose.

For the balance of the ceremony, a sweet peace settled over me.

After dinner, instead of mingling, I sat at the empty table, slipped off my shoes and wiggled my toes. They would never be straight again.

"You've taken off your shoes already?" Ursula fell into the chair next to me.

"Girl, my feet are killing me. I'm not used to dancing all night," I said. "It's been a long time since I've seen you look so happy Anthony must be good for you."

"You and Walter seem… It looks like he's ga-ga over you today. What is that about?"

"Good question, but I'm kinda enjoying it."

"So, you guys are going away on a… little honeymoon, getaway, sex weekend?" She laughed at her joke and I joined her. Then with an introspective look on her face, she asked, "Do you think Max and Crystal will stay married forever?"

I placed my elbows on the table and put my chin in the palm of my hand. "Are you thinking about Crystal or yourself?"

"Me."

"Don't be afraid—you deserve to be happy. Claim it."

"Yeah. You're right. But look at you and Walter." Ursula dropped her elbow on the table, too.

"I've never set good examples for anyone," I joked.

"That's not true. I wouldn't have gone to college if you hadn't," Ursula said.

"Yeah, but then I got pregnant. Some kind of example that was for you."

"Tracy, that wasn't the end of the world. Besides, look at your beautiful daughter." She craned her neck to find Crystal.

I fingered the fork lying on the table. "I think my father forgave me today."

"I think he did that a long time ago. You just have to forgive yourself." She patted my hand.

We sat in silence for several minutes. If being happy was so easy, what was my problem?

Anthony approached the table. "Well, enjoy yourself. Stop thinking about events that you can't change," she said.

"There you are." Anthony reached for her hand, pulled her into his arms.

What was it about weddings that made everyone think love was so attainable?

"Tracy, I'm going to steal her away from you for a little while. I wanna dance."

"Anthony, you go right ahead." I laughed.

I think he said *thanks* before he pulled Ursula into his arms, but they were both laughing and grinning so I couldn't be sure.

I slipped my shoes on to walk over to my parents, who were seated at a table with my aunts and uncles.

"Other than the bride, you are the most beautiful woman in the room."

I turned into his sultry voice and smiled. "Marco, I'm so glad you made it." I brushed my lips across his cheek, holding them in place for a moment too long. He placed his hand on my bare shoulder. A little too familiar for the setting, but I didn't step back. His touch warmed my whole body.

"I mean it. You are stunning. How are you doing?"

I scanned the large room for Walter. He was nowhere in sight. I nodded. He dropped his hands. Only then did I realize I had been holding my breath.

"Did you bring a date?"

"No, I'm alone."

Even though it shouldn't have mattered, I was happy he was alone. It made him more available to me.

"You better go. I'm sure there are guests vying for your attention." He stepped aside. I squeezed his hand before walking away.

I sat at the table with my parents. "I saw you and Mom on the dance floor. You looked pretty good," I said to my father.

"It's not every day I get to dance with your mother." He leaned back in his chair. "You know back in my day we used to go dancing almost every weekend. That was before you were born, of course. Because after you were born all we could do was stay home and try to get you to sleep."

"Dad," I said. "I've heard this story so many times."

"I'm proud of you, Tracy. You're a wonderful daughter." His eyes held mine.

"Your father has been drinking," my mother said.

"Quite a bit I might add." My father slurred his words just a little. "This is the most beautiful wedding I've ever been to."

"What about ours?" My mother nudged him.

"Hey—and what about mine?" I nudged him too.

We laughed. A magical charm touched the evening. I hoped it would never end. The last twenty-four hours had been perfect. The way I always dreamed.

Crystal and Max stood at the chocolate fountain, dipping strawberries into the sweet mixture. My daughter was true to her word, not afraid to eat chocolate in her white wedding dress.

Just before midnight, Crystal and I left the festivities to change into her travel attire.

"Has the day turned out the way you hoped?" I asked her.

She turned and threw her arms around my neck, "Mom..." She planted several dry kisses on my check. "I can't think of anything, *anything,* that could have made this day more special. I wasn't this happy the day Max asked me to marry him. I'm really Mrs. Maxwell Davis." She danced across the room and slipped her dress off her thin frame.

"Are you sure you're going to be okay, Mom?" She thumbed away the tears rolling down my cheek. "You've been crying all day. I'm starting to worry about you. You knew I would grow up one day and move away from home, didn't you?"

"Haven't you heard of happy tears? And when you have my grandbabies and they grow up faster than you think. I give you permission to cry all the tears you want." I reapplied my lipstick. "Besides, your father is taking me on a luxury trip so I won't have time to worry. I'll be sipping

Bahama Mammas by the pool during the day and playing craps into the night." I laughed.

"Just don't lose too much money." She stepped into a street-length white dress. "I'll need your help and your checkbook to decorate our new loft."

"Is that so? Now that you're Mrs. Maxwell Davis, I think you better start hitting *that* checkbook."

"Mom, be happy." Her tone was more serious. "While I'm away we won't talk every day and I want you to—"

"Crystal, I have no intentions of calling you on your honeymoon. I'm fine, honey." I reached for her hand. "Tell you what…I won't worry about you if you promise not to worry about me."

"It's a deal," she said.

We sealed our agreement with a knowing look and smile. In a flash, the instant passed and we finished dressing. Before walking out of the room, I held her and she held on to me until we knew we needed to return to the reception.

"Don't forget your bouquet," I said over my shoulder. She ran to the table and retrieved the white and yellow bundle of calla lilies.

"Do you know how many women in that room are waiting to catch that bouquet and live happily ever after?" she said.

"Yeah, your godmother Ursula is one that comes to mind. Aim it towards her.

"*Mom*, I can't do that," she blushed.

"I was only kidding. Well, maybe I was a little serious; she is your godmother."

Max was out of his tuxedo and in more casual attire too, and waiting for Crystal outside in the hallway. I walked up to him and placed her hand in his.

"Take care of my baby, Max," I said.

"For the rest of my life, Ms. T." He kissed her on the mouth like I wasn't standing in front of them. I would have been embarrassed if his affection wasn't directed towards my daughter. I left them in the hall.

Marco stood in the vestibule of the ornate hall. I saw him from the top of the stairs. Under the dazzling lights of the chandelier, his polished good looks left me awestruck. He spotted me and never took his eyes off me as I descended the stairs. The voice in my head yelled at me to ignore the desire in his eyes, but my heart screamed louder. He smiled at me and my stomach knotted with fear. I wanted him. I wanted him more than I wanted my marriage.

"I'm leaving now." He stood close to me.

Too close.

"Do you have to?" I asked. Knowing he was in the room made me feel happier. I wanted to touch him, kiss him, taste him. Dressed in his dark suit, with his hair slightly tousled, he looked so handsome I wanted to be in his arms. I could live in those arms.

"Yes. But if you need me—"

I shook my head. This was wrong. "I won't, Marco." I bit my lip. "I can't." I placed my hand on his forearm. "I'll be fine."

His eyes locked with mine. The intensity of his stare shook my resolve. I wanted to touch him, press my hand against his heart to see it was beating as fast as mine. Then he turned and walked out.

Walter was seated back at the table. Maybe if I tried harder I could feel for him what I was beginning to feel for Marco. Buried deep inside, maybe there was enough love left for Walter to rekindle.

"You look happy," Walter said when exhaustion tugged me into the chair. The day seemed to run on forever.

"I haven't been this happy in a long time."

"Are you looking forward to our trip?"

He positioned himself closer to me. He wanted me to be happy, excited, maybe even thankful. So I tried. "Yes, very much. What made you decide on a trip? It seemed to come out of nowhere. I thought you were too busy at work to get away."

"You've been fussing so much lately, I think you need a little break." He laughed.

"Yeah, but you've been so distant and the last thing—"

"Tracy, we're going away, okay? So relax and try to enjoy it." He patted my hand.

"I think I can manage to relax, but it will take me some time to get used to your changing moods."

"Can't a man love his wife?"

"A man should love his wife every day, not just on special occasions."

"I do. This is my way of showing it." He pulled me to the dance floor as a slow song began to play and drew me closer. I wrapped my hands around his waist and pressed my body against his, praying for my heart to race or my skin to tingle.

"Okay everyone, the newlyweds are getting ready to leave. We want all the single women on the floor because after Crystal throws the bouquet, we'll all go outside and wish them well," the wedding coordinator announced.

Crystal's single friends pushed to the front of the room. None of them seemed embarrassed to want to catch the bouquet like the men were with the garter. Ursula stood as close to the front as she could without elbowing someone. I gave her a finger wave. Crystal kissed her grandparents and the three of them shared a hug, then she kissed her father on the cheek before she reached me.

"Be happy," she whispered in my ear. She ran halfway up the stairs, turned her back and, without any preamble, tossed the bouquet very high into the air. Several women pushed to grab it. It was snatched out of the air by one of Crystal's friends, who stood almost six feet tall.

***

As soon as I walked in the house I pulled off my shoes. Even though the heel on my sandals was only two inches, I wanted to place my feet flat on the floor. I plopped down in the kitchen chair and propped my feet up in the chair beside me.

"Can I get you something?" Walter asked.

"It's wine o'clock. Give me a glass of wine."

"Don't you think you've had enough wine for one day?" He dangled the bottle of Merlot in front of me.

"Yep, so give me some more."

"I was only kidding, Tracy." He poured two glasses and set them on the table. He lifted my feet and placed them in his lap before he sat in front of me. I'm sure he registered the shocked look on my face when he began massaging my feet.

"What's this going to cost me?" I asked.

268

"It's free for the special lady—and that's not all, either." He gave me a seductive look. I closed my eyes and enjoyed the massage.

"My parents should be safely home now. Your mother should be tucked into her hotel room. I think everything turned out splendid." My eyes were closed, enjoying the attention.

"My mother was on her best behavior."

"Does that mean she didn't jerk your chain today?" I asked.

"She did not. Maybe she's mellowing."

I opened my eyes, sat up, and we clicked our wine glasses.

We sat in the kitchen for two hours, sipping wine and discussing all the funny things that happened during the wedding. Marco's words kept running through my head. Pushing them away seemed useless.

"It's almost two. We need to get to bed." He placed my feet on the floor. I followed him upstairs, slightly intoxicated and so exhausted I couldn't feel my legs.

We dropped our clothes beside the bed and crawled under the sheets. My thigh brushed his, creating warmth. I waited for my heart to rev up. Walter outlined my neck with his index finger. Unhurried, his finger descended down to my breasts. For a fraction of a moment, he hesitated, before running a circle around my navel, where his hand came to rest. His touch telegraphed a spiritual sensation more than a carnal need.

Shame rocketed through me for all the atrocious deeds I'd accused him of, both aloud and in my imagination. I even turned my friends against him. He only needed some time. Crystal getting married had to have an effect on him, too.

I took a quiet breath to erase the negative thoughts and focus on him. I closed my eyes, trying to pay more attention to what was happening to me, now. Not wishing for someone else, somewhere else, or something else. Just Walter and me in this moment. The man I married and vowed to love.

Just having Walter so close to me used to rev me up. My body heating every pore. But my body was hesitant. Every time I thought I was making progress, the feeling disappeared like a ghost through a wall.

Tonight his touch was light and slow. He placed gentle kisses along my shoulder and down the column of my neck. I willed my body to respond, wrapping my arms around his back, and blocking out the images of Marco at the foot of the stairs during the reception, with lust burning in his eyes.

In the darkened room, I found Walter's mouth and kissed him. Gentle at first, but each kiss grew more demanding as I pushed myself toward desire. Walter responded by moaning, a deep sound that vibrated in my ear. He squeezed my breast with just enough pressure to draw me closer to him.

Without releasing his mouth, I gripped his hardened shaft. The familiar feel of his rod throbbed in my palm. I slid my hand up and down until he pulled it away.

He settled between my legs. Without releasing my mouth or my breast. Tonight he took his time. If my head were in the right place, everything would have been perfect.

I squeeze my eyes shut, wrapped my arms around Walter's neck, and allowed him to enter me. All we needed was time. Time fixed everything and it would repair my feelings too.

In the morning, a light rain pulled me out of a fitful sleep. Instead of opening my eyes to greet the day, I feigned sleep, gauging my attitude barometer. I should have been happier, and as soon as I got Marco out of my head, I could get back into my marriage.

"Morning, darling," Walter's voice was husky with sleep. He nuzzled against me.

"Are you golfing today?"

"I'm spending the day with you." He reached for the remote, turned on the television, then plumped his pillow.

I rested my head on his chest. Hope bubbled in my stomach. "This is nice. I remember when we used to do this all the time."

"How about we go to brunch at the country club this morning?" Walter placed his head in my lap.

"That's a good idea, because I sure don't feel like cooking anything," I said as I laid my legs over his.

He kissed my forehead before he got out of bed. "The last one downstairs is a rotten egg."

I watched him head down the hall to the other bathroom. I didn't know where this Walter came from, but I hoped he stayed around. The stress from his job was robbing him of his charm. The charm I fell in love with.

I ignored my suitcases. I dressed, unsure if I was betraying Walter or myself.

By the time we left the house, the rain was falling much heavier. We darted inside the club under one umbrella, laughing like we were carefree and in love. We were seated at a table by a large window overlooking the practice putting green. Walter reached across the table and caressed my hands. "I've missed this." He tilted his head just enough to let me know he was being sincere. "This is our time, Tracy. I know I'm not perfect, but we have a good life. Nothing should come between us. I want to grow old with you."

"We are old, silly." I wanted to lighten the conversation. Making declarations about the future seemed premature.

When the server showed up, we opted for orange juice and coffee instead of mimosas. I wanted something stronger, to numb the edge that competed for my attention, but Walter was trying so hard, I kept my mouth shut.

"How are things at your job?"

"Joe's going to screw me. He told me he'll see what he can do, but I don't trust him." He sipped his coffee as if he were talking about the weather.

"Aren't you worried? You love your job. What will you do? What will we do?"

"Tracy, you worry about everything. If I never work another day, we'll be fine."

"Don't blow me off like that. I'm serious." I fingered my diamond pendant, running my thumb along the gold chain.

"We're fine. I love you and I always have." Walter poured on his charm. "We'll be together forever, you're stuck with me."

"Huh, you're so full of yourself. Where to now?" I leaned back in my chair.

"Let's see, we leave for our trip in two days, so how about I take you shopping before you pack."

"I-I don't believe it. You want to take me shopping?"

He nodded.

"Okay, where is my real husband? What have you done to him?"

"I know I've been a little distant, but I'm here now." He pulled his wallet from his pocket and placed a fifty dollar bill on the table. We walked out of the large dining room. Walter placed his hand at the base of my spine and steered me outside into the light drizzle.

We headed to the mall, where I picked up a couple of casual outfits. Walter even helped me select a pair of navy blue Capri pants and a white top with sailor buttons down the side. By the time we left the mall, the sun was back out.

"Tracy, I'm exhausted, let's head home."

"I figured this would tire you out. You haven't shopped with me in years," I teased him.

"Maybe after I get some sleep we can..." He winked.

"Sounds like a plan to me." I hoped to muster some enthusiasm. Maybe this time it would be different. Maybe he was back to stay, emotionally.

He pulled into the garage.

I dropped my bags on the counter as soon as I entered the house.

"You take that end of the sofa. I'll take this end," Walter said as we nested into the soft fabric.

Sometime during the early evening, just as the sun was setting, the phone pierced the quiet. Walter lifted his arm and moved my head as he reached for the ringing phone.

"Who can that be?" I asked.

Walter swung his feet over the side of the sofa and I rushed off to the bathroom.

"Tracy!" he yelled to me from the family room.

Before I could respond, Walter was standing beside me. The look on his face said that it could only be bad news. My knees buckled. Walter reached for me before I slid to the floor. The sting of tears filled my eyes as I whispered, "Crystal?"

He shook his head, his eyes wide with alarm. I wanted to hear his response, but I knew I wouldn't like it.

"No. It's your Dad." Those are the only words I remember Walter saying. The rest of the day was a numbing blur.

Chapter Twenty-One - Walter

Like melting ice cream, Tracy puddled at my feet. I caught her before her head hit the marble floor. I carried her upstairs to the bedroom and placed her on the bed.

"It's my fault. It's entirely fault. I should have taken him to the doctor before the wedding like my mother asked. It's my fault. It's my fault." She sounded like a wind-up toy as the battery ran down.

"Shhh, shhh. Tracy, you couldn't have known." I tried to calm her, but she threw her head from side to side. A scared, uncertain look filled her eyes, darting around the room as if looking for something to fix on.

I reached for her hand, but she swatted me away. She slumped over the side of the bed, reached in her nightstand and pulled out a bottle of pills. She swallowed two without water and without wincing.

"What are you taking?" I tried to seize the bottle, but she shoved it back in her drawer, and then curled into a tight knot. With her face buried in the pillow, I could only watch her body wrack with sobs.

I stroked her head, moving my fingers through the soft curls. Even in the beginning of our relationship, I remember positioning her head on my chest so that my fingers could move freely through her ringlets.

"I'm so sorry. Your mother said he was gone before the ambulance even got there."

She shifted just enough to look up at me, then released a strained wail that ripped at my heart.

Tracy jerked upright, placed her feet on the floor, and switched into automatic pilot. "I have to get to my mother. She needs me." She showered and dressed without shedding another tear. Her stiff and methodical movements matched the expression on her face.

We drove to Philadelphia in silence. Tracy stared straight ahead. With her hands folded in her lap. I didn't talk to her or attempt to penetrate her shell.

I glimpsed her from the corner of my eyes. "Tracy, are you okay?"

She nodded.

"Can I stop to get you something? Water, coffee?"

"I just need to get to my mother. I need to get there."

Several minutes later I pulled in front of the house. Tracy jumped out before I turned the car off. Her mother leaned against the open door with a wad of tissues buried against her nose. I could hear her howling from the street.

Tracy rushed up the stairs with her arms extended. She enclosed her mother in a hug. Together their resolve evaporated as they sank to their knees on the porch and cried openly.

Frances cried like a cat in pain. The sound of her anguish twisted my heart. I picked her up and carried her inside the house. Her arms tightened around my neck, holding me like she was afraid I'd drop her. Tracy trailed behind me, sniffling.

I placed her mother on the sofa. Tracy knelt beside the couch and clutched her mother's shoulders. "Mom, you're going to make yourself sick." Tears streamed down her face. "We're going to be okay. I promise, we'll get through this." Tracy buried her head between her mother's neck and shoulder.

"No, I won't, Tracy. I might as well die too. I can't…I can't—"

"Shh, don't talk like that."

I stood across the room, my hands in my pockets, feeling useless to help them.

"I'm going to call the hotels. If anyone is still in town, they'll want to know. They might want to stop by."

Tracy dried her mother's tears with her hand, then struggled off the floor. I folded her in my arms and listened as her breathing slowed.

"I'm here for you. Let me help you."

"Okay," she managed. "You call your family, I'll call mine."

***

In a flash, Carla and Ursula arrived at her mother's house. The two of them operated in automatic pilot, too. Food appeared within minutes. Together they pacified Tracy in a way I could not. The tension in her face eased and her breathing came in a natural rhythm without the quick catches like she was having an asthma attack.

"Maybe we should call Crystal together," I said to Tracy when she came out of the kitchen and placed a cake in the center of the dining room table.

278

"No. No, we won't call her." Tracy stiffened. "You only get one chance for a first honeymoon and I don't want to ruin hers."

"But, Tracy." I spoke slow and soft, not wanting to upset her. She threw up her hands and walked back in the kitchen.

I turned to Carla and Ursula. "Can one of you try to talk to her?"

"I'm not so sure I disagree with her." Carla took the seat across the table from me and folded her hands. "Do you want Crystal to always think about her honeymoon and how her grandfather died? Or do you want her to think about her honeymoon and how wonderful it was, and then she returned home to find out her grandfather had died? Her coming home now won't change anything."

Tracy walked into the room carrying a stuffed turkey. Who had time to prepare a turkey on such short notice?

She handed me a piece of paper. "Walter, I need you to go home and get everything on this list. I'm staying here with my mother for a few days." Her tone was short and clipped. "Also, stop at the store and get everything on here." She pushed another list into my hand.

I looked over the items. Everything seemed simple enough. Tracy cleared her throat.

"Okay, I'm going, now." I planted a kiss on her forehead and walked out, happy to get away from the gloom in the stuffy house.

I pulled away from the house and dialed Sasha's number.

"Hello, baby. I was hoping you'd call me," she said.

"I called as soon as I could."

"Are you coming over? I really miss you." The lusty sound of her voice stirred me. "I haven't heard from you in three days."

"You knew I was busy with the wedding, and last night, Carl died."

"Okay, who is Carl and what does that have to do with you and me?"

"Carl is Tracy's father."

She expelled a heavy sigh and didn't disguise it. "Walter, I'm sorry about Tracy's father. I really am. But you know…it always seems to be one thing or another. Does this mean you haven't told her about me yet?"

"When was I supposed to tell her that, Sasha? Before or after I told her that her father was dead?"

"I'm pregnant, Walter. What about that? Where does that fall on your priority list?"

"Sasha, I'm doing everything I can. Her father's dead, dammit. I'm not some heartless bastard."

She didn't reply.

"Sasha!" She'd hung up. Maybe pregnancy hormones were jerking her around. I contemplated stopping by her house, but I couldn't handle two hysterical women.

By the time I got back to Philadelphia, the house was full of relatives. Most of them were already in town for the wedding, but there were new faces I didn't know. Frances sat in the corner, comatose. Not bothering to stem the flow of tears streaming down her face leaving dark spots on her black blouse.

"Hey man, you must be Tracy's husband." A tall man in faded blue jeans and a wrinkled t-shirt shook my hand and gave me a head to toe glance. I threw on clothes so fast this morning I had to look down in order to remember what I was wearing. I had on black pants and a royal blue polo shirt. I was thankful I was better dressed than him, since he thought it was important to give me the eyeball.

"Yes and you're…" His exuberance made me suspicious.

"I'm Mitch. I'm married to Tracy's first cousin, Dee. We talked yesterday at the wedding."

"Man, I talked to so many people yesterday, forgive me. What can I do for you?"

He lowered his voice and glanced over his shoulders. "Dee and I are worried about Tracy and

Frances, they both look like they're…" He searched for a word.

"Yeah, I know."

"In shock or something," he added. "How did Uncle Carl die? What happened? He looked fine last night."

The rest of the morning I saw people gathered around the food-laden tables, trading stories about how they thought Carl died, some people said he died in his sleep. One group had him dead at the wedding. It's a morbid habit, wanting to know the details of death. No matter how it happened, Carl was lying on a slab in some mortuary and nothing was going to change that.

I shifted my bags and took a deep breath. "Last night Frances went to the kitchen to get him some water. When she came out he wouldn't move." It saddened me to sum up the demise of my father-in-law in one tidy sentence. He deserved a much more eloquent pronouncement.

"Oh man, bummer."

I wanted to punch Mitch in the gut. Instead, I excused myself to find Tracy. I left Mitch standing in the middle of the dining room with his hands shoved into his torn jean pockets.

I found Tracy sitting at a table near the back door. I kissed her on the cheek and sat at the table with her.

"Did you get everything?"

"Yeah, I put your clothes in the bedroom and the groceries are in the kitchen."

"Thanks." She nodded towards her mother, who was still seated in the same position from earlier. "I'm worried about Mom. Look at her, she hasn't moved in hours. She can't live in this house alone. It's too big. Do you know she still buys cookies and puts them in the cookie drawer?"

I nodded and didn't try to make sense of her comment. She was still seated at the table too—I doubted if she had moved much. Her eyes were vacant even though she was looking at me.

"The funeral will be later in the week. The mortuary called and they've made the arrangements with the church. Crystal won't be back." She said this last statement with so much longing.

"Do you want me to call her? Have you changed your mind?"

"No. This is the best way. She needs to enjoy her honeymoon. She'll understand. My father would too. I'm sure."

"Are you trying to convince me, or yourself?"

She gave me a weary smile. "Both," she whispered.

There was softness about her, a vulnerability that opened her up and made her available to me. She wore a skirt I couldn't remember seeing before, but the vibrant yellow color reminded me of

sunshine and summer, her shoes were an exact
match to the skirt. How did she manage to look so
attractive under these circumstances? She never let
her guard down, as if doing so signaled failure. I put
my arms around her and held her tight. She went
weak against my chest. I smelled her cologne in the
softness of her neck.

Then just as quickly she pulled away and
scribbled more notes on pieces of paper. Notes for
the mortician. Notes for the church. Notes for
herself. I sat by her side through the next wave of
mourners that descended with their own brand of
grieving.

Chapter Twenty-Two - Walter

I was held prisoner in my mother-in-law's house. Two full days of running errands and circling the small house was maddening. Going to work was unthinkable, but the small confines of the house with all the sad looks and crying was rubbing my nerves raw. Tracy was so distraught, but I hardly seemed needed with all the loud mouths buzzing around her like mother hens.

I wanted to get away from the house for a few hours. That only required a good excuse.

Tracy wasn't asleep. I could tell by her irregular breathing and by the way she kept shifting her position in the small bed that we shared.

I pulled her close and used my arms to hold her still. "I've got to go to the house today. You know, to get the mail, pick up the newspapers, and pay some bills. I need to make sure I cancel our trip, too," I whispered in her ear.

"Uh-huh. Okay." She snuggled closer. My penis throbbed against her soft flesh. She moaned.

"I can't, Walter. I just can't."

"I know, baby. I understand, but that doesn't stop a brother from wanting." I slipped out of bed, dressed quickly, and left the house before another emergency came up, or before another slip of paper was pushed into my hand.

I dialed Sasha from the car, hoping to catch her at home. She picked up the phone and without giving her an opportunity to say anything, I said, "Can you stay home this morning? I'm on my way right now."

"I-I…well."

"I'm on my way now, Sasha. I'll be there in a few minutes."

"I need to get to the store."

"Sasha," I nearly yelled.

"Okay, okay."

Sasha was seated in a straight back chair reading a magazine when I walked in the door. The house was so quiet I could hear the kitchen clock ticking. She didn't move. I knelt at her feet and laid my head in her lap. Her legs were cool against my face.

"I haven't seen you since… How could you leave me for so long?" she whined.

 There wasn't anything to say that I hadn't already said, so I didn't respond. I ran my hand along her thigh.

"Walter." She sounded weak, the resistance gone. I placed the palm of my hand on the swell of her stomach. It was too soon to feel a kick, but a kick would have made this real for me. A kick would have set my life on some sensible track and helped me understand where my allegiance needed to be.

I pulled her face closer and kissed her hard on the mouth. It was easier than trying to talk about what was running through my head. I didn't want to argue with her.

Her large eyes darted across my face. "What's going on, Walter? Are you sick? Did something happen?"

"No, baby. I'm fine. Nothing is wrong. I just missed you so much." I ran my hand under her dress. Tracy may not have been in the mood, but Sasha was always ready. "You're wearing panties?"

"I was going to work," she giggled.

"But, you knew I was on my way over here." I pulled her panties down and stroked between her legs. She sighed so soft I almost didn't hear her pleasure. When she didn't resist my efforts, I pulled her on the floor next to me.

We lay there in a tangle of arms and legs and listened to the quiet of the house. Sasha was on her back, staring up at me. Something was different between us. Again I placed my hand on her stomach. Tears gathered in her eyes.

"What's wrong?"

Her lips trembled as tears rolled into her hairline. "Don't leave me, Walter. I want you to stay," she murmured.

"I have to go to the funeral. You know that." I spoke louder than I needed, but this conversation was becoming an irritant, as if she didn't have the capability to understand my reasoning.

"I'm not talking about the funeral, I'm talking about..." She spoke between jagged sobs. "Leaving Tracy. Are you going to?"

"Nothing has changed, darling. Nothing." My hollow words echoed in the quiet house. She continued to cry and I pulled a fleece throw off the couch and covered her legs, then placed a pillow under her head to make her comfortable. Leaving Tracy wasn't something I was ready to do. I didn't know if I would ever be ready to walk out on her. Tracy wasn't the kind of woman you walked out on. She was the woman you grew old with. My problem was I wasn't ready to grow old yet.

Unlike my brothers, I didn't need a drug to help me get an erection. My sex drive was still as strong as it was when I was twenty-one. Sasha made me feel as close to utopia as being twenty-one. She was supposed to remain free and available to me, not weigh our relationship down with children, mortgages and demands.
We didn't move for over an hour.

"What time is it?"

I shrugged. My limbs were numb; I was too old to lie on the hard floor for long. "I need to get up."

She looked at me without saying anything. Resignation registered on her face. Was I taking more than I gave?

She kissed the palm of my hand and led me upstairs. She slipped off her dress, turned back the sheets on the bed and crawled in on her hands and knees. With her arms extended, I climbed in the bed, too.

"Isn't this why you came here today?"

"Is that what you think?" I asked, as my erection grew.

"Do you love me, Walter?"

I nodded. I didn't trust myself to speak.

"Walter." She started to say more then changed her mind. I stripped off my clothes and climbed on top of her, without putting my weight on her stomach. I ran my tongue down her neck, between her swollen breasts. She arched her body off the bed.

"Oh baby," she moaned.

I found her soft wet core and drove my tongue inside. I continued to stroke her nub until she shuddered uncontrollably and held me tight. For now, everything was okay. I climbed on top of her and pushed into her warm wet center. Her muscles contracted around me, making it hard to hold out. She slammed her hips against me, demanding more and within minutes I answered her call.

I'd slipped away from Tracy every day to spend long, erotic afternoons with Sasha. She was so fanatical about me leaving Tracy, I thought more frequent visits would appease her enough to buy me a little time to settle my life.

Her stomach grew bigger almost overnight. Already Sasha had to adjust her walk to accommodate her fullness. The pregnancy made her radiate a golden glow that was worth looking at all day.

Sasha came into the living room and plopped next to me on the sofa. She rested her head on my shoulder. "You've been here three days in a row." Her voice sounded dreamy and filled with the longing that made me nervous.

"Tracy is so distraught over her father's death, she doesn't miss me. With all the people coming and going, she doesn't know who's in her mother's house. This has been one of the most relaxing weeks I've had in a long time. Like I'm on holiday."

"It's going to be like this all the time. In just a few more days. " She took my hand and placed it over her navel. "I think the baby has started to move. Feel that?"

"When did it start?" Against the palm of my hand I felt the faint push of the baby.

***

The jet stream shifted just enough on the day of the funeral to release us from the grip of humidity that had hung in the air. The temperature was bearable enough to allow us to stand at the gravesite without sweat soaking through our clothes.

Tracy and her mother sat in small white folding chairs facing the coffin-size hole in the ground. From my vantage point behind Tracy, I watched her twist the lace handkerchief around her index finger. She drew the delicate fabric so tight, the tip of her finger grew red. She slowly released the pressure, then began the process all over again. Frances continued to cry. The soft sobs never stopped. It had become white noise to me. Tracy didn't shed a tear.

The blanket of white roses that covered the bronze casket scented the air. Carl would have been impressed with the dignity of the ceremony. The freeloading relatives who kept dropping by the house to gobble up the food would have angered him. While Tracy looked thinner, a couple of relatives looked like they had gained a few pounds.

I tightened my grip on Tracy's shoulder, signaling her to release her finger from the handkerchief tourniquet. She set her finger free and reached up to pat my hand.

I shifted my weight from foot to foot. My week of peace and freedom was coming to an end.

Sasha's words sounded more like a threat than a statement. I was getting closer to the gallows.

Tracy had dropped hints that her mother needed to come live with us now. As much as I cared for Frances, I didn't want to live in the same house with her. Instead of one pair of eyes scrutinizing my activities, there would be two.

The silence in the limousine was broken when Frances released a loud sob, turning up the volume on the white noise. Tracy pressed her nose against the window. Her shoulders tensed, but she ignored her mother.

I slid across the seat. "Frances, we're here for you. You're not going to be alone." I cradled her in my arms and gave her a reassuring pat.

"I can't believe Carl won't come in the house and call my name anymore. Or turn over in bed and rub my back late at night," she managed between sobs. "What am I supposed to do? I'm all alone."

"It might not be easy, Frances, but it can be done. Carl would want you to go on," I tried to reassure her.

After the limousine deposited us in front of the house and disappeared around the corner, I stood between Tracy and her mother. It was time for me to return to my regular life and figure some stuff out.

"I'm going into the office, Tray. I'll come back tonight to pick you up if you want to come home tonight."

She nodded and helped her mother up the stairs.

A neat stack of messages sat on the middle of my desk, and 183 new e-mails demanded my attention when I walked in the office. I threw my briefcase on the corner of my desk and pulled out my chair. It was a huge risk being out of the office for five days during a major restructuring. But being there for Tracy and spending afternoons with Sasha gave me the rest the doctor had prescribed.

Beverly strolled in my office with a stack of folders in her arms. "How is Tracy doing?" Unlike some of the other people who had cornered me on my way inside, Beverly was sincere. She could have been the fourth person in Tracy's loudmouth pack and fit in quite well.

"She's taking it pretty hard. Her mother is a wreck."

"What can I do?"

"Can you clear my e-mail messages?"

"I meant for Tracy." She dropped the folders on top of the other piles of papers on my desk.

"Yeah, that's what I thought. Fill me in on the week."

"It was pretty quiet around here. All the bigwigs were behind closed doors all week. You have a meeting with Joe this afternoon at two. In his office." She spun around and left without saying anything else.

"A meeting with Joe, great," I muttered. The moisture collecting in my armpits accompanied the heavy pressure in my chest. I inhaled a deep breath, trying to remember the relaxed feeling I'd enjoyed before. I pushed away from the desk and placed my arms over my head. After several minutes of standing at my window watching the cars whiz along Trooper Avenue, I picked up the phone and returned calls.

The lunch hour passed and I remained at my desk. I called Tracy at her mother's but after several rings it went to the answering machine. I disconnected without leaving a message, and then dialed Sasha's number.

"How's your wife?" The sarcastic tone said she was trying to pick a fight.

"She's doing fine. She's at her mother's and thinking about going back to work soon."

"Now you can tell her, right? We can be together like we were last week?"

"I have a meeting with Joe in a few minutes," I blurted.

"What about?" I heard her shuffle paper. "Isn't that your boss?"

"Yes. I guess he wants to talk about the office restructuring. I've been out of the office. He needs to fill me in on everything."

"Now that everything is back to normal, you can—"

"Look, you have to trust me. I have every intention of telling her. But, even you can see why I had to wait. Please get off my back, Sasha. It won't be long."

"Fine, Walter. But things are different now. I'm different." Her voice softened. "I know. I know. See you tonight?"

"Yeah, tonight."

"I love you so much Walter," she said.

Her lighter tone eased the tension in my neck. One glance over my shoulder revealed the same messy desk from this morning. I only managed to shuffle papers from one pile to another. With a deep sigh, I picked up a pad and headed for Joe's office. I rubbed my palms against my slacks, ignoring the rumble in my stomach.

"Joe, good afternoon." I stepped in with a fake smile plastered on my face.

"Walter, thank you for coming." He moved away from his desk and sat with me at the conference table. "Sorry to hear about your father-in-law. How is Tracy?"

"She's doing better." I crossed my foot over my knee.

Joe adjusted his tie. "That's good. That's good. I know how hard it is to lose a parent. When my father passed away, I was devastated. I kept wishing I could spend a few more days with him."

I nodded, placed my foot back on the floor and shifted in the hard chair. Joe didn't schedule this meeting to talk about our parents or to find out how Tracy was doing.

"Anyway," he continued. "You know we think highly of you here. This was a very hard decision. We're going to let you go."

My stomach dropped. I straightened my back and picked up my pen. "Excuse me?"

"The incident with that woman a few months ago didn't help your case. This is a small company, we're like family. Your lack of discretion made the partners wonder about other shortcomings. They don't think you'll fit in with the path we're taking for the future.

"It's not a reflection on how you've performed your job. Besides, we've decided to focus on emerging markets in Asia. With your knowledge and experience, you'll find another assignment in no time at all. Of course, you'll receive the very attractive executive exit package."

"A few weeks ago, you said you didn't think I had anything to worry about. I'm forty-two, Joe. I don't want to start looking for a job."

He held his hands, palm sides up. "It's out of my hands. But you have until the end of the month. I wish I had better news." He stood up and walked back to his desk.

By two-thirty, I was back in my office. I shut down my computer but didn't place my laptop in my briefcase. After turning off the lights, I closed the door and walked out of the office past Beverly without a word.

Chapter Twenty-Three – Tracy

I bolted up in bed. Moisture pasted my nightgown against my back. I swung my leg over the side and studied my hands as a flood of memories rushed back to me. All mushed together in my dream was the bridal dress, the five-tiered cake, champagne, flowers, a bronze coffin and a skeleton.

Separating Crystal's wedding from my father's death made my head throb. Every vision I had of my daughter in her beautiful gown was accompanied by a vision of my father in final repose.

I heard Walter fumbling around in the kitchen making his brand of coffee. I jumped off the bed and dashed to the hall.

"Walter, can you make me some coffee too? I'm going to work today," I yelled over the banister.

"Are you sure you're ready? You were pretty restless last night." He walked to the foot of the stairs, still holding a canister of coffee.

"I can't sit around the house any more. Visiting my mother every day won't help her to pull her life back together either. Yeah, I'm sure." I couldn't tell him I wanted to see Marco. The guilt of wanting to talk to Marco stabbed at my conscience, but I could squash the need.

I showered as quickly as I could. My favorite pair of black Ralph Lauren slacks slipped on with ease. They were loose enough in the waist for me to grab a handful of material. They didn't cut me in the crotch. Not eating for over a week agreed with me. I found a cream capped-sleeve shirt and pulled it on.

I checked my image in the mirror and swiped my cheeks with blush. The puffiness under my eyes had subsided. Gone were the darkened circles that labeled me a tragedy. I looked normal.

I wanted to talk to Walter before he left. He was a new man. Maybe one I could love again. When I walked into the kitchen he handed me a mug of coffee. "I expected you to take another week off," he said.

"I know, but what would I do?" I blew into the cup before taking a sip. He fixed it just the way I liked, mild and sweet. "You were my savior. I don't know what we would have done if you couldn't have taken off to help me and Mother." I snuggled against his shoulder.

"No problem. I love you." He looked down at me.

"My family kept you on your toes. There were times when you were gone for hours. I hope you got frequent flyer points for all those trips to the grocery store."

He set his cup on the counter and picked up his briefcase.

"Hey, how about we reschedule that trip after I get my mother settled?"

"Mmm, we'll see."

"Don't you still want to get away? Don't you need a little rest and relaxation too?" I stroked his back and rested my chin on his shoulder. I could make my marriage work, if I just tried.

"Yeah, but I need to get back to my desk now. Maybe in the fall. We'll see." He shrugged his shoulders to remove my chin. In a split second I was sent reeling right back to where we started to slip away from each other.

"I really need to get away. Do you think we can do it in September or October?"

"You may have to go without me," he said.

"Without you? It was your idea, remember? Your gift to me. " I backed away from him.

"Tracy, I lost my job. The last thing on my mind is laying in the sun, drinking sweet liquor."

My head began to throb. "What about all that talk about us being fine, Tracy? No need to worry, Tracy. Trust me, Tracy." I was shaking.

"Wasn't I the perfect husband while we were dealing with your father's death? I was by your side every single day. What do you want from me?"

"What do you want, Walter? A medal? Do you think being a husband is a part-time job? Do you want time off for good behavior?"

"I just need some time."

"Okay. Okay. I understand. I just thought we might want to stoke this special feeling between us. Besides, I need to rest and see something other than interior walls and sad faces. I'm falling apart. My dad's gone, Crystal's moving, Ursula's left, and Carla's so busy trying to make a baby she can't see straight. I want to spend more time with you."

"Everybody wants a little piece of me. I'm being picked to pieces, Tracy. We'll get away, when I get a chance. Now I've got to go to work."

"You're being picked to pieces? By whom? I don't think I asked you for much. I certainly don't get much. So if you're being picked to pieces, you need to be having that conversation with whoever is doing the picking. The little bit of yourself that you give to this relationship could hardly be defined as enough to cause you any discomfort."

"Well, I'm uncomfortable. I'll schedule something when I see my way clear. Until then…" Without another word he walked out the door.

My cheeks stung. I dropped the cup in the sink, coffee splashed across the granite counter. Where was the sensitive man who stood by my side last week? Where was the man who stood up in front of our families and friends a few weeks ago and professed his love for me, his sweet, endearing wife?

I stared at the closed door for several minutes, willing him to come back inside and apologize, to hold me for just a moment. But his car roared as he backed down the driveway.

A knot formed in my stomach as a familiar sadness settled around me. I reached for my purse and pills. I needed to feel better and little else mattered.

At nine-thirty I sat behind my desk facing the dark computer screen while my computer booted up. Exhaustion filled my bones.

"You have to turn that thing on to get it to work." My breath caught at the sound of his voice. Marco leaned in my doorway looking like he just finished a magazine cover shoot. The argument with Walter faded the moment I set eyes on Marco. An ember of hot desire flared in my core. I was being silly, but I missed him.

"Very funny," I tried not to sound like a goofy teenager.

With one quick stride he stepped into my office and gathered me in his arms. He smelled good. Without meaning to, I rested my head on his chest and let out a deep breath.

He relaxed his arms and gave me a long look. "How ya doing? You look like you could use some coffee. Come walk with me to the cafeteria.

I'll treat." He grabbed my hand and led me down the hall before I could object.

"It feels good to be back in the office."

"You've been missed around here." He looked down at me and I knew he meant he missed me. My insides turned warm, just like a girl with her first crush.

"Yeah, right." I nudged his arm.

Sitting at the table with Marco brought me a level of comfort I hadn't felt since Walter told me about my father. Tears rushed down my face. He pressed a tissue into the palm of my hand, and then gently brushed his thumb over my knuckles.

I wiped my nose. "I didn't expect to see you at the funeral. It was nice of you to come all the way to Philly."

"I figured you needed the moral support."

"I was pretty much out of it. Did we talk at all?"

"We talked plenty, but you weren't coherent." He chuckled. "It's okay. I didn't expect you to be your bubbly self."

"You think I'm bubbly? I haven't felt bubbly in…"

"You're just going through a tough time."

I nodded and sipped my coffee. "Has your life ever been slightly out of sync and you haven't been able to put your finger on the reason why?"

"Let's see, my wife and I spent a year going through the motions before either one of us would admit our marriage was over. Then there was the year we spent dividing up the property and deciding on how we'd share Briana before the divorce was final. I haven't lost a parent, but I think some of what I've been through qualifies as being out of sync." He rested his elbows on the table and leaned closer. The dimples in his cheeks deepened.

"Tell me what I need to do."

"What's wrong? You know it's normal to feel a little out of sorts after the death of someone you love.

"No, it's not my father's death. If that was it, I could get it right." I shook my head. "I…I don't know what it is." I sipped my coffee. "Tell me something, Marco. Do you believe in happily ever after?"

"I do. I absolutely do. My parents have been married for forty-five years and they still look at each other like it's brand new. The next time around for me is going to be forever." He punctuated his affirmation with a smile.

"You sound so sure. I can't even find a word to describe my marriage. I'm contemplating leaving Walter." I swallowed. "Crystal's not a little girl anymore. Maybe…"

"Tracy, you know how I feel about you. I'm not qualified to give you advice. I probably shouldn't even hear this or I might take advantage of you right now."

I rested my chin in the palm of my hand. "If I were going to have an affair, it would be with you." I watched his face for a response.

His smile broadened. "*Si grazie*. I'm flattered."

"Oh, then it's on."

He laughed with me.

We sat for a few more minutes before strolling toward my office. My mind didn't feel as foggy as it had earlier at my desk.

We made our way through the lobby and scooted around a group of gentlemen at the receptionist desk. A woman sat off in the corner with her purse in her lap.

"Lots of visitors today." Marco looked around the lobby.

"Tracy, there's someone here to see you," the receptionist called to me. She pointed past the gentlemen gathered around her desk and indicated the woman standing with her arms beside her protruding belly. Fear inched up my spine, settling in my throat. Making it hard to breathe.

"To see me?" I pointed at my chest.

"Do you want me to stay around?" Marco placed his hand on my shoulder. His touch felt hot on my skin.

My hands shook. "No, I'll be fine."

He looked at the woman and back to me. "You don't look fine."

"I am." I nodded, hoping he'd leave.

I held my shoulders high and made my way across the lobby. The woman pushed her purse onto her shoulder, exposing her round belly. She leaned forward, her fullness tightened my heart. I gulped for air. The sun from the palladium window slanted across half of her face, giving her an odd look. Several questions flitted through my head in the seconds it took me to reach her. Should I ask her into my office? Was she looking for a job? Was she a friend of Crystal's?

"Tracy." She extended her hand.

Her informality shocked me. "Do I know you?"

"We've never met, but I've heard so much about you." She sounded very proper, like she was giving a canned speech.

I sat in the chair in front of her. Only a few feet of space separated us.

"Do I know you?" I asked again.

"I'm Sasha Samuels. Look, this is very hard for me so I'm going to just say what I came here to say. Walter doesn't know I'm here." She rolled her hand over her swollen stomach as if she coveted some youthful secret I was no longer privy to.

"Walter? What does this have to do with Walter? Your name is familiar. You helped with the wedding?" I placed my hands at my sides, anchoring me to the chair. The lobby felt warmer. Hot. A feeling of dread pricked every pore in my body. The wedding planner never mentioned anyone named Sasha. The door in my head that kept all the scary things locked away flew open, spilling the contents on my heart.

"No, it's not that. He doesn't know how to tell you. The stress is… The stress… Just a week before the wedding he was in the hospital overnight. The doctors said it might have been an anxiety attack. Look Tracy, this is Walter's baby." She rubbed her stomach again, her large engagement ring glittered. "You've got to let him go, but you seem to go from one crisis or family drama to the next. And Walter doesn't know how to tell you."

My eyes were fixed on her mouth, but I couldn't say anything. Words jumbled in my head. Every breath was a struggle.

"We're engaged. Well, sorta. But we do plan to get married." She stuck her ring finger out for me. A diamond the size of a melon sparkled against the sun in the atrium. I looked down at my own ring. In comparison, mine looked like the third place prize.

"Are you sure we're talking about the same person? Walter Baptiste is my husband. He can't be engaged." My voice sounded far away and oddly calm.

"I know it sounds strange. But he wanted to show his commitment to me, so he bought me a ring."

"Walter sent you to talk to me?"

"No. He's been promising to tell you he was leaving for months, but you…something kept coming up."

"So, this is his baby?" I pointed to her stomach.

"Yes. He's promised I won't have to go through this pregnancy alone."

"Promised. Walter promised…" I suppressed the urge to laugh at the sublime absurdity of what was unfolding right in front of me. Walter had painted me as a woman moving from crisis to crisis. I wondered if he'd told her he was the architect of most of those crises. He just might have a few for her as well.

A sense of knowing flowed through me, my instincts about Walter's activities were right. That constant gnawing in my stomach had been my warning. Sasha's confession punched a hole in my gut and dragged my heart out.

She looked fantastic, her skin still plump with youth. "I guess you love him?"

"Yes, I love him and he loves me. He really wants to be with me."

"I imagine he does."

She stood up. "So you'll let him go? He wants a divorce."

"We've been married over twenty years. Surely you don't expect me to hand him over to you based on this little conversation?" I waved my finger between us. "How about I have a talk with Walter and get back to you on that?" My tone was firm, matter-of-fact, just like hers. I spoke like a woman entitled to my indignation.

"I hope you understand why I had to come here today." She stood and the sun streaming through the window bounced off her diamond pendant necklace, an identical match to the one around my neck. My knees trembled with her truth. All the pieces of the puzzle nestled together perfectly.

I squared my shoulders, mustering strength I didn't possess.

From the oversized windows in the lobby, I saw her hurry down the curved sidewalk. She walked up to Walter's new Lexus and got in the driver's seat.

My chest constricted as I gasped for air. My legs went numb. But I made it to my office and fell into the chair. I grabbed my pills and swallowed without counting.

My husband had a family on the other side of town. I had a zillion different thoughts at once. The onslaught of emotion paralyzed me.

It was almost as if I had been waiting on just this thing to happen. My world started to crumble months ago, but all I did was pack my bags and look in on them every day. What kind of lame plan was that?

How would Crystal accept the news that she had a sibling who would be born in a few months? And in that moment, I was thankful she was moving to New York. At least this way she would be away from some of the ugliness as it unraveled over the next several months and it would be harder for her to bond with her father's new family.

I was ashamed of myself for relishing that thought. It was as if my mind had been taken over by some unknown force. My life was disjointed. I was a stranger to myself.

I picked up the phone and put it back on the base. I picked it up again and punched in Walter's number, which was more instinct than anything else. I couldn't think of anything to say to him. I hung up the phone and looked over my desk. It was nice and neat. Nothing was out of place. A message from the receptionist lay in the center of the desk telling me I had a visitor in the lobby. I folded the note and stuffed it into my purse and decided to take a few more pills. The other pills weren't working. Maybe the longer you took them the less effective they became.

My phone rang. It was Marco. Instead of picking up, I waited for him to hang up. I sat in my office for an hour, watching the minutes tick off. Too numb to move. Too numb to care. Too numb to try.

After several tries I managed to dial Ursula.

"Meet me at my house," I said when she answered the phone.

"Why? What's going on?" Ursula asked.

"Just meet me, please. I'll be there in a few minutes."

"Tracy, you know I just started this new job—is everything okay? You sound funny. What's wrong?"

"Call Carla too, she'll need to be there."

"Tracy. Tracy slow down and tell me what happened." When I didn't respond, she said, "Where are you now?"

"Mmm, I'm leaving the office. Call Carla. Call Carla." My voice was calm, balancing the rage roaring in my head.

"Tracy, what happened?"

"Ursula, I'm not feeling too good. Just come, okay? Come, okay." I hung up the phone, collected my purse, and pulled my keys out of the side pocket. My head throbbed like the base drum at a rock concert. The constant boom, boom, boom pounded in time with my heart.

I stumbled out of the building. Nothing felt real. A vortex of whirling color blurred my vision, becoming more vibrant the farther I walked. Finally the pills were working. The loneliness and deceit blurred. The notion that I had been so supremely duped ricocheted around in my head. My body revolted at the news.

I walked out of the same door as Sasha Samuels, down the winding sidewalk just as she had. I thought I could still smell her cologne lingering in the air. With the sun in my eyes, all the cars looked the same.

The same color.

The same make.

The same model. I stepped off the curb toward the car that should have been mine. I wasn't fast enough to jump back on the sidewalk. I tried, but the curb was too high.

So high.

A car struck me so hard I landed on the hood. I rolled off into a big ball and landed hard on the asphalt.

The pain hit me with so much intensity I couldn't move. The driver yelled to someone and came to stand over me. His hands flapped in several different directions. I refused to get up, maybe because I couldn't or because it felt good to just lie down. I wanted to stay there.

Forever.

Marco's face hovered over mine. "Tracy, *Cosa c'e che non va?* Are you hurt?"

"All over."

"An ambulance is coming. Don't move."

"Can't you just help me to my car? I need to get home. I have to check his office drawer."

"Ma'am, I think you need to get to a hospital. Please just be still." The driver's voice was shaky.

"Marco, help me up please. Please."

Instead of giving me a hand, he got down on his knees and spoke into my ear. "Tracy, you are going to the hospital so they can take a look at you. I'll go with you. Take my hand and hold on to it. I'll be here."

I grabbed his hand and held on to it as I tried to straighten my legs. "Her name was Sasha. Why do I know that name?"

"Shhh, Tracy it's going to be all right."

The siren got closer.

"I'm going to close my eyes, Marco, for a moment, but I'm not going to die, okay?"

Chapter Twenty-Four - Tracy

"Ms. Baptiste, I'm Dr. Ali." She sat in the chair beside the bed and crossed her legs. "How are you feeling?"

"My throat is sore." It came out more like a croak than actual words.

"Yes, we had to pump your stomach. Are you aware that you had a very high dosage of anti-anxiety medication in your system? Do you know how many you took?"

My head pounded like a freight train was running through it. I shook my head. I had bigger problems that needed solving.

"Did you take more than what was prescribed?"

I used my elbows to lift up in the bed. I spoke slowly. "Do you think I did it on purpose?" When she didn't reply, I asked her again.

"I have to ask these questions. It's routine."

"Well, I can assure you I didn't take them on purpose. I mean… I know I took them…but the pain… It was an accident. My father died, I found out my husband is a big fat liar. It was an accident."

"Do you feel like you need more pills?"

"I'm sore, all over, but I'm fine. Fine."

The doctor gave me a firm look before scribbling on her pad and walking out. Ursula rushed into the room before the door closed. She threw her arms around me and held me while she rocked back and forth.

"Marco called me." Tears glistened in her eyes. "He's outside the door. He told me a little bit. What happened? Did you…" Ursula seldom cried. "Did you try to commit suicide, Tracy?"

"Oh, Ursula, no. You know me better than that. You sound like that psychologist—doctor—person who just walked out of here. Why would you think I tried to kill myself?"

"The pills and stepping in front of that car." Her high-pitched voice was full of fear. "And when you called me you weren't very coherent." She sat in the chair. "Tracy you gotta do something. Honey you can't keep this up."

Carla banged the door against the wall when she stormed into the room. "What happened to you? You don't look so good."

"Thanks, Carla."

"You know what I mean." She threw her purse on the foot of the bed. "What did the jackass do this time?"

"Huh. You got that right," Ursula quipped.

Both of them stared at me.

"He's been having an affair for years. Years." I swallowed against the roughness in my throat and told them the whole story. My heartbeat increased with each detail. Their eyes grew bigger.

We sat in silence for a few moments while they absorbed the gritty truth.

I had to stop this. Stop dragging my friends through the bowels of my relationship. It was bad enough that it was tearing me apart.

"I knew it. I knew it." Carla slapped the bed. "That no good S.O.B. We should've kicked his ass after that first time." She stood up and faced the window. Ursula continued to look at me with sadness in her eyes.

"Soooo, what's next?" Ursula let out a deep breath.

"Well, now I go to my house, pack up his stuff so he can move out, then I move on. It's really as simple as that."

"It's never that simple," Ursula said.

Carla turned around. Her eyes were damp with tears. "Oh, yes it is. It's as simple as that. It's time she took a walk, without looking back. What kind of man does a thing like this? How can he…" Carla pointed her finger at me. "It's time you got angry enough to pull yourself together."

Ursula reached across the bed and touched my leg. "The more important fact we need to talk about is how…why the pills, Tracy? And why did you step in front of that car?"

"Look, you two have known me a long time, you know I wouldn't try to kill myself." I cried freely. "I was just trying to stop the pain. I didn't do this on purpose. It's been…look at all the stuff I've been going through. I didn't see that car. Really, I didn't. I just wanted to feel better. That's all."

"Honey walking in front of cars never made anyone feel better. You won't feel better until you start fixing your life," Carla said.

"You know what I mean…I was going home to prepare to confront him. My head was just…just so full of all the stuff that that woman said, and the incidents I've ignored or pretended not to see, that I wasn't paying attention," My confession eased some of the pain sitting on my heart.

"She's right, Tracy, you've got to change something. You can't keep doing what you've been doing. Honey…honey, I'm not trying to be mean, but—"

I put my hand up to stop her from the painful statement she thought she needed to make. "I know. I know I've got to do something different and I will. I promise."

"You think he's going to just walk away? It can get ugly and it probably will. I don't think you're strong enough to handle all this right now. Let me call your mother or Crystal."

"No," I snapped. "No, Ursula. My mother definitely can't handle this right now and Crystal will be home in a few days." I paused. "I won't lean on anyone but myself. I can handle this, and I will."

"Suppose Walter decides he's not moving out?" Carla asked.

"I'll deal with that when the time comes."

"By taking more pills?" Carla placed her hands on her hips.

"My bags are packed. I'll go. Maybe I need to change the scenery, anyway." I twirled my thumbs and avoided her eyes.

"Don't act tough for me, Tracy. You don't need to be tough, I'm here for you." Ursula rubbed my leg. Her touch reminded me of our college years when we cried together over our disappointments.

"Ursula, I'll be fine."

Carla folded her hands and nodded.

Walter hurried into the room with his hand shoved so deep in his pockets I thought his pants might come down. His annoyed look said I'd interrupted his busy day and needed to be swatted. He rushed to the bed and planted a dry kiss on my forehead. His affection was as artificial as the smile pasted on Carla's face.

Carla and Ursula hugged and kissed me then scurried out of the room. Ursula shot me a thumbs-up before she disappeared through the door.

"What the hell happened?" Walter asked.

I stared at my husband, the stranger. Impeccably dressed and as handsome as ever but little else about him was recognizable. The distance between us was too wide to be filled with flowers, sex or romantic weekends in the Caribbean.

"They are releasing me in a few minutes. You might as well sit and wait until I sign the release forms."

"What the fuck did you do, Tracy? I knew you were popping too many pills, like they were candy or something." He walked around the bed.

"You might as well sit," I repeated, while searching his face for a hint of his duplicity.

He circled the bed again, slower this time, without taking his hands out of his pockets. "Are you going to tell me what happened?"

"Eventually."

"What the hell does eventually mean, Tracy?"

"It means, when I feel up to it I'll tell you all about it. And right now, I'm not up to it. But we'll talk. We'll talk. By the way, did you ever find out any more about that check for five thousand dollars?"

"Are you shitting me? We're in the hospital because you got hit by a car, they had to pump your stomach, and you're asking me about some damn check? Maybe that psychologist needs to come back in here and talk to you a little more," he huffed.

"Maybe she does." I shrugged. "Because I sure need to have my head examined."

"What the hell does that mean?" He glared at me.

I clasped my hands tight, holding in the hostility bubbling in my gut.

Chapter Twenty-Five – Walter

Tracy was in a daze. She couldn't answer any of my questions. The whole idea of being hit by a car and overdosing on drugs didn't seem to faze her.

I held her elbow as I guided her through the door of the house. She groaned as I eased her onto the couch. Her mouth twisted with pain.

"I'm going upstairs to change. I'll be right back."

She adjusted her position, but didn't respond.

After spending a week running nuisance errands while she mourned her father, I had no intentions of playing nursemaid to her for another week. Those loudmouth friends should be putting her to bed, holding her hand, and talking nice to her.

"Did you hear me?" I asked again.

"I did." She folded her arms over her chest. "I'll be here."

Upstairs, I closed the bathroom door and dialed Sasha's number. No use having her yakking in my ear about stopping by after work. My call transferred to voice mail. I was saved the hassle she was going to dish out.

I stepped into my neat closet and examined the wire shelf. Tracy knew exactly how I liked my shirts folded. I pulled my lucky blue golf shirt from the pile and pulled it on. Eighteen holes of golf called my name.

Tracy was probably asleep. I planned to leave her a note instead of looking at those sad brown eyes and tell her I was going golfing. I was so happy about playing golf, I whistled as I bounded down the stairs.

Tracy was seated in the center of the family room sofa, clutching a bunch of papers while a steady stream of fat tears rolled down her cheeks. *Good lord, if she's still upset about her father or her mishap today, then I'll have to skip my golf game and sit with her.*

"Shit," I muttered as my dream game evaporated. "What's the matter, Tracy?" I tried to hide my exasperation as I sat down beside her. "Are you in pain?"

She flung the papers in my face, just missing my eye.

"What the hell is wrong with you?" I yelled. I gathered the papers from the floor. "These are my cell phone statements. Why…" My heart hammered in my ears. "What the hell are you doing going through my office drawers? Do I need to call the doctor because you must be losing your damn mind?"

"Why don't *you* answer some questions for a change? Why don't you tell me who Sasha

Samuels is, Walter? Tell me why you wrote her a check for five thousand dollars? Tell me the story again about taking your pregnant secretary to the doctor. Tell me about the house on 108 Academy Drive. Tell me why she's driving your car and carrying your baby."

"I don't know what the hell you're talking about." I jumped off the couch. Beads of sweat pricked my forehead and upper lip. My chest contracted. I moved away from her. I needed another panic attack, but I couldn't will an episode to strike me down, to get me out of the mess.

"It's nothing, Tracy. It's not what you think."

"Don't tell me what I should be thinking. Your Sasha Samuels visited my office today. She had a very interesting story to tell. I can see from these bills you call her a lot. A lot. Shit, Walter, you call her more than you call me. Look at the bills, it's all right there." She stabbed a finger at one of the bills in her lap. "So if it's nothing, then tell me what it is." Her eyes were red and tears continued to roll down her face, but she seemed calm. "Tell me, dammit," she hissed.

During our marriage, I had told so many lies, I couldn't keep up with them. What made this beautiful, intelligent woman love me the way she did? She could have—and maybe she should have—walked out years ago. The hurt engraved on her face ripped me apart. I needed to get it out in the open. I owed her the truth. She would understand. She'd always been there for me. I had to trust her to help me work through this situation.

"Tracy," I started. "Tracy, I never meant for this thing to get so carried away. It started out as just…you know, sex." I hunched my shoulders waiting for her to nod in agreement. She didn't. "It wasn't supposed to get this far. I'm going to end it with her."

"She came to my office today."

"Who?"

"Who are we talking about? Sooner or later you'll be honest with yourself and maybe, just maybe, you'll be honest with me."

"What?" I threw my hands up. There was a tightness in my chest. My mind searched for a way out. "Who, Tracy?"

"Sasha." Her shrill voice was unrecognizable.

"She wouldn't."

"She did."

"Why?" I shook my head and sat next to her.

"My God, Walter she's barely older than Crystal. What are you trying to prove? Your girlfriend, your lover—or should I say your fiancée—says you want to leave me, but don't know how to tell me. That I won't let you go. It was quite obvious she's pregnant with your child. You are the one who needs to see a doctor." Her sarcastic truth was hurtful to hear. The pain in her voice was audible.

I never thought I'd admit the truth, even when I dreamed of this moment, I always had a handy explanation to tell Tracy, but not the truth.

"I'm so sorry. You know I'm too old to raise another family…I'll take care of the baby. I promise you it won't have an impact on our lives. I really didn't mean for this to happen, and I didn't mean to hurt you. Honestly. You have to believe me. This wasn't supposed to happen." I wasn't sure which part of this statement was true and which part was a lie. I'd enjoyed every minute I spent with Sasha. I hadn't intentionally set out to hurt Tracy. "I can fix this, Tracy. Just bear with me and I'll fix everything."

"How can you sit there and tell me this was something casual and that you'll fix it? Maybe what the two of you had was more real than what we've had. So real that she felt she had to come to me and claim you." She bowed her head and studied her hands.

"How long?"

"How long what?"

"Please don't disrespect me anymore. You know exactly what I mean. How long have the two of you been together? How many years, Walter?"

"Don't."

"How long," she shouted. "How many years, you bastard?"

"Tracy…I-I don't…it's…three years." I dropped my head when her eyes grew larger, and she started crying uncontrollably. She tried to say something, but she couldn't catch her breath long enough to get the words out. I wanted to pull her into my arms, but I didn't dare touch her.

"What about me, where do I fit in here?" she finally said.

"I still love you. I always have and I always will. We'll get through this, just like we've gotten through other difficult times."

"Do you love her?"

I didn't expect this question. She wanted me to say no, but I couldn't. I nodded.

"We'll get through this."

"No…not this time, Walter. We won't get through this." She shook her head and struggled to stand up. "Get out," she yelled. "You have to leave now. I don't want to look at you another minute." She pointed to the door like I didn't know where it was. "Get out."

I didn't move.

"Did you hear me? I said get out, Walter. Now. Get out now."

"Tracy, I don't think you need to be alone right now."

"I've been alone for years. I can't stand the sight of you. Get the hell out of here." She pointed to the door again.

"Where am I supposed to go?" I held out my hands.

"The hell if I care. You must think I'm an idiot." Her words hung between us.

"Were you ever going to tell me?"

"Tell you what?"

She cocked her head to one side but didn't say anything.

"No, I don't think I ever would. You know how I am. Eventually I would have come back home. I think this is just a phase. I love you, Tracy."

"Go to 108 Academy Drive." She started up the stairs. "And don't you ever set foot in this house again. I'll have every single thing in this house that belongs to you sent there. If I come across anything I don't want, I'll send that to you, too. Now get the hell out of here."

"I lost my job."

"And I'm supposed to care…because?"

"Come on Tracy, this isn't like you. You've been through a lot and you're probably not thinking clearly right now."

"Is that what you think? I'm not thinking clearly. And the day of Crystal's wedding, when you talked about taking your dear wife away because I was the love of your life…Was I thinking clearly then or was I just foolish?"

"Tracy."

"No, I think I get it now." She descended a couple of stairs. "Let me make this clear to you. I finally get it. Walter, I get it. This marriage is over. It's done. I'm done. My bags have been packed and sitting in my closet for months. But I kept thinking I needed to give our marriage one more try, that maybe there was one little thing I could do to feel something for you again." I shook my head. "Go to your fiancée and be happy, you bastard."

"Aah come on, let's talk about it." I threw my hands in the air. I wanted to hold her in my arms and make this better. The cold stare in her eyes sliced me in two, making me back up.

"Good bye, Walter." She walked up the stairs without looking back.

Chapter Twenty-Six – Tracy

Such an artful liar. His dark brown eyes never shifted while he professed his commitment to me. For twenty years of marriage, I'd managed to overlook his arrogance, his selfishness, and a whole host of character deficiencies, until he closed the door leading to the garage. All his imperfections sailed back to me like a wave at high tide. The thick veil that shielded me from seeing the ugly side of my marriage lifted, revealing the real man I married. His charming good looks and sleek physique couldn't hide his shortcomings any longer. His narcissism clawed at the wound that was our marriage.

I climbed the stairs, my body screamed with each step. I felt like I had been torn apart and glued back together. It was hard to identify what hurt most—Walter's betrayal or my own stupidity.

Outrage at his guile and duplicity pushed me up the stairs and into our bedroom. I stood in the darkened room with my fists clenched at my sides and wrath coursing through my veins.

"I did this to me. I closed my eyes and ignored the signs. For what?" I shouted as I yanked open my closet door. I pushed aside the clothes and managed to drag the two large bags out of the closet and deposit them in the middle of the floor. The trappings of middle class were more than I could tolerate to stay in this marriage. Even protecting Crystal seemed to be less important as I threw my makeup bag into the opened suitcase.

It took over an hour to finish packing my toiletries. With frequent stops to massage my back, I finally threw the last of my things into the stuffed bag. I found a tissue on the nightstand and wiped my nose before plopping down on the edge of the bed.

I couldn't call Ursula or Carla. Seeing my sadness mirrored in their eyes would rip me apart. There was a limit to the number of times I could expect them to rescue me. My mother was in no state to assist me. She still needed me to hold her together.

The outline of the telephone blurred as I stared at it. With a heavy sigh I dialed Marco's number. He answered immediately. "I was hoping I'd hear from you," he said without waiting for me to identify myself.

"I didn't know who else to call. I can't stay in this house tonight, I swear the walls are laughing at me and I can't drive."

"I'm on my way," he said.

I placed the phone on the receiver and looked around the room. The huge suite had everything I thought I wanted. I shook my head, turned out the light, and headed downstairs. My energy gave out on the bottom step. I settled on the last rung, and waited. My clothes were damp with perspiration, and clung to my skin, making me shiver.

My stomach twisted and settled like a cast iron anchor in my gut. I wrapped my arms around my waist, holding in what little strength remained. For several minutes I stared at the intricate glass in the front door, following the lines that made up the design. What should have been a sad, devastating moment actually felt calm and serene.

All my questions had been revealed as the universe coughed up the massive hairball with the answers. At some point, Walter had loved me. I wish I could pinpoint when he stopped, and saw me more as an accessory instead of a partner. I covered my face with my hands and cried. The quiet stream of tears didn't bring the relief I expected. It wasn't until the sobs rumbled in my stomach, did I accept the truth. The sadness closed over me and for once I didn't fight it. I'd earned every morsel.

Calling Marco may have been another dumb thing to do, but it felt right. I was so numb I couldn't tell if my feelings for him were a true emotional connection or a need to fill the hole left of my marriage?

Without my marriage to hide behind, I wasn't sure who I'd be. I wanted to be the person who followed her instincts. There was only one way to go now.

Forward.

Even if I had to take baby steps, at least it was away from the pain and toward a new life. A better life.

What would I tell Crystal? I closed my eyes and prayed that by the time she returned home, some of the emotions would have settled. Walter would have to provide his version of what happened. Either way, I couldn't smooth this out for her.

Marco rang the doorbell, jarring me back to the present.

"Come in, it's open," I yelled without moving.

The knob turned and slowly the door opened. He stepped into the foyer without seeing me seated on the stairs.

"I'm here." I waved my hand to get his attention.

"Are you okay?" He rushed to my side; his six-foot frame towered over me. "Are you hurt?" He scanned my body from head to toe.

"I feel like a baseball in a world series game. I need to get out of this house. My bags are in the bedroom. First door on the left."

He dashed up the stairs and was back in seconds. After loading the bags in the car, he lifted me off the steps. I was getting stiffer, my body rebelling from the accident.

Marco backed to the end of the driveway and stopped, putting the car in Park. "Do you want to talk about what happened?" he asked.

"Okay, let's see…where should I start? I could start with the secretary or the college fling, but you already know those stories. I should cut right to the chase and tell you the pregnant woman in the lobby is his new love. She's expecting his child," I said without masking my sarcasm. "Oh yeah, and get this. They're engaged." I emitted a sound that could have been confused with laughter but it was too harsh.

"If it upsets you, we don't have to talk about it." He glanced at me.

"I want to say it out loud, to make it real. If I hear it in my own voice it gives me the push I need to do what I've been ignoring for so long." I took a deep breath. "I called her tonight. She said he bought her that car she drove to the office. I thought it was his, but they have matching cars. Can you believe that? After over twenty years he and I don't have anything that match. Aagghh! And…and she's only twenty-seven years old."

"Go ahead. Let it out. Are you sure this is helping you?"

"I don't know. I'm just so…so wound up. Are we going to your house?

"*Si bella*. I'm taking you to my house where I can take care of you."

"Maybe I shouldn't stay there. I'm a wreck and maybe I should be alone. Besides, what will people think?" My thoughts boomeranged in my head with rapid speed. Staying at Marco's house suddenly seemed impulsive. "Maybe I should go to a hotel or Ursula's."

"What people are you worried about?"

"Well…" I paused. My father was dead. Crystal was away, my mother lived miles away. Who cared where I spent the night or with whom? Certainly I didn't care what Walter thought.

"You can sleep in the spare bedroom. I promise I won't sneak in and take advantage of you during the night."

"Then I might as well go stay with Carla and Javier," I teased.

He gave me a disapproving look. "Don't tempt me. My feelings for you are too strong. It won't take much for me to cross that line."

"I know. But I've got to get my life together before I can embark on anything else. You understand, don't you?" I placed my hand on his thigh. My goal to be level-headed evaporated.

"But you've made so many sacrifices. When do you put Tracy first?" He shifted into gear and backed into the street.

"Now. Starting now." I gave his thigh a tight squeeze.

He placed his hand on top of mine. "I'll do anything you ask."

"Would you take a hit out on Walter?"

"Anything but that."

We rode in silence for a few miles. Going to his place may have been a bad decision but it was what I wanted.

He pulled into the parking garage and walked around to my side of the car. I held on to him, gripping his solid forearm. The elevator to his floor was small but elegant.

His huge living room had large windows spanning the length of one wall. Lights from the city sparkled in the distance. The opposite red brick wall housed a massive wood-burning fireplace that looked big enough to heat the whole condo. A large flat-screen television and state of the art stereo equipment occupied one wall. His home looked like I pictured it, very masculine but very organized. I sank into the lush chocolate leather sectional.

"What can I get for you?" he asked over his shoulder on his way to the kitchen.

"I need some water." I rummaged through my pocketbook until I located my pills. The amber vial warmed my hand, promising me euphoria within minutes. I almost had the lid off before the vision of the car smacking into my hip came into view.

The pills were an old friend—just like Walter used to be my husband. They felt good for a little while, but they'd sent me crashing without a safety net. I put them back in my purse and folded my hands in my lap. Marco stood against the doorjamb, watching me.

"How long have you been standing there?" I asked.

"Long enough." He placed the glass of ice water in my hand and sat beside me. The tenderness in his voice belied the worry in his eyes. "Are you okay?" His voice was both soothing and reassuring.

"I think so." I gulped the water and looked away. He sat so close I could feel the heat from his body. My lust twenty-two years ago had changed the direction of my life. This time I needed to act differently. I wanted the comfort of his arms around me, cuddling my head against his chest would have been the perfect prescription.

"I'm really tired. I think I ought to lie down."

He helped me up, supporting my weight on his forearm. The most I would allow myself was to lean against him. My body felt like a mass of aches and soreness.

"Can I get you something else?"

"I'll be fine."

"Everything is going to be okay." He spoke with the assurance of a man who'd been in my place. It happened for a reason."

"My pride is hurt more than anything. Before Crystal's wedding, I was planning to leave him and somehow I got sucked back into that maze of crazy."

He nodded and disappeared down the hall.

I found the pills in my purse, walked into the adjoining bathroom and flushed them down the toilet. I watched them swirl their way out of existence. I'd expected them to erase the unhappiness and my guilt. Instead, they only delayed the inevitable. For the first time in months I was able to think clearly. Walter's actions shouldn't have surprised me. He showed me who he was years ago, with that first affair. I just refused to see it.

I stripped down to my bra and panties before climbing into bed. With the cell on vibrate, I placed it next to me in the bed. I didn't expect any calls, but I didn't want to disturb Marco.

My mind raced as thoughts pushed around demanding attention. In college I had sprained my arm doing a cartwheel in gym class. The doctor said a sprain was worse than a break because it took more time to heal. All the time I spent trying to figure out what was wrong with Walter and me was like walking around with my arm in a sling, nursing

a sprain. Now that I knew my marriage was broken,
I could get on with the business of healing.

Chapter Twenty-Seven – Tracy

The phone vibrated just as I was falling asleep. It pulsed several inches across the bed before I decided to talk to Carla.

"How ya doing, sweetie?" Her voice could make a baby coo.

"I-I'm okay." I told her I put Walter out of the house.

"Do you need me to stay with you tonight? I can come over right now."

"No. I'm fine." I didn't tell her I was staying at Marco's. "I'm fine tonight. I'll give you a call tomorrow." As long as I had friends like Carla and Ursula, my life would have some measure of happiness and contentment.

"You know this will get easier. It will only hurt for a while," she said.

"I've been hurting for so long, I think I'm numb. Look how many years I've wasted."

"Honey, you can't move forward until you're ready. You were thinking of Crystal," she assured me.

"Was I a fool?"

"Not at all! Now you can walk away with a clear conscious, knowing you tried."

After we hung up, I punched the pillow and burrowed under the sheet. Several minutes later, I flipped over and scrunched the pillow under my head. Without the pills, I was wide awake. My thoughts raced from Crystal, to my mother, then back to Crystal.

When the sun came up, I sat on the edge of the bed. My body ached in places I hadn't known existed. A small penance to pay for the way I'd ignored all the symptoms that indicated something was wrong with my marriage.

Marco knocked on the door. I ran my fingers through my hair, and pulled the sheet around me.

He stepped inside the room but kept his distance. I adored him for understanding I needed a little privacy and distance first thing in the morning. "Rough night, huh? You cried most of the night. I heard you."

"Are you sure it was me?"

He nodded.

"I'm sorry if I kept you up."

His eyes fell on my thighs and I tugged the sheet tighter.

"No, you didn't. I wanted to come in here." His heavy Italian accent was coated with a tenderness I hadn't experienced in years. My heart opened up to him in a way I didn't think was possible.

"It's probably best you didn't. It wasn't a pretty sight."

"You've never looked more beautiful."

I bit my lip and combed my hair with my fingers again.

"What would you like to do today? I'll take off from work."

"No. You go to work. I've got to do this alone. Just drop me off at the house before you go to work. I'll call Carla for breakfast." I spread my hands wide to encompass the whole room. "I kinda like this room, so if it's okay with you, I'd like to come back tonight. I promise to be quieter."

"Not a problem. You can use the room for as long as you want."

"I'll be gone by Christmas. I don't want to wear out my welcome."

He took a step forward. "I wish you would." The fire behind his eyes made me want to rush into his arms, but being half naked I didn't dare move.

***

My life was about to change. The thought didn't scare me like it had in the past. I stuck the key in the lock, opened the front door, and stepped into the house. It was exactly the way I'd left it, but it seemed lifeless.

In the kitchen I poured myself a glass of orange juice, and dialed Carla.

"I've been waiting on you to call. Can I come over? I got someone to sub for my spinning class so I can spend the whole day with you."

"I'll leave the door unlocked. When you get here, come up to the bedroom."

I hung up and opened the refrigerator. There were leftovers from the wedding breakfast and a huge hunk of wedding cake. After more than a week, the breakfast leftovers had to be scrapped. I wrapped the cake, then placed it in the freezer.

Seated at the kitchen table, I nibbled dry toast and stared at the blinking message light. Walter, no doubt. But I ignored it. There was so much I needed to get done and he would just have to wait, maybe for the rest of my life.

Crystal would have to be told, and so would my mother. The thought of those conversations made my heart race. Instead of reaching for the extra bottle of pills I stored in the cabinet, I poured a glass of water, then dialed my mother's number. Thankfully, Crystal was away, it gave me a few more days to figure out how to tell her.

"Tracy, I've been trying to get in touch with you," my mother said. "It's been a few days."

"I'm sorry. Is everything okay?"

"I'm doing the best I can. Sometimes I'll see something or hear something and think I have to share that with Carl, and then I remember—" She stopped. I heard her fight back a sob. "I'm selling the house. I've been here for over fifty years, but they were all with your dad.

I imagined her sitting at her kitchen table with her coffee cup. My guilt for not visiting her for several days rested on my chest, but I hadn't been frolicking around having fun.

"Mom, I'm leaving Walter," I said.

"What?"

"It's a long story. I promise to tell you all about it. But for now, all I can say is my marriage is over."

For a long moment neither of us said anything.

Then with a sharp intake of air, my mother said, "You know best. You've never been impulsive. You know you two looked so content and happy at the wedding that I thought things were getting better. Well..." I could tell she was having difficulty compartmentalizing the information. I wished there was some way I could have spared her this disappointment, too.

"You need me to come down there?"

"You're sweet, but no. I'll be okay. I'll come up before the end of the week and tell you all about it."

"Does Crystal know?" she asked.

"No."

"That poor girl goes away on a honeymoon and comes back to a totally different world."

"This wasn't part of my planning. But Crystal will be fine. You and I will see to it."

I hung up and pushed out of the chair. In the garage I found the box of extra-large trash bags and carried them under my arms as I managed the stairs. I went straight to Walter's closet and pulled his starched white shirts from the hangers and stuffed them into one of the bags.

I ignored the cell phone when it rang. When the house phone rang, I let it to go to the recorder. I continued stuffing his clothes into the trash bags. Each handful I shoved in the bag shored up my resolve. For once, I was doing something instead of having something done to me.

My body ached, but I refused to take a pain reliever. By the time Carla walked into the bedroom, I had eleven bags lined against the wall.

"Girl, what are you doing?" Carla looked around the room, her hands on her hips.

"Something I should have done the very first time he cheated on me."

"Girl, please let me help." Carla threw her purse on the bed.

"Those are his drawers, just take everything out and put it in a bag. When that's empty, just move to the next one."

"All right, this is up my alley." Carla yanked Walter's underwear out of the dresser and shoved them into the bag like she was trying to win an Olympic medal. She made me laugh.

The sound of rustling bags filled the room for thirty minutes. We used hand signals to indicate where we could find more of his belongings. When the bags were all gone, we fell on the bed to catch our breath.

"Now what? Should we drag this shit outside and burn it in the driveway 'Waiting to Exhale' style?"

"No, Carla. I'm going to call someone to pick all his stuff up and take it to his new home. If I give him absolutely everything, then he will have no reason to come back to this house or near me."

The phone rang again. "Want me to get that for you?"

"No, let the recorder get it. Walter's been calling all morning. But Carla…I'm telling you, I don't want to see him and I don't want to talk to him." I put my hands behind my head and crossed my feet at the ankles.

"What will my life look like once I'm divorced?"

"You'll go back to being that fun person I met in college. The girl who laughed a lot and smiled all the time." She cradled her head in her hand, too.

"I didn't stay here last night. I stayed at Marco's."

"Marco's house?" Carla turned over on her stomach, her mouth slightly open. "You barely get one man out of your life and you invite another one in?"

"It wasn't like that, Carla. I just couldn't stay here. I'm not sure I'll ever spend another night in this house. Ursula's in Philly, you and Javier are busy. Besides, could you really say Walter was in my life? I think I was hanging on to the fringes of his life."

"Girl, you know I'm always there for you no matter what." She reached across the bed and touched my hand.

My eyes locked with hers. "How are you doing, Carla?" I hoped she knew I was asking about the whole baby business.

Her mouth opened like trying to form an answer to my question was exhausting. I wanted to retract the question, but it lingered between us.

"I'm trying to accept the idea that maybe it won't happen. And even though he's been very supportive and would never say otherwise, Sometimes when Javier thinks I'm not paying attention he gets a sad, distant look in his eye."

I squeezed her hand and wondered if it was the same look I saw in her eyes.

I climbed off the bed. "It's time to change the scenery. Ready to hit his office? I'm sure we'll find lots of good incriminating stuff down there."

"Yeah, you're calling the shots and I'm your girl." She jumped off the bed and any traces of sadness fell away. "There may be some stuff you want to hold on to. It could be useful if he decides to act crazy later on."

I snapped my fingers. "Good idea." I nodded remembering the cell phone bills I found in his desk drawer. "Very good idea."

Chapter Twenty-Eight – Tracy

"I think I hate this house." We made our way to Walter's office. Everything was neatly organized and pristine, except for the paper I'd scattered on the floor the night before.

"Will you be able to live here, you know…after?" Carla asked.

"When I first saw this house, I begged Walter to buy it because I loved it so much…"

"Where should we start?" Carla glanced around the immaculate space.

"I'll take this bottom drawer. The important stuff is in here. You take the rest."

I found enough evidence to indict Walter for being a lousy husband.

Receipts for expensive jewelry I never received.

Hotel bills for rooms I never stayed in.

Statements for an investment account I knew nothing about.

His betrayal ran deep, and I'd allowed him free range to lie to me. With a hefty sum.

"Have you told Ms. Frances or Crystal what you're planning?" Carla heaved a sandwich bag full of pen refills into the trashcan.

"I told Mom today. I'll tell Crystal when she gets home. I haven't spoken to Ursula since I left the hospital. So when you get home tonight, before you jump Javier's bones, call her and tell her."

"I'm on it." Carla laughed.

"My body's screaming for a rest."

"Okay, I'll get us something to drink."

"Water for me," I said.

In the family room, Carla sipped wine. I drank water.

The house phone rang again.

"Sooner or later, you're going to have to talk with Walter. He's been blowing up your phone all day. Get it over with." Carla held the receiver out to me.

"I'm not ready yet. I'm still so angry and can't say anything constructive. This anger gives me an edge and I like it."

"Let me tell him to stop calling, it's driving me crazy."

When the phone stopped ringing, Carla hit the message play button. "Let's hear what he's got to say, the poor bastard." She depressed the speaker button and Walter's voice permeated the room.

"Tracy, I know you're upset and you have every right to be. But baby, we can get past this."

"Did he call me baby?" I whispered.

Carla put her index finger to her lips to quiet me.

"I know I messed up pretty bad this time, but I love you. I really love you and I know you need a little time to calm down. Listen, I'm going to my office tonight, so please call me there. I'm sorry, Tracy…I never meant for things to get this far. Baby, I can make this up to you. I'll spend the rest of my life making this up to you. Give me a chance."

The phone beeped, cutting him off. I sat back against the sofa and laced my fingers together.

Walter's third message played. "Tracy, if you're there please pick up. We can talk about this. It's not what you think. Let me come home. I'll be different, you'll see. Think about what this will do to Crystal."

"That sucker hasn't talked that nice to me in probably five or six years. I don't believe he called me baby. You know, if he was here right now I'd gash his eyes out."

"No, you wouldn't, Tracy. You're not like that." She sat next to me and placed her hand on my back. "You've got to have faith in what you're doing."

"I know I'm doing the right thing, but it doesn't lessen my anger."

My cell phone rang. I expelled a heavy sigh. The ringing phones exhausted me. Carla picked up my cell phone and glanced at it quickly then handed it to me. "It's Marco," she sang.

"How's it going?" His smooth baritone voice eased my tension. I flipped my hand at Carla, but she refused to leave the room.

"Hey. Carla and I are cleaning house."

"Are you ready for me to pick you up?"

"I'll drive over to your place this evening. I need my car." I stretched my legs out in front of me.

"How 'bout dinner tonight?"

"I…um…okay. I guess we can," I stuttered. "Sooner or later I have to go out in public."

"Is that the only reason you're saying yes?" he asked.

"Certainly not. I'd love to have dinner with you," I replied.

"Good. You have the key I gave you. I'll be there at six."

Carla's eyes grew large and she placed a hand on her hip.

We agreed to meet at his place at seven and ended the call.

Carla crossed her arms over her chest and stared at me. "What was that all about?"

"Girl, you need to quit. You're acting like we're still in college and trying to decide which guy to take to the dance."

"Anyway." She rolled her eyes. "Dinner, tonight?"

"I feel like I've been living under a shoe. Maybe getting out in public will pull me up."

She nodded in agreement.

"Between my father's death and this, my life has been all red lights. I'm so tired of being sad and crying and wanting something more but settling for less."

"Then go out tonight and enjoy your dinner with Marco. Have rambunctious sex with him if that's what you feel like doing."

"What does rambunctious sex feel like?"

"If you don't know, then you really need it."

***

Marco walked in the house. "Wow! You look fantastic." He held my hand above my head and spun me around.

"You're being nice," I said.

"*Cha, bella.*" He leaned in so close I thought he was going to kiss me. Instead, he extended his elbow for me. "We're going to have dinner at the restaurant at Penn's Landing in Philly. Not because we needed to hide, but because this dinner is to be special.

"What makes it so special?"

"You're going to be a single woman and I don't have to pretend I want to be your friend anymore."

"I…I—What…?"

"Shh. Don't say anything. I'm willing to wait as long as it takes, or two weeks, whichever comes first."

I jabbed his arm and laughed.

"See, my plan is working, already. You're laughing." He helped me in the car, walked to the driver side and started the engine. Chatting with Marco during the drive to Philly was easy.

Once we were seated in the restaurant I said, "Okay, tell me what they're saying about me at work."

"It's ugly, you know how gossip is. *Sono davvero spiacente.*"

"Don't be sorry. It's my life. Tell me."

He shared the details.

"It sounds like the gossip mills have my story about right. My husband cheated, his mistress confronted me at work, I snapped. That's pretty much my story." I took a sip of water and swirled the liquid in the glass.

He rearranged the salt and pepper grinders on the table. "Does that bother you?"

"Not as much as I thought it would."

When the server arrived at our table, Marco ordered a bottle of wine, then sat back in his chair. "You know I can't be objective here. I think you should have left Walter a long time ago. So you'll understand if I don't try to give you any guidance as you go through this thing. If it frees you up and makes room for me, then I'm all for it."

"I need somebody to listen."

"I'll always listen. You can even lay your head on my shoulder." He reached for my hand and caressed my fingers. The warmth from his palm penetrated my heart. The ice around my heart melted. Was it cheating to want Marco so much when I had unfinished business with Walter?

We lingered over dinner, stretching it out until I released a string of uncontrollable yawns. Even though I didn't want the night to end, I couldn't keep my eyes open.

"Time to get you home." He paid the check and led me out of the restaurant.

During the drive, I tried to stay awake. I realized I hadn't made it when Marco shook my shoulder.

"Time to wake up sleepy-head."

We were at his house, in the garage.

"I'm sorry. I guess I wasn't very good company on the way here, was I?"

"You were great company." He leaned over, his mouth inches away from mine. I focused on his lip, wishing and wanting. My heart picked up speed, accelerating beyond my control. Placing his mouth over mine. His warm, thick tongue immediately woke me up. My body came to life at the core as I placed my hand on the back of his neck to draw him closer. Suddenly the interior of the car felt warm.

After a full minute, he pulled away. "I couldn't wait another minute." His eyes searched my face. "You get it, don't you?"

"I get it." My voice sounded thick and sweet.

"If not now, Tracy, then when? Haven't you been living on hold long enough?"

"I need to be fair to you, but I need to be fair to myself this time too. I need to make sure I'm not with you because I'm sad, depressed, rebounding, or just plain stupid."

"If that's important to you, I'll wait. But I'd want you even if you were doing it for any of those three reasons. You know that, don't you?" His eyes held a warm yearning.

"I know, and that's what makes you so incredibly sweet."

"I think we'd better get you to bed before…" He got out of the car and walked around to open my door.

"Thank you for dinner, it was a lovely evening." He held my hand and searched my eyes. This couldn't be happening. I should have been broken up over my failed marriage. Instead, I wanted to fall into Marco's arms. When he released my hand, I rushed off to my room. Leaning against the closed door, I took a deep breath. My mouth watered. My body screamed for attention.

The light knock on the door startled me. "Can I come in?"

I stepped back, closed my eyes and bit my lip. "Marco, if I open that door I can't be responsible for anything I say or do."

He cracked the door and slipped inside. "I'll be responsible enough for the both of us."

He pressed his tongue between my lips. My heart fluttered and threatened to stop as he gathered me in his arms.

Chapter Twenty-Nine – Walter

The narrow couch dug into my back. A sharp pain slid across my chest, forcing me to sit upright. I rubbed my breastbone with my fingertips, coaxing the spasm to release me.

After trying to fall asleep for several hours, and dialing Tracy's phones through the night, I gave up. I swung my legs off the couch. My shoes sat side by side next to the couch like mates are supposed to.

I dropped my head and rubbed my face hard, much harder than I intended. The discomfort was a distraction.

A thin film of perspiration covered my body. This was bad. The anger in Tracy's voice and eyes were new to me. Even after the second time I cheated, she cried, never had she yelled. I wrung my hands then stared into my empty palms.

Without my permission, everything was changing. My personal belongings from my desk were packed in boxes and stacked at the door. The office was hardly recognizable after all my years of employment. Beverly needed to be thanked for packing up my items. She would be glad to see me go. Another woman I failed to please.

I had to start over again, find another job. It wouldn't be easy at my age. But Tracy was patient.

She'd give me time to look around until I found the right fit.

I shrugged and stood up on stiff legs. I felt old, like a grizzly senior.

It wasn't like Tracy not to answer the phone. Her voice and the directness of her eyes made me believe she was capable of getting through the night without me. Waiting for her to change her mind was my best plan of action.

I woke Sasha while my anger festered.

"Why are you calling in the middle of the night, Walter?"

"Why didn't you pick up when I called earlier?"

"Where are you? I thought you'd be coming here."

"I'll bet you did."

We fell silent. Exhaustion and anger circled my brain like sharks.

"Why, Sasha?" I asked when she didn't volunteer any information.

"Because you wouldn't. Because you couldn't," she hissed.

"Dammit, Sasha. I don't fucking believe you did this. You had no right. What the hell were you thinking going to Tracy like that?" I walked around the room, making sure to avoid the boxes.

"I was thinking about our child. I was thinking about getting… getting this done, over.

Don't you see…it's really better now that it's out in the open? I—we don't have to sneak around anymore. We can go out in public, have a meal in a restaurant." She paused. "What choice did I have, Walter? What choice did you leave me? I'm different from Tracy. I can't live on promises."

"You were only thinking about yourself and what you wanted," I shouted.

"Is that what you think?" Before I could respond she rushed on. "If I was thinking only of myself, then who were you thinking about? Who were you thinking about?"

I bit my tongue. I didn't know what to say to make her see the damage she caused. The fight drained out of me. For a moment, neither of us said anything. It was an uncomfortable silence.

"It's late, Walter and I'm tired. Let's talk in the morning."

"Sasha, do you ever think about anyone other than yourself?"

"Yeah, I think about the baby on the way. I want you to do the same."

Outside, someone lay on their car horn and tires screeched. Even in this early morning hour, life moved on.

In a voice that was more conciliatory, Sasha asked again, "Where are you?"

"In my office."

"Why are you there so late?"

"Tracy put me out."

"Why didn't you come here? I don't understand—why would you go there and not here?"

"Sasha, I—"

"Walter, why didn't you come here? What's going on?"

"Look, I need some time."

"Walter?"

I hung up. Never had I been angry with her. She called me back. I ignored the ringing phone and stretched out on the couch again.

Light came through the slits in the office blinds, crossing the floor in thin ribbons. I couldn't block out the light. Instead of sleeping, I stared at the ceiling. What could I say to Tracy to get her to forgive me this time? I couldn't picture a life with us all intertwined: Tracy, Crystal, Sasha, and the new baby. I could see bits and pieces, but the puzzle never came together.

I pushed off the sofa, showered in the corporate bathroom, and dressed. I didn't want the whole office to know I slept on my couch. Beverly stepped in my office and closed the door.

"I don't know if you heard yet." She sat like there were thorns in the chair. "I'm going to be the admin assistant for Thompson effective next month." She looked pained.

"Thompson!" Her betrayal socked me. I couldn't tolerate the little weasel of a man. "Thompson's name was on my list, he's being let go, too."

"Joe decided to promote him. He's the new Vice President of Sales and Marketing."

"I guess he's better at the political game than I am." I tried to hide my discomfort. "Beverly, sorry about that, but I guess it could be worse. You could be out on the street like me."

"He's not so bad. He never works late and his offices will be in the new wing with the new furniture." She shrugged one shoulder. Beverly didn't approve of my choices. She'd be quite delighted to know Tracy kicked me out of the house. "Besides, you'll get a nice little package plus all the executive perks. You won't have to work again if you don't want to."

"Yeah, but…" I didn't know how to respond. "This might be my last week in the office. I don't see a need to hang around."

"I'll call and make arrangements to have your boxes sent to your house."

"Give me the number and I'll handle the arrangements." She gave me a quizzical look. I didn't want her to know where my belongings would end up.

I dialed my home number after Beverly walked out. The phone went to the recorder again. I left another message and hung up.

I busied myself deleting personal emails and shredding documents. At the end of the day, well after Beverly had left, I prepared to leave the office. I couldn't spend another night on the narrow couch.

No word from Tracy all day, so I drove home to check on her. As I pulled into the cul-de-sac I saw lights on in the house. I pushed the button and waited while the garage door went up. The house was quiet. I searched downstairs; she wasn't there. I took the stairs two at a time to see if she was in the bedroom.

The ransacked master bedroom was empty. My clothes cluttered the bed. Along the wall were trash bags, lots of trash bags. Drawers on my chest hung half open, they were all empty. I opened my closet door, it was empty, even my shoes were missing.

With a sinking feeling, I opened a few of the bags and recognized my belongings. My worldly possessions were in a state of transition from one place to the next. My office was in boxes. Now my home belongings were in bags.

Tracy had to be out with the loudmouths. I went downstairs to the wet bar and opened a bottle of Duckhorn Estate Grown Merlot. We had saved that bottle for a special occasion. I couldn't think of a better time to drink the wine. I sat in the kitchen and poured the wine in a glass. My BlackBerry vibrated and I pulled it off the clip. It was Sasha. I pondered taking her call.

"Yeah," I said.

"Where are you? She said she was letting you go. Aren't you coming here?"

While Sasha droned on I sipped my wine. I thought my anger would have subsided, but seeing my clothes squished into trash bags unsettled my emotions.

"Walter? Are you there?"

"Yeah, I'm here," I sighed.

"So what's up? What's happening?"

"I'll be there. I have a few things to take care of, then I'll come."

"Tonight?"

"Yeah, I'm coming tonight. I'll see you shortly." I ended the conversation and thought about calling Ursula or Carla to find out where Tracy was staying. I sipped my wine in the noiseless house. There was no need to hurry. I had plenty of time. I walked into my office; it was in the same disarray as my clothes. Tracy had a busy day.

Even the family pictures I had placed around the desk and bookcase had been packed away. Nothing that belonged solely to me was in sight. I forced my emotions down. The last thing I needed was for Tracy to walk through the door and see me crying like a pussy.

I scribbled a note for her and left it on the kitchen counter. I apologized again and assured her I could change. After an hour and a half and an empty bottle of wine, I left the house. My drive across town was slow.

Sasha met me at the door. Her big frightened eyes were full of tears. She fell into my arms as soon as I walked into the house. Without giving it much thought, I folded my arms around her. Her stomach kept some distance between us, but her skin was soft and warm.

"Are you hungry?" she asked when I released her. A hopeful look filled her eyes. Tonight I needed more than food.

"No, let's just go to bed."

Chapter Thirty – Tracy

"*Buon giorno*, Antonio. Marco gripped the restaurant owner's hand and pointed to me. *Questa e Tracy.*"

"*Ciao*," I responded when Antonio kissed my cheek.

"I'm very hungry, Antonio, so I hope you're making homemade biscuits this morning." Marco patted the owner on the back and flashed his beautiful smile.

"Yes. With your hearty appetite, you'll probably want your usual three egg omelet and apple butter, too," the owner laughed.

"You know it." Marco held my chair.

"And the little lady? Her the same?" he asked with his thick Italian accent.

"Oh no, not for me. I'll have one egg and toast."

"*Cet un munu per bambini*?" Marco teased.

"I don't need a children's menu. I'm just not as hungry as a horse." I nudged him.

The owner scurried into the kitchen. Marco reached across the table, taking my hands in his. "*Grazie*." He squeezed my fingers.

"For what?" I angled my body to face him.

"For this time, for spending it with me."

"You've been my lifeline. I feel like you've pulled me from under a shoe and breathed life back into me."

"I adore you, *bella*." He closed the distance between us and kissed my mouth.

"I love it when you speak Italian. Even if I can't understand some of it."

"Then I'll speak less English and more Italian. That should keep you in my bed, yes?"

"Yes." I breathed heavily. "That, along with your warm caresses, the slow kisses and—"

"It has been even more enjoyable for me. I'm a lucky man." He rolled his thumb across the back of my hand.

"We're both lucky. I hardly recognize myself now when I look in the mirror."

A server set several heaping platters in front of us. The rich aroma of butter and sugar made my mouth water. I snuck several bits off Marco's plate while the waters of the Chesapeake Bay played behind us.

Marco finally set his fork down. "I'm stuffed."

"You know, I've got to go to the house today. I have to talk to Walter."

"Yes. I think it's time. I didn't want to push you." He smiled sympathetically.

"I dread going there. It's been a month, but I think I need to go." I put my napkin on the table.

"When I told Crystal about her grandfather, she sobbed, when I told her about the divorce, she yelled like a two-year-old. I've never seen her like this."

Marco slid his chair closer and pulled me into his arms.

"She finally agreed to talk to Walter and me tomorrow. She sounded so angry."

"She'll get past it. Give her time," Marco assured me.

I couldn't stop thinking about Crystal as we drove back to Delaware. She worried me. Getting her to agree to dinner with Walter and me was difficult.

Marco pulled into my driveway.

"Are you sure you're ready to do this?" he asked as we sat in the car.

"I'm ready." His hand rested on my thigh. "I'm going to handle a couple of things and make a few calls. I'm afraid if I don't keep moving forward I might lose my momentum."

"Want me to hang around…just in case?" He gestured with his hand.

"I do, but I need to do this myself."

"But not by yourself. I love you, Tracy." His eyes were intense.

I never got tired of hearing him say it. He said it several times a day and every time my heart spun around like a kid's toy. "I love you, too."

He gave me the half smile that I adored. "Call if you need me," he said as I got out of the car, and his eyes lingered on me. I was reluctant to leave the comfort and harmony of his presence.

I let myself into the house by the front door. In the five years that we'd lived in this house, I only went in through the front door a few times. This was a defiant act for me. I needed to start accumulating more brave acts.

I hadn't been back in the house since I packed up Walter's belongings. I felt like a stranger as I wandered through the rooms. The last several years I guess I was a visitor, only pretending to have a life here.

A half-empty wine bottle sat on the kitchen table along with a note from Walter. I balled it in my hand and tossed it in the trash. There wasn't a single word or phrase he could say that was worth my time to stop and read. Stepping back into my marriage would be like severing my coronary arteries and serving them up on a hot plate.

I'd asked him not to come back, but he did. He always did whatever he wanted, which reinforced my decision to let his selfish ass go.

I punched his number into the phone. He picked up before the second ring.

"Are you available for lunch today?" I asked without preamble.

"Yes. I've been calling you."

"I know. I've been ignoring you."

"What's up? What are you going to do? Why did you send me all my stuff?"

"I told you, it's over."

"Baby, let's talk." His tone was different, less intense.

"We'll talk at lunch. Meet you at Union Grill at noon." Before he could ask another question, I hung up.

In the living room, I faced the crystal butterfly perched on the center of the sofa table. Walter and I had purchased it one spring while in Venice. We found it on a side street not far from Saint Marc's Square. I wanted to keep the butterfly, not to remember Walter, but to remember the beauty of Venice and to celebrate how happy I was at that time in spite of him. The hand-blown cobalt blue vase he gave me for our fifteenth wedding anniversary was going to the Goodwill. Very little of what was in this house would follow me to my new life. I planned to collect new memories.

In the bedroom, the drapes fluttered as the air conditioner roared. I positioned myself on the chaise and looked out the window onto the garden. I hadn't seen one hummingbird all summer. Usually one or two of the tiny birds fed on the daylilies or phlox. This year they were strangely absent. I hadn't filled the sugar-water feeder that swung from the pole in the center of the garden. My attention had been focused elsewhere.

I made a mental note of the few things that needed attention before the sale sign was stuck in the yard. There weren't many things that needed to be done. The house was ready to be put on the market.

It was easy to erase Walter's presence from my life. "You can't miss what you never had," I murmured and crossed my arms over my chest with satisfaction.

The ringing phone harassed me. But it was Ursula.

"Hey, it's been weeks since I talked to you. What's up?" I said.

"Girl, what is up with you? Carla told me you and Marco are talking marriage!" she shrieked.

"That's right. Later, next year, in Italy," I laughed.

"I've never been to Italy. This is going to be great," she gushed.

"Oh no, we're not doing the big wedding thing. It'll be him and me, one witness and a priest on some small piazza in Florence. I'll send pictures."

"Okay. If that's what you want, I understand." She sounded disappointed.

"I'll let you and Anthony do the big wedding thing." I tried to coax a smile out of her.

"You sound so happy. I haven't heard you this content in a long time."

"Ursula, happy doesn't come close to describing my state of mind." I blushed with excitement. "I feel guilty for being this happy when Crystal seems so miserable with the whole idea."

"She's speaking to you now?" Ursula asked.

"A little. Last night she told me she loved me, so we're making progress." I sat on the edge of the bed.

"You know, Carla left this morning for Guatemala."

"Yes, to pick up her baby girl. I don't know if I understand how it happened so fast, but I'm glad she and Javier are getting a baby. She couldn't stop smiling when she told me her good news." I shifted the phone to my opposite ear. "Maybe there is such a thing as happy endings."

We chatted a few more minutes and promised to spend some time together later in the week. Now that she was working in Philadelphia, I missed popping in and out of her office and seeing her every time something worth chatting about came up. But after all the years between us, I knew I could count on her.

Her relationship with Anthony was growing stronger. She was giddy with that new relationship excitement. I prayed her happiness would last her a lifetime. Time is only good for aging wine; time alone does nothing to nurture a relationship.

I took my time getting to the restaurant. Keeping Walter waiting wasn't ever done; nothing made him angrier than waiting on others. But if he left the restaurant before I got there, then he could talk to my lawyer. God knows I'd waited on him for years. I slowed my pace and relaxed my shoulders.

I prepared a speech in my head. This was my moment and I planned to purge my soul.

I sashayed into the restaurant on my four-inch heels, my shoulders back, my head high, and an air of confidence reminiscent of my college persona. Walter was already seated at a booth along the wall of the restaurant. A glass of wine sat in front of him. I took a deep breath and pushed past my anxiety.

I slid into the booth, with my back to the door. Exhaustion showed in Walter's face, dark coloring puddled under his eyes. Salt and pepper stubble peppered his chin. Impeccably dressed as usual, but there was something missing from his arrogant air. I couldn't put my finger on it, but that was no longer my concern. I only had to focus on me. I only had to make myself happy. I suppressed a big whoop as that realization settled over me.

"You're late," he said, without hiding his annoyance.

I ignored him. "I'll have a glass of iced tea and a Caesar salad," I said to the server who rushed to the table.

"I've been trying to get in touch with you." Walter balled his fingers into a fist.

"I know."

"No one would tell me where you were." He released his fingers and placed them on the table. "Look, I know you're upset and you have every right to be. But we've been through more than this. We can get over this and have a happy life. You know we can." He clenched his fingers again.

"Walter, I don't want to be married to you anymore."

"But…all those years, you can't walk away from them."

"I didn't, you did. And every time you did, I forgave you. But not this time." I smacked the table. Walter sat back. "It's over."

"No, not yet." He rubbed his chest. "I can't do it, Tracy. I can't raise a child. I'm too old." He ran his hand over his close-cropped hair. "I've lost my job. I need you, Tracy. Please understand."

"Tell me something, Walter. A few months ago, when you didn't come home, were you really called into a meeting?"

He dropped his eyes and shifted his fork. "Of course I was. Remember, I left you the message?"

I shook my head. "You've made your bed, Walter, get comfortable."

"Is it because you don't believe I was in a meeting?"

"According to your Ms. Sasha, you spent several nights with her, playing house. She even told me about a trip to Paris and to the emergency room."

His face turned gray. "You're being mean. That's not like you."

"No I'm not. What you've done is mean. I'm finally seeing my marriage—what I thought was a marriage—with fresh eyes." I restrained my anger. "What did you think when you were making that baby? They need a father. They deserve a father, so forget what you want and step up."

"I can't do it, Tracy. I can't." He dropped his head. "These should be my golden years, I don't want to do parent-teacher conferences and all that stuff again. I'm miserable just thinking about it."

"Walter, I don't know what to tell you. Our marriage is over. It's been over for years. There's no going back. This is your problem, you'll figure it out." We sat in silence for several moments.

"Where have you been? I went past the house several times."

"I'm staying with Marco."

His eyes narrowed. "Are you fucking him?"

"Now let me see," I taunted. "That's none of your business." I stirred sweetener into my iced tea. "If I was, what would you say? What would you do?" I placed my chin in the palm of my hand and leaned forward. "What would you have to say about that, Walter?"

He didn't respond.

"That's what I thought." I sat back.

"Tracy, I'm really sorry, but think about what you're saying, what you're doing. We've been through tougher times. We're both too old to start over again."

Poor Walter was still trapped in his own haze. Thinking he loved me or wanted me. My haze vanished when I stopped the pills. I had no compassion or empathy for him. I took a deep breath and slowly released it. I could move on without looking back. "Maybe you're too old, but I feel like my young self again. Maybe better than I've felt in years."

He reached for my hand, but I placed it in my lap. I looked around for our server to cancel my salad. What I needed to say was said in the time it took to drink a glass of iced tea.

"Walter, I've filed for divorce. I'll have my lawyer call yours. You can keep your pension and I'll keep mine. Everything else we'll split down the middle." Never had so few words felt so liberating. I wasn't daddy's little girl or Walter's wife.

"But Tracy…"

"We get together with Crystal tomorrow. You can tell her… Well, you might want to work on that story." I reached for my wallet, extracted twenty dollars and laid it on the table. "I think this should take care of my salad and tea." As I stood, he poised his mouth to say something, but I turned away from the booth and walked out.

ABOUT THE AUTHOR

Jacki Kelly has written dozens of short stories and several books. She lives in the North East with her husband and one loveable dog. She loves hearing from her readers so please contact her.

Connect with her online:
http://www.jackikelly.com
Twitter - @jackikellybooks
http://facebook.com/jackikellyauthor

If you enjoyed reading Packed And Ready To Go, please tell everyone you know. Please post a review for other readers on Amazon, Barnes and Nobles or Goodreads or other forums.

JOIN THE JACKI KELLY NEWSLETTER! So you can stay tuned to new releases, appearance and events and prizes.

EXCERPT FROM GOING BACKWARDS

Chapter One - Crystal

I was turning into my mother. For some people that would have been a happy thought. I would rather tear open my chest and pull my heart out with my bare hands than let someone walk all over it and tell me they love me at the same time.

It was a reality I could have done without.

I ran my hand down Max's chest. We had just enough time for a quickie before he left for work. I caressed his morning woody, massaging it slowly enough to arouse him.

"Crystal, I can't this morning. I have to go in early. If I don't finish the deposition on the Royal case, I can't tell the firm it was because my wife wouldn't let me out of bed." He placed his hand over mine and pulled it away before climbing over me and heading toward the bathroom. "It would be nice if my wife could have breakfast ready before I leave the apartment." He was everything I wanted in a man, tall, handsome enough to turn heads, dark hair and eyes that accentuated his chocolate complexion, but lately I didn't seem to be enough for him. Maybe he no longer found my skinny legs or narrow hips attractive.

Max's rejection was so nice I didn't want to cry this time. Marrying the most polite man on the east coast had its benefits. It softened the blow when I slipped from being the star in his life to being the woman he dragged home to so late at night, when he was too tired to see I'd waxed every part of my body just for him. Stayed up late with heavy eye lids just for him. Would do anything, even look foolish, just for him.

This wasn't the life I thought I would be living at twenty-two. The two of us should be still combing the bars into the wee morning hours and heading off to work too hung-over to care about mortgages and or savings funds.

Swinging my legs over the side of the bed, I asked, "What time will you be home tonight?"

"Don't wait up for me. It might be late," he yelled through the door.

"That's the same thing you said last night, and the night before, and the night before that."

"You knew there would be days like this. I warned you." His response sounded like my concerns were the least of his worries.

When had our marriage become such a burden for him? The fun carefree Max disappeared for weeks at a time, leaving behind a conservative stranger I hardly recognized. He was so obsessed with saving money and making partner and getting a larger apartment that he seemed to forget the promises we'd made on the warm sands during our honeymoon. We weren't going to become our parents and we were always going to put each other first, but now that sounded like a different couple in a different place at a different time.

I was growing impatient with all the waiting. If my mother had been a little less patient and a lot more diligent she could have saved herself a lot of heartache. I had no intention of being just like my mother.

Walking from the bedroom to the kitchen took seconds, but it was long enough to remember all the good stuff. The good stuff that had walked with us down the aisle of the church, went to Hawaii on our honeymoon, moved into the tiny two bedroom apartment on New York's east side with us. But all the good stuff was gone, used up by neglect.

The kitchen, like every other room in the apartment with a window, looked out on the brick wall of the building next door. I cracked the window to allow the smell of fresh bread from the bakery to tickle my nose. It seemed like such a small thing, but it always made me smile.

From the cabinet over the refrigerator I removed a box of Cheerios and set it on the table next to the quart of skim milk. I was almost out of the kitchen when I remembered the bowl and spoon. I returned and placed them on the table next to the cereal.

In the bedroom, I pulled on my sweats and running shoes. I was tying my hair in a bun when Max called me from the kitchen.

He had his back to me when I walked in. "Yeah, babe?"

"Is this your idea of breakfast?" He spun around and shoved a spoonful of cereal into his mouth.

"You said you were in a hurry." I shrugged a shoulder. My tone should have let him know we were having a silent tug of war, again.

He put the empty bowl into the sink, then pulled me close, wrapping his arms around my waist.

"I'll make dinner reservations at your favorite

restaurant, BoBo. Let's meet there at seven tonight. Will that put a smile on your face?"

"Yes, yes." My voice was squeaky with delight. "But I thought you had to work late. You just said—"

"My beautiful wife comes first." He looked down in my eyes and pushed my hair off my forehead. And just like that I forgave him. I draped my arms around his neck and he kissed my lips, then slipped his tongue in my mouth. The sweet taste of milk lingered on his tongue.

I drew back and looked up at him. "We haven't been out in a long time. I'm so excited."

"Crystal, we went to the Chelsea Market last week. You even bought brownies. Remember?"

"If we buy groceries for the house, it doesn't count. Tonight, I get to dress up."

He made the face that said he thought I was being bratty before kissing my forehead.

"Oh, okay. Don't be late." He pulled on his suit jacket, picked up his briefcase, and was out the door before I could think of a witty retort.

I'm never late. We missed the movie last week because by the time he got home the show had already started.

I laced up my sneakers, then shoved the apartment key and my ID into my pocket. With my phone in my hand, I was out the door.

I hit my favorite path in Central Park and all the fussing from this morning disappeared. All I needed was a job to fill my empty days. It shouldn't have taken so long to find something. I had experience, a degree, impeccable references, and nobody was perkier than me.

I rounded the path and almost ran into Dexter. Several times a week we jogged together if our paths crossed. Someone at Max's firm had recommended him to paint our condo when we moved in. He introduced me to colors I would never have thought about for the kitchen and the bedroom. The warmest shades of gray and pink gave the bedroom a romantic aura even though there was very little romance going on in it.

Dexter was the boyfriend in my head. With his olive complexion and shoulder length blond hair, I couldn't explain the attraction, but I couldn't ignore it either. He was having a backup man just in case I grew bored, or just in case Max slipped into an endless coma or even worse just in case Max dropped dead. As long as he stayed in my fantasies it was acceptable and I didn't need to do any Hail Mary's.

"Hello gorgeous. Are you trying to increase your pace? You almost blew right past me?" Dexter had the sexiest grin outside of Max. But Dexter was carefree and always available. There were a few drawbacks with the little fantasy I often unleashed in my head. I was married, I loved Max and even though Dexter was tall and Hollywood handsome, his ambition was on par with a dog with a limp. He was only interested if it was placed right at the tip of his nose. How he kept his small house painting business afloat was a mystery. He never seemed to work.

At the end of three miles my clothes were soaked, my hair was plastered against my head, and

I was drained.

"Calling it quits already?" Dexter jogged around me. He didn't even sound winded. He stopped, bent at the waist to look in my face. His lips were just inches from mine. I could have pretended to fall right into their lushness. "What is it? What's bothering you?"

I rested my hands on my knees. "Everything and nothing. How's that for an answer?"

"Tell me more."

"Living in New York was supposed to be glamorous. Nothing I dreamt has turned out the way I imagined. And Max doesn't seem to care and he's never home."

Dexter grabbed me by the hand and tugged me toward the little cafe where we often shared bear claws after our run.

When we were seated, he poured two packs of raw brown sugar into his black coffee without taking his eyes off me. "How long are we going to sit here before you let loose?"

"I gave you the whole story. I'm supposed to be happy and I'm not. We haven't been married long enough for it to be falling apart already."

"Are you upset you don't have a job or has Max done something?" He leaned back in his chair as if my reply required lots of space.

I picked up several artificial sugar packets and stacked them on top of each other. "I've told you about my parents and the ugly mess they made of their lives. I've only just started talking to my Dad again and that's only because of my little sister, Kia." I shook my head. "Anyway, I feel like we're becoming like my parents."

"You think Max is cheating on you?" Dexter sounded more interested now.

His words hit me in the gut. "I don't know what I think. I…I…he wouldn't, not after what my father put us through."

Dexter shrugged his shoulders. He wasn't buying my reasoning, but he wouldn't tell me so. "Always verify, Crystal. Always." He picked up his cup, drained it, then leaned back in his chair and dropped the cup in the trash. "If you need a job, I could use some help."

"Yeah, right. I can't paint the back side of a barn."

"I wasn't talking about painting. I need an assistant. Someone to keep track of the appointments, the colors, the payments. It pays better than minimum wage." He rested his elbows on the table and locked eyes with me. I knew I should say no. Dexter's intentions weren't purely altruistic and I should know. The way he always let his hand linger on my back wasn't for moral support.

"Look, I've got to run, think about it and give me a call. You've got my number." He kissed me on the mouth and disappeared out the door.

####

The last time I'd dressed up for Max was for one of his firm's dinner parties. I remember feeling very prim and proper all night. He was adamant that I not reveal too much, so I was buttoned up and zipped up so tight I could hardly breathe. Tonight I didn't have to look like a recovering nun, so I slipped on the sexiest dress in my tiny closet. The deep V-cut exposed my breasts. My best assets. The emerald green color made me sparkle, and tonight I wanted to remind Max of all the things he said he loved about me.

The dress was much too revealing for the subway, so I splurged and hailed a cab on the corner. The excitement in my stomach reminded me of our first date. Max had been just as excited. He stumbled over his words all night. But his persistence won me over. Somewhere behind all the cases, the briefs, the court appearances, and the long hours that same person still existed. I saw it in the fleeting moments when he relaxed.

In the West Village traffic slowed and grew thick as we neared Sheridan Square. I tapped on the plastic shield and asked to be let out. Even in my four-inch heels I could walk the two blocks to BoBo's. I paid the fare and hopped out.

The small restaurant located in what used to be a townhouse was known for its fine French food. True to his word, Max had made the reservation and, even though I was twenty minutes late, he wasn't there yet. Not surprising. Something always held him up. It used to be me, now it was his career.

I was escorted upstairs to a small table jammed in a corner. Every time we came, we were seated at the same table. I wondered if Max had requested it for our romantic evening.

I ordered two Manhattans and waited.

Dexter's job offer wasn't something to get

excited about, but it would give me something to fill my days until my career took off. I was beginning to wonder if that was ever going to happen. The publishing industry was in such turmoil maybe I needed to reconsider my choices. But working with Dexter was just as crazy. What would Max think of the idea? He didn't really know Dexter. He was too busy at work to care what color I painted the condo. But I'd given him enough stories about Dexter's antics. He always half-listened and nodded his head until I grew silent.

Over the roar of conversation in the congested space, I picked up the chime of my phone. I hesitated before opening my clutch.

Max was an hour late.

"Where are you?" I whispered into the phone.

"Don't get mad, Crystal, but I'm still at the office. I don't think I'm going to make it. I've been trying to call you for twenty minutes."

"I have the ringer down low, so I couldn't hear it. Do you mean you're not coming at all?" I didn't want to sound like a whiny child, but my disappointment edged out my ability to restrain it.

"Go ahead and have dinner. Since you're there it makes sense. Order the same thing for me, but get it to go. I'll eat when I get home. I'm sorry, Crystal. I'll make it up to you." The phones ringing in the background validated he was in the office, the constant ringing always drove me crazy.

I nodded and pushed back tears.

"Crystal, did you hear me?" He sounded rushed.

"Yes. I heard you." I ended the call without a good-bye. I paid for the drinks and walked out.

It took me almost a half an hour to catch a cab. The night was cool and my attempt to look sexy only looked crazy as I pulled my flimsy scarf tight around my shoulders.

"Where to?" the cab driver asked over his shoulder.

"West 78th street…no change that. Please take me to the corner of Wall Street and Water Street. And please hurry." The skin at the base of my back itched. I'd promised I wouldn't do this anymore, but every instinct in my body wanted me to. I had no desire to cause a scene, or yell at the top of my lungs, or scratch or kick. I only wanted to know if Max was bent over his desk, cluttered in papers and stacked with his expensive law books.

Once I witnessed that with my own eyes, I could go home, go to bed and not become a raging lunatic obsessing about what I thought was going on. My mother would have gone home and waited—a glass of wine at her fingertips and a box of tissues on her bed side table.

The more I thought about what my mother wouldn't do, the more I knew I was doing the right thing.

Since it was after nine, traffic wasn't nearly as thick. The closer we got, the faster my heart raced. By the time the driver slowed and turned on Water Street, I was breathing, I was gasping. If Max was behind his desk working, he'd be so angry at me, he'd probably want a divorce—that's what he threatened the last time I showed up unannounced. If he wasn't there, this might just be the push I needed to walk away.

I paid the driver. "Can you wait for me?"

"How long are you going to be?"

I gave him an extra twenty. "If I'm not back by the time this is used up, you can leave."

He nodded and I hopped out. The small parking lot out front was empty. There weren't even any cars from the service waiting to take the late night lawyers home. Didn't he know I'd check? How long did he think he could fool me? Twenty years?

"Good evening, ma'am who are you hear to see this time of night?"

"I'm going up to Walchoff and Finestein, to see my husband." I scribbled my name on the log without looking at the guard.

"The offices are all closed. There's no one up there. We just did a sweep of those floors and shut down the Teleprompters."

"Are you sure? My husband said he was working late." I looked around the lobby. Usually this building was teaming with people, tonight it was strangely quiet, locked down, buttoned up like a vault.

"Yeah. I'm sure." His gruff tone left no room to contest him. It was enough to make me drop the pen and hurry back to the cab.

.

Trademarks:
True Religion; True Religion Apparel, Inc.
Corvette; General Motors Company
Manolo Blahnik; Manolo Blahnik
Birkin; Hermès International S.A.
Friends; Warner Bros. Television
Corona; Grupo Modelo, Anheuser Busch InBev
iPod; Apple Inc.